D0481347

BEAST & CROWN

ALSO BY JOEL ROSS

The Fog Diver
The Lost Compass

BEAST & CROWN

JOEL ROSS

HARPER
An Imprint of HarperCollins*Publishers*

Beast & Crown

Copyright © 2017 by Joel Ross

All rights reserved. Printed in the United States of America.

No part of this book may be used or reproduced in any manner whatsoever without written permission except in the case of brief quotations embodied in critical articles and reviews. For information address HarperCollins Children's Books, a division of HarperCollins Publishers, 195 Broadway, New York, NY 10007.

www.harpercollinschildrens.com

ISBN 978-0-06-248459-8 (trade bdg.)

Typography by Joel Tippie

17 18 19 20 21   CG/LSCH   10 9 8 7 6 5 4 3 2 1

First Edition

BEAST & CROWN

1

EVERY EVENING, FILTHY boots appeared in the elegant hallways of Primstone Manor. Riding boots, dueling boots, dancing boots. Boots made of bull hide and boots made of snakeskin, boots with glass buttons and boots with silk flowers.

But they all looked like mud clots and dung stains to Ji—because it was his job to clean them.

When he'd been hired as a boot boy three years earlier, his mother had beamed. "We're so proud of you, Ginaro!"

"I'm Jiyong," he'd reminded her. He was the youngest of fourteen kids, and his mother only called him the right name by accident.

"You lucky brat!" his third-oldest brother had said, punching his arm. "Just think, you're wiping mud from *noble* boots!"

"Yeah, what an honor," he'd muttered.

His oldest sister had ruffled his hair. "If you work hard and never talk back, maybe one day you'll become a footman! Or even a butler!"

Ji hadn't told her that getting promoted from *boot* boy to *foot*man didn't sound so great. Either way, you were still down around the toes. And even though butlers ruled the servants, Ji didn't want to buttle. Sure, he was only thirteen now, but he already knew there was more to life than buttling.

And there was more to life than filthy footwear, too.

Ji rubbed his aching neck and peered down the elegant hallway. Paper lanterns dangled from the ceiling and a painting of the Summer Queen hung over a flower vase, but he barely saw them. Instead, he focused on the rows of dirty boots slumped outside the bedroom doors.

He trudged along, collecting pair after pair. Dozens of wellborn guests were staying at Primstone Manor, which meant ten times as much work for him. They'd come from the city to enjoy the rolling hills, the soothing streams . . . the swan poop.

Ji smelled them before he saw them: a pair of dainty boots smeared with green-black slime. One of the guests must've stepped in a pile of swan droppings . . . and *slid*. Wrinkling his nose, he reached for the boots. They were made of calfskin, with silver baubles shimmering on chains at the ankles, and they reeked.

"Yech," he muttered, stuffing them into the "extra gross" section of his boot bag.

He'd get a beating if he tracked that stench through the house, so he opened a discreet door in the wood paneling and slipped into a gloomy passage that ran between the walls. Primstone Manor was honeycombed with cramped corridors and stairways, so servants could get around without bothering their betters.

Ji nodded to a chambermaid but didn't say anything—no one was allowed to speak in the passages—then picked his way down the stairs that plunged into the bowels of the manor.

Below the ground floor, the respectful hush of the upper house turned into a raucous clamor. A visiting nursemaid played cards with three footmen near the rice-wine cellar, and a valet wept to a laundress at the side door. In the kitchen, cleavers chopped, fires crackled, and a scullery maid mashed refried beans.

The hubbub reminded Ji of the old days, when his whole family lived at the same hacienda. He'd missed that sometimes, when he'd first come to Primstone Manor. But everyone knew that servants' younger kids didn't stay with their parents for long. At ten or eleven, they were sent to work elsewhere: there was no reason to cry about it.

Ji scurried through the chaos. Cook snapped at an under-cook, who snarled at a kitchen maid. Someone cuffed Ji's head, but he didn't stop to see who—or why.

He just slipped into the next room.

The scullery was normally used for dishwashing and laundry but served as an extra kitchen when guests came. With all the copper tubs and washing drums shoved against the wall to make room for cooking, Ji had to crawl beneath a trestle table to reach the chimney, the cramped alcove where he worked and slept.

Once inside, he stood to a hunch. The chimney was an abandoned hearth, deep enough to roast a boar. The stone walls were stained with soot, the floor was black with grease, and the ceiling sloped just above Ji's bowed head.

Still, after staying there for three years, it felt like home.

He sat at his workbench and kicked off his shoes, a pair of crude sandals with leather strips. He eyed his brushes and rags, polish and oil, needles and thread. Then he reached for his second-most-prized possession, a tin box overflowing with shoe decorations: laces, buttons, beads, clips, bangles, and pins.

"Hey, Ji!" Sally's voice called from the scullery. "Are you in there?"

"No," he called back.

She crawled into the chimney. "Can I sleep here again?"

"Sure." Ji frowned at her bloody lip. "You got in another fight?"

"It wasn't a fight." Sally wiped her mouth. "It was a duel of honor."

"Against who? Big Min?"

"Yeah."

"Then it wasn't a duel either—it was you getting stomped."

Sally flopped onto the pile of rags where she slept when she needed to get away from the stables. "He cheated at dice."

"Who cares? You don't play for real money."

"That doesn't matter. It's the principle that counts."

"He's twice your size, Sal."

She was smaller than Ji, and lighter skinned, with wild curly hair. Everyone had expected her to become a maid like her mothers, but instead, she'd snuck into the stables every morning for months to muck out the stalls. After the grooms got tired of chasing her away, the stablemaster hired her.

"You can't let that stop you," she said.

"Of course *I* could," Ji told her. "And I would've, too."

"I don't like cheaters," she said.

"And yet I'm your best friend."

"You're more of a thief than a cheater." Sally wiped her mouth again, then looked at the dirty boots. "Is that your last bunch tonight?"

"Nah," Ji told her. "There's at least two more."

"Did you find . . ." She wrinkled her nose. "Anything valuable?"

"Not yet."

5

"Oh, good!"

Ji frowned. "What do you mean, 'good'?"

"Well . . ." Sally lifted one shoulder. "I'm kind of hoping you won't find anything."

"You *need* me to find something."

"And I want you to," Sally told him. "I'm just hoping you don't."

Ji looked up at her. "You're doolally."

"Roz says I'm conflicted."

Ji gaped at her. "You told *Rozario*?"

"Yes?" Sally said, in a little voice.

"About *this*?" Ji gestured angrily. "You told her what we're doing?"

"Only because she asked!"

"If someone asks, you're supposed to lie."

Sally glared. "You know I'm not good at lying."

"Lying is easy! Just think about the truth and say literally anything else."

"You said you trust Roz."

"I do, but—"

"You said she's the smartest person you know."

"She's the *only* smart person I know," Ji snapped.

He turned away from Sally and cleaned a pair of knee boots, scrubbing extra hard so she'd know he was mad. Though he wasn't that mad, not really. More like terrified. If Butler found out that Ji was stealing boot ornaments, he'd be sent to the gallows. He'd watched a hanging once,

6

and he still saw the woman's bare feet kicking in his night-mares. Sometimes, he dreamed that it was *him* hanging from his neck; then he'd wake up in a sweat, gulping for breath.

After finishing the knee boots, he looked at Sally. "What does 'conflicted' mean?"

"That's what I asked Roz," Sally said, half buried in rags. "It means that I disagree with myself. Like, I want you to find valuable stuff, but I also don't want you to."

"That's not conflicted," Ji said. "That's cactus brained."

Sally toyed with her leather bracelet. "You know I hate stealing."

"Do you have a better idea?"

"No," Sally admitted.

"Anyway, you're not stealing," Ji told her. "I'm stealing."

"And if they catch you," Sally said, a stubborn glint in her eyes, "I'll tell them *why* you're stealing."

"That's stupid," he said. "You'd just get yourself hanged, too."

"I don't care."

"What would happen to your brother then?"

She glowered at him and didn't answer. She knew that if she were hanged, her little brother wouldn't have a tiny sliver of a ghost of a chance of living to his next birthday.

2

JI WORKED IN silence, scrubbing dung, oiling leather, polishing buckles, and mending tassels. His back and neck throbbed, but that was nothing new. Bits of him had ached every day for the past three years, from hunching over boots.

"What're they having a house party for, anyway?" Sally asked.

"Who knows?"

"Fun, I guess," Sally said.

"Stupid fun," Ji muttered.

Sally snorted in agreement, though she actually liked fun—just not as much as she liked truth and justice. She should've been born a knight with a gleaming sword and spent her life riding into battle against the mountain ogres. Instead, she'd been born a servant.

After Sally's mothers disappeared from Primstone, she'd raised her little brother, Chibo, all by herself. She dreamed of becoming a squire, but shoveling horse manure every day didn't leave much time for battling monsters . . . though she wasn't afraid to fight. When the tapestry weavers dragged Chibo away last year, she'd tried to stop them with a pitchfork. They'd broken one of her arms and she'd barely even cried.

Ji took the dainty boots from his bag, and the stench filled the chimney. His eyes watered and he wanted to spit.

"What *is* that?" Sally asked.

"Swan poop."

"Gross."

"Look who's talking." Ji breathed through his mouth as he wiped the filthy boot. "You smell like horse manure."

"Horse manure doesn't stink."

"Only you think that."

Ji rubbed the leather with lavender oil until the stench faded. He picked the seams clean, then wiped and polished every surface. He rinsed and dried the laces, rethreaded them, and finally eyed the decorative bangles at the ankles.

"Hmmm," he said, jingling them with his fingertip.

"Uh-oh," Sally said.

"What?"

"Are they silver?" she asked. "I'm feeling conflicted again."

"They're not only silver," he said, feeling a spark of excitement. "They're *pure* silver."

"If they're worth that much, maybe you should leave them alone."

He jingled the bangles again. "Why?"

"Because, y'know . . ." She shrugged. "Stealing's a crime?"

"Who cares? With this much silver, we're done. We'll have enough to save Chibo!"

Sally tugged at her frizzy hair. She needed the money to buy her brother from the tapestry weavers before he died. That was what happened to kids who worked at the looms all day: if exhaustion didn't kill Chibo, the fumes would.

As the youngest of fourteen, Ji had always been the baby—until he'd met cheerful, impish, reckless seven-year-old Chibo. Finally, he'd felt like a big brother. Chibo was ten now, but he'd always seemed younger. Ji had taught him how to snag food from the kitchen and where to hide from Butler. He'd taught him how to play dice and tie knots and catch eels. He'd always wanted a little brother, and he'd finally had one—until the tapestry weavers dragged him away.

So Ji had started stealing boot ornaments to pay for Chibo's freedom.

"Nobles don't need fancy beads and buckles on their shoes," he'd told Sally. "They don't even care. They drag them through the mud."

"Stealing is wrong," she'd said.

"So is leaving Chibo to die at the looms."

"We can't steal stuff that doesn't belong to us!"

"We can't steal stuff that *does* belong to us," Ji had pointed out. "That's not stealing."

"You know what I mean!" She'd narrowed her eyes. "It's wrong, Ji. It's dishonorable."

"Honor's useless," he'd told her. "Just like boot beads."

She'd glowered at him. "What if they catch you? I won't let you hang, not for me and Chibo."

So Ji had told her the truth: "I'm not just doing it for you and Chibo."

"What are you talking about?"

"You know my brother Tomás?"

"Which one is he?"

"The oldest. Pa says I look just like him. He started as a tea boy and rose all the way to footman before he caught the fever. His lord and lady wouldn't let him rest, because they liked how he served soup. He got sicker and sicker . . . ." Ji scowled at the floor. "Until he died. So they hired a new footman. They replaced him like a worn heel. And in Tomás's whole life, he never did anything that mattered."

"Like what?" Sally asked.

"Like trying to save a friend, no matter what it takes. Or like . . . breaking free of all this."

"All what?"

"All the bowing and scraping," Ji said, his face suddenly hot. "All the stupid boots and stupid rules. Trying to help Chibo is the only worthwhile thing I've ever done, Sally. That's what I mean. I'm doing this for me. Because otherwise, I'll just live and die and never *matter*."

A tangle of silken cords bound the silver bangles to the dainty boots. "This is the most fashionable knot this season," Ji said, tugging at a loop.

"You'll never unravel that," Sally said.

"Want to bet?"

"Not without cutting through the—"

Ji flicked the untied cords. "Done."

"Whoa! Not bad."

"I'm a boot boy. I'm good with knots." He tossed the silver bangles to Sally. "Here. The first part of our crime spree is done."

She made a face but stood and pulled a stone from the fireplace wall. She tucked the bangles in a hollow niche packed with beads, ribbons, and even a tiny pearl. Those were Ji's *most* prized possessions.

Working fast, Ji tied a pair of cheap tin bangles from his box in place of the silver ones, copying the elaborate knot.

"You really think we have enough loot to save Chibo?"

Sally asked, shoving the stone back in place.

"I'm pretty sure."

"If we can find someone to buy it."

Ji finished the knot. "I heard you can sell anything in the city. In the rough neighborhoods."

"Because they're full of criminals."

"Right," he said.

"And we're bringing stolen stuff there," she continued, "which means *we're* criminals too."

"Only because we have to be."

"That's what all criminals think!"

Ji started packing the clean boots. "Yeah, but there's one big difference."

"What's that?"

"We're right."

"It's not funny, Ji."

He thought it was a *little* funny, but he kept that to himself. "So how do we get to the city?"

She glared at him. "We are *not* going to steal horses."

"Some of us can't even ride them." He kneaded his aching forearm. "But what I meant was, there's no way they'll give us a week off, to get there and back."

"We'll probably have to lie and cheat," she grumbled.

"And steal!" Ji said. "Don't forget stealing."

"Jerk," she said, and threw a candle stub at him.

So he tossed the swan-poop rag at her and fled.

3

JI SPENT THE next two days scrubbing dishes and sharpening knives until sunset, then cleaning boots past midnight. A snarl of pain settled between his shoulder blades, and his eyes felt gritty with exhaustion.

As he picked at a pebble jammed in a boot sole, he longed for the olden days. Roz said that centuries ago, before the first Summer Queen, every human had a *little* magic. Not much, just enough to keep a bonfire burning, keep a bouquet fresh—or keep a pair of boots clean.

But when the monstrous hordes attacked, those little tricks couldn't protect them. With humankind on the brink of extinction, the Summer Queen gathered all the human magic into herself. She defeated the monsters and saved humanity . . . but nobody had magic anymore, except for queens and kings and their chosen mages.

Which meant that bonfires died, bouquets wilted—and freshly polished boots were soon caked with thick, horrible mud.

On the second evening, Ji headed for a fancy corridor where the highest-ranking guests stayed. He tucked four pairs of boots into his bag, stifled a yawn, and heard voices in the curving stairway.

He stepped against the wall and lowered his head. That was what servants did when nobles came near. And in return, nobles ignored servants completely, like they were uncomfortable chairs or bad breath.

So Ji wasn't surprised when the nobles kept talking as they strolled along the hallway toward him. One was Baroness Primstone—Ji recognized the rubies on her house slippers. She was a tiny woman with a pile of braided hair that looked like a shoelace knot, except half of the Baroness's braids were painted gold every morning.

". . . young Brace is an *exceedingly* fortunate boy," she was saying. "We've shown him *every* kindness."

"I'm sure you have," the gentleman with her murmured.

"I'd never say this myself," Baroness Primstone said, "but I am *widely* known for my kindness, Proctor."

With his head still bowed, Ji inspected Proctor's soft-soled walking boots. Even from down the hall, he could tell that they'd been crafted by An-Hank Cordwainer, the finest boot maker in the city. He raised his gaze slightly and saw a hearty-looking gentleman with curly hair, a bushy beard, and twinkling eyes, wearing a green linen shirt and embroidered black trousers with a silken sash.

"Your generosity is the talk of the city, my lady," Proctor told the baroness, his voice faintly teasing. "And your kindness is a byword."

Ji almost laughed. Proctor was making fun of the baroness! Right to her face. He stayed silent, though. An undergardener had once giggled when the baron tripped on a tree root, and they'd tied him to the tree for three days as punishment.

"I've raised my nephew, Brace, like he was one of my own," the baroness explained, pausing in front of a painting of the first Summer Queen. "Although I am too humble to admit it, I am *far too good* to do anything less for my poor sister."

"If you were any farther good, my lady," Proctor said solemnly, "you'd make the angels jealous."

"I told my sister not to marry *that man*," the baroness sniffed. "He was beneath her."

"Brace's father was related to the third Summer Queen, was he not?"

Ji wrinkled his nose. He'd never heard that before: he mostly thought of Brace as a gawky noble kid who played strategy games and hid in closets.

"Only in the *lowest* branch of Her Majesty's family tree. Still, in the end, everything worked out."

"You mean after your sister and her husband died?"

"Precisely!" the baroness said with a bright smile. "That's when Brace came to live here, as a rather ill-mannered eight-year-old. At least his arrival brought good omens. Our desert lotus blossomed, which is an *excellent* portent. And what more could my nephew want than to live at Primstone Manor?"

His parents? Ji thought.

"His parents?" Proctor suggested. "Or he may want the crown."

A hush filled the hallway. The ache throbbed in Ji's back, but he didn't move. He barely breathed.

"The Summer Queen wears the crown," Baroness Primstone said, frowning at the painting on the wall beside her. "She always has, since my great-grandmother's time."

"And yet, for the past five years," Proctor told her, "she's held a Deedledum Rite every year. To choose an heir to her throne."

A *what?* Ji squinted at his sandals. A "Deedledum Rite"? That didn't sound like a way to choose the heir to anything bigger than a pigsty.

"So far, no candidate has passed the rite," Proctor continued. "Her Highness is now inviting another three young people with the proper ancestry."

"She's inviting *Brace?* But he's such a frail boy, and the Deedledum Rite is rather *dangerous*, is it not?"

17

"That is why I must get your permission to let him join me in the city."

The city! Ji felt his breath catch, his exhaustion forgotten. *He* needed to get to the city, to sell his loot. Maybe he could tag along with Brace. . . .

"I'm quite sorry." The baroness sighed. "But I'm afraid that is not possible."

"And why is that?" Proctor asked, a hint of steel in his mild voice.

"As I mentioned," the baroness said, "a desert lotus bloomed in the mausoleum when Brace arrived. That unlucky boy brought good luck to our household."

"The ogres are restless, my lady. There are rumblings from the mountains."

"The ogres? They are weak and feeble—a mere shadow of the threat they once posed."

"The realm needs an heir," Proctor told her. "And a Deedledum Rite is far more important than silly superstitions about lotus vines and blossoms—"

"My dear sir!" the baroness interrupted. "So long as that *blessed* flower blooms, Brace will remain here."

A vague discomfort filled the corridor, like a sliver of apple peel caught between your teeth. Ji peeked between his eyelashes at Proctor and watched his bearded face.

"Perhaps the bloom will suddenly die," Proctor said, his gaze flicking toward Ji. "Now that the queen needs Brace."

Ji flushed at Proctor's attention. Why was he looking at Ji? And what was he saying? That if the bloom suddenly died for no reason, Brace could leave Primstone?

"Perhaps it will shrivel in the next few days," Proctor continued with a wink at Ji. "And the young gentleman will be free to join me in the city."

Ji ducked his head at the wink and tried to melt into the wall. *In the city.* The words echoed in his mind despite his nervousness. If the lotus blossom died, Brace would join Proctor in the city. Which was exactly where Ji needed to go. He kept his eyes down and his mouth shut . . . and started to make a plan.

When Ji returned to the chimney, Sally was snoring softly. Sometimes, when she stayed the night, he'd hear her whimpering in her sleep. She'd say her brother's name, and *sorry* or *no!* or *please.* Either begging the tapestry weavers to release Chibo, or begging his forgiveness for not having saved him yet.

Ji sat at his workbench and thought about what he'd heard. And what he'd seen. There was no way that a fancy gentleman like Proctor had actually winked at a boot boy. No way. Ji must've imagined the wink . . . but he definitely hadn't imagined the conversation.

So he dropped a boot beside Sally's head.

"Bridle!" she yelped, sitting upright. Then she saw Ji. "Oh."

"I've got an idea."

She rubbed her eyes. "Not again."

"I know how to get to the city," he said. "I think."

"I was asleep," she grumbled.

"Because you're lazy."

"I start working at dawn!"

"Horses are even worse than boots," he told her. "I heard the baroness talking with a nobleman named Proctor. He wants to teach Brace—"

"*Master* Brace," Sally corrected sleepily. "And horses are not worse than boots."

"Of course they are. They bite."

"Not usually."

"And sneeze in your face." Ji tugged on the strap of his bag. "Anyway, this Proctor guy wants to bring *Master* Brace to the city. So we just need Brace to take us along."

Sally yawned. "You think he will?"

"Sure. I mean, we're almost friends." Ji half smiled, remembering. "I met him my first week at Primstone, before I even met you. I thought he was just some scared kid at the creek, hiding from the twins and playing with a toy catapult. So I built these twig houses and he launched pinecones at them."

"Mm," Sally said.

"Anyway, he'll need servants in the city," Ji told her. "That's where we come in."

"Mm," Sally repeated.

"You can groom his horses, and I can clean his boots." Ji rubbed the ache from his neck. "Only one problem. Did you ever hear Nosey and Pickle talking about the desert lotus flower that bloomed after Brace showed up?"

Sally didn't say anything. She didn't approve of Ji nick-naming nobles, not even ones as annoying as the Baron and Baroness's fifteen-year-old twins. But their names were Posey and Nichol, so Ji couldn't resist calling them Nosey and Pickle. Especially because Posey's nose was always stuck up in the air, and Nichol was as sour as brine.

"Fine," Ji grumbled. "Did you ever hear *Lady* Posey and *Lord* Nichol talking?"

Sally stayed quiet.

"The baroness thinks the flower is a sign of good luck," Ji told her. "She won't let Brace leave while it's blooming. Which means—"

Sally snored. Oh. She'd fallen asleep.

"Which means," he repeated, more softly, "that I've got to convince Brace to sneak through the goblin pen into the bone crypts—and kill that flower."

21

4

AFTER JI FINISHED cleaning the boots, he packed them in his boot bag and slunk through the scullery—and a bony hand grabbed his neck.

"Hey!" he said, trying to pull away. "You chuckle-knuckle!"

The hand pinched harder. "What did you call me, boy?" Butler's voice rasped from behind him.

"Oh," Ji mumbled. "Sorry."

"Leave the clean boots outside the guests' rooms, you laggard, then get to sleep."

"That's what I'm trying to do!"

"And none of your lip," Butler snapped. "You have a big day coming."

Ji lowered his head to hide his glare. "Yes, Butler."

"Help the kitchen maids before you start the boots tomorrow."

"Yes, Butler."

"And wash your face!" Butler grabbed Ji's hair in one hand and scoured his cheek with a rough cloth. "You're filthy."

Butler's breath smelled like pickled eels. His nostrils flared and his fist tightened in Ji's hair. Tears sprang to Ji's eyes, but he clamped his teeth and didn't make a sound.

"That's not dirt," Butler said, releasing him. "That's just *you*. Get moving! Lazy mutt."

Ji wiped his eyes and trudged toward the fourth floor, where poor relations and unwanted guests stayed. Stupid Butler. He rubbed his stinging cheek, exhaustion weighing him down like a pair of punishment shoes. He usually only worked twelve hours a day, but with this house party, it was more like sixteen. There were endless boots, and instead of doing laundry twice a month, they did it twice a week.

When he reached the fourth floor, he passed a painting of the long-dead Summer King. His Majesty stood above a crowd of half-human beasts with curved tusks and weird wings who knelt to serve him, monstrous heads bowed.

Ji considered the picture. Maybe Butler knocked him around a bit, but at least he didn't have tentacles. On the other hand, imagine how easy boot cleaning would be with a few tentacles.

His mood a little lighter, Ji tapped on a plain door at the end of the hall. A shuffling sounded and the dead bolt rattled, like the person inside was checking that it was locked.

"Master Brace?" Ji said, softly. "It's me, Jiyong."

"Ji?" Brace asked, a hitch in his voice.

"Yeah," Ji said. "I mean, yes, my lord."

"Are you alone? Is anyone else there?"

"Just me."

The bolt rattled again and the door opened an inch. One of Brace's blue eyes appeared, and he scanned the hallway behind Ji.

"Come in!" he blurted, when he didn't spot any threats. "Quickly."

Ji slipped inside. Compared to the chimney, Brace's bedroom was airy and luxurious, with a bed, a dresser, and even a window. But for a member of a noble family, it was cramped and dingy.

Brace locked the door behind Ji. "Whew."

"Are the twins picking on you again?" Ji asked.

"None of your business!" Brace snapped.

"Sorry, m'lord," Ji said, bowing his head. Because showing disrespect to your betters could get you whipped.

Brace chewed his knuckle and probably would've said *sorry*, if nobles were allowed to apologize to servants. Instead he just stood there, nervous as a newborn colt on a frozen pond. His long face, sharp chin, and bony shoulders looked horsey, too—but for some reason, the chambermaids all thought he was handsome.

"Um . . ." Brace gestured toward his bed. "I'm fighting the Siege of Mount Atra."

Which was as close as he could come to apologizing to a servant. Ji eyed the bed, where toy knights and soldiers were positioned on blanket-mound hillsides, surrounding a few strips of leather that represented ogres.

"Looks like you won," he told Brace, which was as close as he could come to saying *apology accepted.*

"Nah," Brace said. "I can't take the caves."

Ji frowned at the toy battle. "What caves?"

"They're underground." Brace lifted a blanket to reveal more strips of leather. "I can't flush them out."

"Send your troops after them."

"I tried that. I don't mind sacrificing knights as long as I *win*. But I lost them all for nothing."

Ji considered the bed. "The mountains are snowy, right? What if your guys melt the snow and flood the caves?"

"Huh." Brace's eyes gleamed. "That might actually work."

Ji used to sneak into Brace's room every few days, to reenact skirmishes with him, using toy soldiers. Mostly for fun, but also because he felt sorry for Brace. Which was stupid. A boot boy feeling sorry for a noble was like an earthworm feeling sorry for a hawk. Still, Brace was so scrawny and meek that Ji felt like he needed to stick up for him—and befriend him, as much as a servant could.

Plus, Ji liked playing strategy games and reenacting battles.

They'd almost become actual friends, until Butler caught Ji slinking into Brace's room. Nobody cared that he'd been invited: Butler belted him for not knowing his place. Brace didn't get off unpunished, either. Baron Primstone had given his favorite horse, the only thing his parents had left him, to the twins. And in the past two months, Brace had been afraid to even look at Ji.

"You shouldn't be here," Brace said, probably remembering his lost horse.

"If anyone asks, I just came for these." Ji grabbed a pair of boots from the floor. "So, uh, do you know Proctor?"

"I've met him," Brace said. "He's the reason for all these guests."

"He is?"

"Yeah, they're having a party so nobody will realize that Proctor's here on palace business. A proctor is a sort of fancy teacher. I guess he came for the twins. Everyone wants their kids to be taught by a proctor instead of an ordinary tutor. That's how you get closer to the queen."

"He didn't come for the twins," Ji told Brace. "He came for you."

Brace gaped at him. "For me? No way."

"I heard the whole thing!"

Suspicion flickered in Brace's eyes. "Did the twins tell you to say that, just so they can laugh at me for believing it?"

"Do you really think I'd do that?" Ji asked.

"Well . . . no." A gleam of hope replaced Brace's suspicion. "So it's true?"

"Yep. I heard Proctor talking to the baroness."

"Whoa. He's going to train *me*? Why?"

"Uh, for the 'deedledum'? I'm not really sure."

"Who cares?" A smile curled at Brace's mouth. "Taught by a real proctor! I'll learn sword fighting and strategy and everything!"

"He wants to take you to the city, too."

"No way!"

"There's only one problem."

Brace's smile froze. "What? What problem?"

"The baroness won't let you go while the desert lotus vine's still blooming in the mausoleum."

"That dumb flower never brought *me* any luck."

Ji cleared his throat. "Um, there's one solution."

"What?"

"Sneak into the mausoleum and kill the flower."

Brace paled. "The mausoleum?"

"Yeah."

"By myself? Are you coming?"

"I can't! They'd hang me." Ji swallowed. "They'll hang any commoner they catch trespassing. Maybe the twins will go with you?"

"They'd rather throw me down a well!" Brace looked like he wanted to cry. "Lady Posey says they're going to lock me on the roof again."

Ji winced. A few months earlier, the twins had shoved Brace onto the roof after his bath. He'd been stuck there for hours before a chambermaid spotted him, naked and shivering. And a week later, they'd poured a barrel of lard over his head and shoved him onto a hill of ant lions.

"You'll have to convince them," Ji told him. "Or sneak through the bone crypt alone."

At the words "bone crypt," a sense of danger shivered in the air. Danger and dread, like that moment after a glass bowl topples off a shelf but before it hits the ground.

5

"I CAN'T!" BRACE flopped onto his bed, sending toy soldiers tumbling to the floor. "The bone crypt is crawling
with goblins."

For hundreds of years, every member of the Primstone
family had been buried beneath a mausoleum with three
marble walls. The fourth wall—a jade wall facing a serene
courtyard—was carved into curlicues, with gaps the size
of a man's fist. You could see through the latticework into
the mausoleum, where desert lotus vines twined around
hundreds of decorative burial urns . . . but you couldn't
enter. There was no doorway in the jade wall, because it
symbolized the separation of the living and the dead.

The only way into the mausoleum was through a jade-
studded door in the rear wall, which opened into an

enclosed stone chamber. A flight of stairs in the chamber led downward into the bone crypt, a maze of tunnels where goblins lurked. Ji shuddered at the thought. Goblins had pale, wrinkly skin and teeth like beavers, strong enough to crack rock. They walked upright like humans, on two legs. But they had two pairs of arms: one short, muscular pair with bony shovel-claws and one spindly pair that sprouted from their bellies.

Noble families kept goblin slaves for digging cellars and ditches and burial chambers. A crypt in an old hacienda like Primstone branched into hundreds of tunnels, all tended by the goblins who lived in a pen on the grounds. Nobody human entered the crypt, except for priests during funerals.

If commoners set foot in the mausoleum—much less messed with the lotus vines—they'd be hanged for desecration. Things were different for nobles, though. They'd get punished, but not too badly. That was why Brace needed Nosey and Pickle to help him: the three of them together could brave the crypts.

"Yeah, but the twins want to explore the tunnels," Ji told Brace, crouching for the fallen toys. "Maybe they'll help for once."

"They pretend they want to explore, but even *they're* scared," Brace said, his voice trembling. "And we're not allowed. I—I wouldn't want to upset the baroness."

"Not even if it means getting trained in the city?"

Brace bit his lower lip. "I can't. I can't."

Ji grabbed the last toy soldier from the floor. He knew what he had to do, but he kept thinking about lightless tunnels and goblin eyes. About rotting corpses and bottomless pits. He set the toy on the bureau, then rubbed his neck, mostly to keep his hands from shaking.

"I'll go," he said.

"You will?"

Ji nodded, unable to speak.

"You mean . . ." Brace looked scared and hopeful at the same time. "You'll sneak through the crypts and kill the flower?"

Ji took a steadying breath. "Yeah."

"I—I can't go with you!" Brace blurted, then looked down for a second. "I mean, not because I'm afraid. Only I promised the baroness that I wouldn't misbehave, and I can't break my word. It's different for you. You're a commoner."

"That's okay." Ji didn't actually want Brace to come along, panicking at every shadow. He could do *that* all by himself. "I'll bring Sally."

"That frizzy-headed stable girl?"

"Yeah."

Brace fiddled with a toy soldier. "But why? Why risk it?"

"Because you and I are . . ." Ji shrugged. "We're sort of friends, aren't we?"

"Sort of, yeah."

"And because then Proctor will take you to the city. And when he does, I want you to bring me and Sally along."

Brace chewed his lower lip. "But there are *goblins* in the crypts."

"They're tame." At least, Ji hoped they were. "Probably."

"No. No, this is nuts. They'll hang you!"

"Only if they catch me."

"You're totally forbidden to go in there."

"Are you going to tell on me?"

"And miss my only chance to get trained? To leave Primstone Manor? No way." Brace chewed his lower lip. "You really think you're brave enough?"

"No," Ji admitted. "But Sally's brave enough for both of us."

"And in return," Brace said, "I'll bring you to the city?"

"Yeah."

"If you don't get eaten by goblins first," Brace said. "Or hanged."

Ji gulped. "So do we have a deal?"

"We do," Brace said, and stuck his hand out.

After his chores the next evening, Ji headed for the library, a horseshoe-shaped room packed with bookcases. Leather couches scattered the floor, flanked by low tables with ornate glass lanterns. Servants weren't allowed to enter, unless they were, well, serving: bringing drinks, dusting books, polishing shelves. Which was why Ji's heart hammered in fear every time he snuck in.

Still, he needed to snag a book for Roz. She loved books, for some reason. Maybe they were more fun if you knew how to read.

Ji slunk inside and eyed the shelves. He couldn't read the titles, so he ran his fingers across the spines. When he saw a book that looked good, he pulled it from the stacks. Roz had once told him, *You can't judge a book by its cover,* which just proved that even smart people said stupid things. Judging a book was what covers were *for.*

The first book smelled like pickled goat, so he shoved it back onto the shelf. The second was full of sketches of noses. Big noses, small noses, hairy noses, warty noses. Ji flipped through, looking for his own nose. He found But-ler's instead, a bony spigot with thin nostrils.

Ji started tucking the book into his bag, but stopped when he noticed that a few pages were torn. Forget that; Roz went berserk when people abused books.

He replaced the nose book, grabbed one with a leopard on the cover . . . and spotted a thick tome splayed open on an end table. Drawings covered the open pages—in *color,* which was amazing. Though the pictures themselves were horrible.

At the top of the page, a woman and a man stood beneath a leafless tree. A little lower, the woman hunched painfully and the man's face turned bright red. In the next picture, skinny arms burst from the woman's stomach, and fangs sprouted from the man's mouth. Below that, the drawings showed the couple turning into monsters: she looked like a half goblin and he looked like a half ogre. And at the bottom of the page, they slumped across the tree's roots, malformed and dead.

"Gross," Ji muttered.

What kind of freaky guest was reading this stuff? He turned away—and heard murmuring from the hallway.

His stomach twisted. Someone was coming!

He jammed the leopard book into his bag and ran to the library door. He didn't see anyone, but the chattering sounded louder. He trotted into the hallway—and a bunch of noble kids stampeded down the grand stairway.

Ji scuttled against the wall and bowed his head. The noise tumbled closer and Ji peeked toward the stairs and saw a gangly noble boy tossing a fluffy white doll over the head of a little girl.

"Give her back!" the girl sobbed.

An older girl caught the doll. "If you want her, come get her," she said, tossing the doll back to the boy.

The doll peeped, *Pwoh!*

It wasn't a doll. It was a fuzzy white kitten. They were throwing a *kitten* around. Anger pounded in Ji's temples. The ache in his shoulders faded, and he lifted his head. He shouldn't get involved—he *couldn't* get involved—but he also couldn't let them hurt a kitten.

He wanted to say something. He wanted to punch the

stupid gangly boy in his stupid gangly face. Instead, he unsnapped his bag. Once he dumped dirty boots on the floor, the noble boneheads would focus on beating him and leave the kitten alone.

But before he opened the flap, a new girl's voice said, "Stop teasing her."

The noble kids looked higher on the stairs, watching Nosey and Pickle descend from the landing, as petite and graceful as their mother. Three tendrils of gold-painted hair glinted among Nosey's ebony waves, and the dragon embroidered on her silken pants matched the one on Pickle's shirt.

Pickle extended his hand to the gangly boy. The boy gulped and handed the white fuzzball over.

"Shall we get her a saucer of cream?" Nosey asked, taking the crying girl's hand.

The girl whispered, "Yes, please, Lady Posey."

Nosey and Pickle led the girl away . . . and Ji got even angrier. Nosey and Pickle were horrible. They were *always* horrible. Cruel, selfish, and proud. They had no right to suddenly start acting kind, saving a kitten and helping a little girl. They should be horrible all the way through, so Ji could *enjoy* hating them.

He glowered at the floor. For once he didn't feel sore and tired. All he felt was bitter.

After the noble kids wandered away, Ji exhaled. Forget Nosey and Pickle. He still needed to learn about this

Deedledum Rite, just in case it mattered. He still needed to talk to Roz about the goblin pen, and learn how to sneak into the mausoleum. And he still needed to survive the bone crypts without getting eaten or hanged.

He crept toward the servants' door, rubbing his neck. Some days he felt like a tiny kitten in the hands of deranged giants. You never knew if they'd toss you downstairs or bring you a saucer of cream.

IN THE NURSERY on the top floor, Ji wove between rocking horses and toy chests. He tucked away his bitterness and headed for the door to the governess's room.

Governesses weren't quite servants, because they always came from wellborn families. But they weren't quite guests, because they came from wellborn *poor* families. Which meant they didn't fit in anywhere. They were the loneliest people Ji had ever seen.

And Roz wasn't even a governess. She was only a little older than Ji, the younger sister of the previous governess, who'd left for a new position when Nosey and Pickle had outgrown the nursery. Roz had wanted to go with her sister, but the new employer said no, so she'd had to stay at Primstone Manor.

"The baron and baroness are extremely kind to let me

stay," she'd once told Ji, with a brittle smile.

"I thought you hated when they . . ." He'd trailed off.

"Trot me out during fancy dinners," Roz asked, "and tell their guests that I'm a charity case? To make themselves feel generous?"

"Yeah, that."

"I do," Roz admitted. "But it's true. I *am* a charity case."

"You look after the little cousins when they visit," he'd said. "And anyway, what else are they going to do? Throw you out on the street?"

"Exactly," Roz had said, with a flash of fear in her eyes.

In some ways, the life of a girl like Roz was just as hard as Ji and Sally's. Sure, she didn't have to work that hard, but what would happen if they *did* throw her onto the street? She'd probably starve.

Ji stepped past a toy model of the Royal Menagerie— which was a fancy word for "zoo"—and tapped at the door.

"One moment!" Roz called from inside. "I'm just setting down a cup of hibiscus tea! Who is it, please?"

"It's Ji," he said. "And *I'm* just wondering why you told me what kind of tea you're drinking!"

Roz opened the door and smiled at him, and he felt himself smile back. Roz was pretty and kind and big for her age. The chambermaids called her "husky," and Pickle and Nosey called her "fat." She wasn't skinny like Nosey, but she was ten times cleverer and a hundred times sweeter and a thousand times *better*, and anyway, what was so good about being skinny? Everyone except nobles knew that being skinny just meant you didn't eat enough.

Stupid nobles.

"An evening visit!" Roz declared, stepping aside to let Ji enter. "Is this house party running you ragged? What brings you visiting so late?"

"What do you think?" Ji asked. "Boots, the same as every night."

"I don't own any boots."

"You don't own boots *yet*." Ji slouched into her brightly lit sitting room. "Maybe I'll sell you some."

"You're a scoundrel," she said, closing the door. "And a reprobate, but even *you* aren't going to sell me boots that you snaffled from downstairs."

"What's a reprobate?" Ji asked. At least he knew that "snaffled" meant "stole."

"A troublemaker."

"I never make trouble."

Roz lowered her voice. "Sally mentioned that you're *fixing* boots."

"Well, that's part of my job! I also untangle laces and daydream about drowning Butler in a vat of shoe polish."

"By 'fixing,' I mean stealing bangles and baubles." Roz made a snipping motion with two fingers. "Cutting off ribbons? Replacing pearls with pebbles?"

Ji felt a twinge of worry at Roz's reaction to his thieving. "Oh, er . . ."

"And you're planning to sell your ill-gotten gains in the city?"

"Well," Ji said, rubbing a twinge in his forearm. "Yeah?"

"That is very wrong of you," Roz said primly. "What are you thinking? Aren't you afraid? What if they catch you? . . . I'm so *very* glad you're doing it."

He blinked. "Wait, what?"

"You can't simply leave Chibo with the tapestry weavers," Roz told him, sitting at her tea table. "He won't survive long in those conditions. You're a good friend to him, Ji. And to Sally, too."

"Nah," he said. "I just need to do *something*, you know?"

"I do know." Roz patted the chair beside her. "But of all the possible somethings, you chose one that helps your friends. You think that buying Chibo's freedom is worth the risk."

Ji plopped onto the chair. "I know Chibo's a pest and all, but sure . . . freedom's worth anything."

"Even getting hanged?"

Ji felt his cheeks heating. "What else am I supposed to do?"

"You could do nothing," she said. "Like everyone else."

"Sounds boring. Like hibiscus tea."

"Hibiscus tea is delicious! And you're a good friend to me, too. You . . . retrieved another book, didn't you?"

"Of course I did!" he said, relieved by the change of topic. "I just snaffled it a few minutes ago, like a proper reprobate."

He'd started bringing Roz books three months earlier.

Before that, she'd been allowed into the library; then the baron realized that she knew more than Nosey and Pickle, and banned her, because "A governess's sister knowing more than my own children makes my skin crawl."

"You shouldn't sneak into the library," Roz told Ji, with mock severity. "What if someone sees you? What if you knock over a vase? What if there's a guest napping on a couch? What if you knock a vase onto a guest napping on a couch?"

"How else am I supposed to get books?"

"That's easy for you to say! What happens if they whip you? Imagine how bad *I'd* feel!" Her lips curved into a mischievous smile. "Especially if you bled on a book. Do you ever think of all the tears I'd cry if you ruined a page? It would ruin my whole entire day."

He snorted a laugh. "Not your whole entire day!"

"Possibly a full week! I really should get my own books, though." She smoothed her dress over her lap. "Except I'm not particularly well suited for sneaking."

"You just need a good pair of sneaking boots."

"I don't think my problem is footwear," she said.

"*All* my problems are footwear," he told her. "I like your slippers, though."

She wiggled her feet at him. She was wearing pointy-toed slippers with ribbons that looped around her ankles. "My sister sent them."

"You miss her, huh?"

"I do," Roz admitted.

A thought occurred to Ji. "You're kind of trapped here too, aren't you?"

"Perhaps. Still, if this is a trap, at least it's a comfortable one."

Ji wasn't sure how much that mattered, but he just looked at her slippers and said, "I like the stitch work."

"They're too small for me." Roz sighed. "Everything is too small for me."

"Is not," he muttered, and shoved the leopard book at her. "Here."

"Ha!" She beamed at the cover. "Now *this* fits me perfectly!"

Her smile reminded him of the sun coming out from behind clouds. Roz loved reading. Half the time, when he came to her door, she was curled in the chair beside a lantern, lost in the pages. She'd read him the story, or recite poems or recipes or riddles. And even though his life usually felt cramped and small, listening to Roz made it feel big and roomy and free.

"What's a Deedledum Rite?" he asked.

"The opposite of a deedledum left." She opened the book. "Or a tweedledum wrong?"

"I'm serious, Roz!"

She giggled. "Sorry. Where'd you hear it?"

"That visiting Proctor said—" Ji stopped at the look on Roz's face. "What?"

"Proctor's scary," she said with a shiver. "His eyes are

like black ice."

"He's not that bad," Ji said. "His boots are made by An-Hank Cordwainer."

"You can't judge a man by his boots."

Ji snorted. "You and your rules about judging. Anyway, I heard him talking to the baroness about training Brace."

"A proctor for Brace? That doesn't make sense. Unless . . ." Roz gazed at her bookshelf. "What kind of rite, did you say?"

"Deedledum."

"Diadem!" she said. "The Diadem Rite!"

"That's what I said!"

"*Die-uh-dem*," she repeated, more slowly.

"What's that?"

"A crown that looks like a metal headband."

"Weird. Crowns are supposed to be big and golden with jewels and stuff."

Roz tapped the book with a fingertip. "What do you know about the Summer Queen?"

"The same as everyone," Ji told her. "She's been around forever. She's the only thing that keeps the ogres and trolls and goblins from attacking."

"She hasn't been around forever. Her reign started less than two hundred years ago."

"Oh, is that all?"

"I mean, there were other kings and queens before her.

Royals live for hundreds of years, so she's not the first, and she won't be the last. The Diadem Rite is how the crown finds an heir."

Ji frowned. "So this rite chooses the next queen?"

"Or king, yes."

"Wait," Ji said. "Brace could become king? He can't even keep the twins from locking him on the roof."

"Well, the rite tests many candidates, so he probably won't be chosen." Roz frowned faintly. "This is unsettling news, Ji. A queen only calls a rite when she feels her power ebbing."

"What do you mean, 'ebbing'?"

"I mean, toward the end of her life. She summons noble children to the Diadem Rite every year until an heir is chosen. Then she trains her heir until . . ."

"Until she dies?"

Roz nodded. "At which point the heir takes the throne, wields the royal magic, and lives for hundreds of years."

"A servant's lucky to reach sixty," Ji said. "So the Summer Queen's reign is ending? That's kind of scary."

"We won't notice any changes. The new king or queen will take the crown and everything will stay exactly the same."

"Oh, that's good. I guess." He rubbed his neck. "Well, I hope Brace is chosen, but all I really care about is getting to the city."

"To sell your baubles to a 'fence'?" Roz said. "A loot merchant? A receiver of stolen goods?"

"Once I find one," he said. "Yeah."

"I would dearly love to visit the city. Ti-Lin-Su once lived there." She gestured to the books on the bedside table. "She's my favorite scholar. She's the leading authority on zozology."

"Zozology?"

"The study of nonhuman creatures."

"That's thrilling," Ji said, pretending to yawn. "The thing is, I made a deal with Brace. If I kill the desert lotus flower, he'll take me to the city."

Roz gaped at him. "You're going into the *mausoleum*?"

"Yeah."

"Past the *goblins*?"

"Yeah."

"When do we *go*?"

"What?" Ji gaped at her. "We what? What? We?"

Roz's eyes brightened. "I've always wanted to see a goblin crypt."

"Why?"

"The tunnels must be fascinating."

"They're holes in the ground!"

"Built by goblins."

"Yeah," he said. "That's not a good thing."

"Goblins are fascinating, too."

Ji scoffed. "Have you *seen* them?"

"I didn't say they were pretty," Roz said. "Just fascinating."

"No," Ji said.

"'No' what?"

"No, you can't come."

Roz shot him a governess-y look. "The crypts are a maze of dark, twisting tunnels. Once you get past the goblin pen and inside the crypts, how will you find the mausoleum?"

"Um, you'll tell me where to look," Ji said. "That doesn't mean you need to come with me."

"Well, I do know a thing or two about goblins—"

Ji exhaled in relief. "Perfect!"

"*However*," she continued, "if I don't join you, I can't help you. There's no map, Ji. Still, I'm halfway certain that I might possibly find the lotus vines if I come along."

"So you're halfway certain that it's almost possible?"

"Precisely," she said, and fixed him with her clever gaze. "And Ji? You're not the only one whose life is empty. You're not the only one who dreams of better things."

"Better things?" Ji swallowed the knot in his throat. "You mean like hibiscus tea with *honey*?"

"You know precisely what I mean," she said.

And he did. She wanted more than her cramped, airless life. She wanted more than meek obedience. Roz was coming to the crypts.

7

THE TRICK TO sneaking away from work was simple: you didn't *sneak*. You didn't hide, you didn't tiptoe. You did the opposite.

So at sunset on the next day, Ji marched into the kitchen, called friendly insults to a footman and a page, and headed for the "buffet." Lower servants like him ate leftovers from the upper servants' meals, which were leftovers from the nobles' table.

He took a bite of pickled radish and told a kitchen maid, "Yuck. Spicy."

She whacked his butt with a ladle. "Shut your teeth, boot boy."

"Tastes like bootlaces," he said, "with too much jalapeño."

The kitchen maid swung her ladle again, but Ji darted

past. He burst through the side door into the evening. As the maid shouted from inside, Ji grinned and ambled away. He felt taller outside the manor. It was as close to freedom as he got.

The autumn air smelled cool and flowery. The sunset glowed pink over the distant mountains, and a couple of the brighter moons already hung in the evening sky. A swarm of blue-bats, each the size of Ji's thumb, bumbled past his face. He waved them away and followed the scent of manure to the stable yard.

When Ji slunk past the burro stalls, two of the tough little donkeys eyed him suspiciously. He showed them his palms to prove he meant no harm, and one brayed like a bugle with a stuffy nose.

Ji rushed onward, trotting around the stables until he spotted Sally. She was smashing what looked like a scarecrow with the flat edge of a shovel. He didn't know why. Some kind of horse business, maybe. Horses were weird.

He frowned at the stable boys mucking out the stalls nearby, stepped behind a tree, and whispered Sally's name. She didn't hear him. He gave a low whistle, but she still didn't hear. He thought about laughing, because she'd told him that one of the burros freaked out whenever it heard laughter. But a crazed burro didn't sound like a great plan.

So he cupped his mouth. "Hoo! Hoo-hoo! Hooooo!"

"What are you doing?" Sally asked, from the other side of the tree.

"Ya!" Ji grabbed his chest to keep his heart from exploding. "You scared me!"

"I'm not the one making ghost noises."

"They're owl hoots!" Ji took a breath. "Come on, we're meeting at the Folly."

According to Roz, most noble haciendas had follies: scale models of ruined castles and citadels, about a quarter the size of the real things. The Folly at Primstone was a ruined pagoda, a six-sided tower with angled roofs. A cracked ramp rose to the front doors, and ivy climbed the crumbling walls, but on the inside, the pagoda contained an airy ballroom for costume parties and special occasions.

Smaller fake ruins dotted the parkland beyond the main Folly, built to look like battlements and towers and temples. The nobles used some for picnics, some for festivals, and some for romantic strolls.

But one of the ruins was different. One was part of the goblin pen.

When the baroness wanted to thrill her guests, she'd dress her goblins as mountain ogres and make them lurk in the towers and forts, even though goblins looked nothing like ogres. For one thing, goblins were only about Ji's size, while Brace said ogres were shaggy beasts that walked on two legs, with curved horns and tusks. Though according to Roz, some were more like scarlet-skinned humans, with pointy ears that jingled with rings.

Still, even goblins playing dress-up were enough to make the guests shriek. And Ji couldn't blame them. The sight of nonhuman eyes peering from the fake ruins gave him a chill every time he'd snuck away to see them. Usually, though, the goblins stayed in their pen inside a ruined temple near the bamboo garden, with their creepy faces and chisel teeth and wiggly belly-arms.

Ji shuddered as he followed the carriage path toward the Folly. "Maybe this is a bad idea."

"Don't be silly." Sally propped her shovel on her shoulder. "It's worse than bad."

"Why did you bring a shovel?"

"Because I couldn't find a battle-ax," she said. "You know, in case of goblins."

Ji groaned. "We're so dead."

"Are you scared?"

"Are you *not* scared?"

"Not enough to stop me," she said.

"That's the whole point of scared!" he told her. "To stop you from doing stupid things."

"Not me!" She gave her shovel a twirl. "Getting scared just makes me extra determined."

"We're so dead," Ji repeated.

"Stop worrying so much."

"We're so dead that skeletons look at us and think, wow, now *that's* dead."

Sally smiled in the light of the lanterns lining the path. "Where's Roz?"

"She's meeting us there," he said. "In the bony grave-yard of the extremely dead."

"I can't believe you let her come," Sally said.

"Roz knows more than you and me combined. How else are we going to find the mausoleum?"

"We could take prisoners," Sally suggested. "Like knights do in battles."

"We're not going to fight anyone, Sally. We probably won't even see the goblins. Roz will get us in and out without a whisper."

"I'll never become a squire if I don't fight anyone," Sally grumbled.

They headed past the trout ponds, then crossed a stone bridge with three little arches. After the carriage path curved through a stand of hydrangeas, the Folly rose overhead, a craggy pagoda that looked like a relic of a for-gotten time.

Ji barely noticed it. Instead, his gaze snagged on a light splotch in the dusk: a pale-pink gown. Because Roz was sitting on the steps, reading a book in the fading light, dressed for a fancy ball.

"What is she *wearing*?" Sally asked.

"That's her lucky dress."

"She's got a handbag!"

"That's her favorite bag."

"We're not having green tea and sweet rolls! We're crawling through underground crypts with hungry goblins trying to eat us!"

"At least you brought them a big spoon," he said, glancing at Sally's shovel.

"I wish it was a big knife."

Ji stopped in front of Roz. "Hey, Roz."

She didn't look up from her book.

"Roz!"

She jerked. "Oh! Sorry! This is Ti-Lin-Su's book about goblins. Well, mostly about them. There's a little about hobgoblins. Did you know they're small and furry, with foxlike tails? Or that bugbears migrate to snowcapped mountains? Oh! And ogre cubs aren't boys or girls!"

"Of course not," Sally said. "They're ogres."

"I mean they're not male or female," Roz said. "Not until they grow up. Then they choose which they want to be. And there's a chapter about dragons, too."

"I *love* dragons," Sally said, her eyes glinting.

"You're not going to slay a dragon," Ji told her.

"I might."

"Yeah? When?"

"When the time is right."

Ji shot her a dubious look. "With your shovel?"

"Dragons are old magic," Roz interrupted, leaning forward. "They're not huge, like in the stories: they're more like big water buffalo, except with tails longer than their bodies. And scales and claws and so on."

"Sounds pretty huge to me," Ji said.

"And they're the subject of what Ti-Lin-Su calls her 'outstanding question.' Why do dragons hoard treasure?"

"'Cause it's *treasure*?" Ji asked.

"Right," Sally said. "They could buy all kinds of swords and castles and stuff."

"They can't spend it!" Roz said. "They're dragons. So why collect it? Oh! And here's a sketch of what's either a sprite or an extremely glowy butterfly, with—"

"Roz!" Ji said, eyeing the sunset anxiously. "What did you learn about goblin tunnels?"

"Oh, right, yes. Goblins." Roz flipped a few pages. "During the wars, when the survival of humankind was hanging by a thread . . ." She peered at Ji and Sally. "Do you know the history?"

"Of course we do," Ji said, though he was fuzzy on the details.

"Not really," Sally said. "You mean back when everyone had magic?"

Roz nodded. "Before the first Summer Queen collected all the human magic into herself."

"What magic would you want?" Sally asked Ji. "A way to clean boots with a wave of your hand?"

"Nah," he said. "I'd just want to stop aching all the time."

"I'd want a sword that could cut through stone."

"That's too big," he told her. "People only had little magics."

"I'd want to be able to forget my favorite books," Roz said. "So I could read them again for the first time."

Ji gave a snort of laughter, but Sally said, "You know what I'd really want? To always know where Chibo was."

Nobody spoke for a minute. Then Ji said, "So, um, what's the history?"

"Many hundreds of years ago," Roz said, smoothing her dress, "the ogre hordes rampaged down from the mountains while the goblins swarmed up from the south. They clawed and killed and feasted, and drove the entire human nation into Summer Valley. Half of us died during the final battle, before the first Summer Queen turned the tide and defeated them."

"Yeah, yeah." Ji rubbed the back of his neck. "Get to the bone crypts."

"Oh! Didn't I say? During the war, human soldiers scouted the goblin burrows. Most were eaten, but a few returned. Goblins find humans delicious. We're like candy to them."

"Fascinating," Ji said faintly.

"I know!" Roz riffled through the pages of her book. "There are a few words of Goblish in here, and the word for 'human' is the same as the word for 'tasty'!"

"What's 'Goblish'?" Sally asked.

"Goblin language," Roz told her. "Like 'ka-shin' means

54

sister and 'sut' means rock and—oh, this one's neat! 'Kultultul' means goblin."

"'Goblin' means goblin," Sally said.

"They call themselves Kultultul," Roz explained. "Which also means the people."

"They can't be people," Sally said. "*We're* people."

"Who cares?" Ji looked to Roz. "Forget history. Do you know how to get to the mausoleum or not?"

Roz nodded slowly. "Yes. Probably. I think so. I'm not sure. Maybe?"

"I'm glad that's settled," he said. "Let's go."

8

FROM HIS HIDING spot in the bamboo garden, Ji eyed the ruined temple inside the sturdy fence of the goblin pen. Torches flickered in the dusk, and his breath caught when he saw the gate wide open beside a row of wheelbarrows. If the fence wasn't keeping the goblins in their pen, what was?

Then he saw motion near a rickety trough beside the temple. Two goblins wearing dingy collars stuffed food into their mouths with their spindly belly-arms, while a third hunched forward to join them. Watching goblins walk made Ji's stomach twist. Their legs bent in unexpected places. As far as he was concerned, two was a perfectly good number of knees.

Sally peered at the open gate. "Why don't they just leave?"

"And go where?" Roz asked. "They're a hundred leagues from the goblin lands, and they don't exactly blend in. If they escaped, they'd be caught in days."

"Let's distract them," Ji whispered, "then sneak in."

"That's cheating," Sally said.

"What do you think we should do?"

She wielded her shovel like a sword. "Vanquish them."

"*What*?"

"Vanquish means beat."

"I know what it means!" Ji said. "That's not the point!"

"We should face them in open combat." She nodded firmly. "That's the only honorable way."

"There are a hundred more of them inside the pen!"

"There are nine more," Roz said. "I checked the estate books this afternoon. There are exactly twelve goblins at Primstone."

"Even if there were only three," Ji said, "we couldn't chase them off."

"It can't hurt to try," Sally said, with a jab of her shovel.

"Actually, that's exactly what it could do," Ji told her. "Especially if they eat us."

"Better to lose with honor than win without."

"No!" Ji said. "No, it's not! Where do you get these doolally ideas?"

"That's not doolally, that's what all the squires think!"

"Then the next time you see all the squires, tell them I said they're doolally."

Sally lowered her shovel. "I hate sneaking around."

"Sneaking around is going to save your brother's life," he reminded her. "We'll sneak through the bone crypts and kill the flower. Then we'll get to the city, sell our loot, and free Chibo. Done."

"Fine," Sally said. "But how are you going to distract the goblins? Ghost noises?"

"They were *owl* noises!" Ji rubbed his shoulder. "Maybe we should . . . I don't know. Start a fire?"

Sally looked dubious. "A fire would attract too much attention."

"Roz could throw rocks."

"She does have a deadly arm," Sally said. "She throws like a catapult wearing a beaded handbag."

"Yeah, and then—" Ji stopped, as a pink shape drifted through the dusk light. "Roz!"

She'd left the cover of the bamboo garden and was walking openly toward the goblins, her pale dress impossible to miss in the light of the flickering torches.

"See?" Sally said, trotting after her. "Even *Roz* knows we should charge."

"She's not charging," Ji said. "She's strolling."

Then he swore under his breath and followed, his mind whirling with half-formed excuses. But what kind of excuse worked with a *goblin*?

Roz marched through the open gate into the pen. The three goblins at the trough turned, beady eyes narrowing and shoulder-arms pawing the air. Ji's throat shriveled in fear. He wanted to run away, but instead he trotted closer to Roz.

"Good evening," Roz said, stopping in front of the goblins. "My name is Rozario. I'm very pleased to meet you, and on such a lovely night! I do enjoy these autumn sunsets, don't you?"

Three sets of belly-arms waved; then a one-eyed goblin wearing a copper collar shuffled closer to Roz.

"Ka-lo," the goblin said in a gravelly voice. "Miss Kazario."

"And, uh, ka-lo to you, too." Roz curtsied, slightly unsteady. "W-what a nice home!"

"Not a home," the goblin said. "A pen."

"Oh!" Roz said, gulping. "Yes. I'm s-sorry."

The other goblins hunched forward, and Sally stepped beside Roz, looking small and fierce. Ji wanted to keep his distance, but he slunk to Roz's other side, suddenly wishing he had a shovel of his own.

"But underground, where you dig, is th-that more of a home?" Roz asked, her voice fake-bright. "I'm sure you burrow deep, all the way to the, um, secret heart of the earth, where only the bravest Kultultul dare to venture."

The one-eyed goblin made a coughing noise, and three more goblins shambled from the archway in the fake temple, their collars glinting in the torchlight.

Sally shifted her grip on her shovel and Ji got ready to grab Roz and drag her to safety. Maybe he wasn't good at battling evil, but he'd mastered the art of running away.

The one-eyed goblin didn't attack, though. It ground its teeth and said, "Than-ka you, Miss Ka-zario. Our tunnels are deep. You are polite. Very good ka-manners."

"Thank *you*," she said.

"And you loo-ka very tasty," the goblin continued.

"Hey!" Ji said, his hands clenching into fists. "Back off, beaver-face."

"Or we'll vanquish you," Sally growled, raising her shovel.

The goblins cringed, making pitiful barking sounds, and Roz stepped forward and told them, "I'm very sorry. My friends are sorry, too. They didn't mean to startle you." She shot a quick glare at Ji. "*Did* you?"

"Uh, what?" Ji said, squinting in confusion. "He said you're tasty."

The goblins peered at him nervously—like *they* were afraid of *him*—and a little one raised all four arms in surrender.

"That's a compliment!" Roz whispered to Ji. "Goblins like politeness and manners!"

"Manners? *Them?*"

"That's what I read in the book," she told him. "That's my plan."

He gaped at her. Her plan was to ask *politely*?

"Now apologize properly!" she said, giving him an un-Roz-like glare.

"I—I didn't mean to startle you," Ji told the goblins, with a tentative bow. "I'm very sorry. I beg your pardon. Please excuse me?"

After a moment, the little goblin lowered its hands, and Roz smiled at the one-eyed goblin. "You are polite, too," she said.

"Very good ka-manners," Ji said, trying to help.

The goblin bared its front teeth—and in a flash of panic, Ji thought that it was about to gnaw his eyeballs out. But the goblin didn't attack. Instead it sort of cocked its head, and a different explanation occurred to him.

Maybe that was a goblin *smile.*

So he bared his own front teeth, and the goblins made another barking sound, a happier one. They were laughing! He snapped his teeth tentatively, and they woofled again. Which didn't sound polite to Ji, mocking his tiny human teeth . . . but it was better than eyeball gnawing.

"We wonder," Roz told the possibly smiling goblins, "if you'd be so kind as to let us into your burrow. We would be very grateful."

The goblins stopped woofling and started muttering to one another in Goblish. One of them shook its head. Another waved its belly-arms. It looked like they were arguing about what to do with Ji and the others. Let them into the burrow, or cook them in a creamy worm sauce?

"Ka-vel?" the one-eyed goblin asked Sally, as the muttering continued.

"Hello, Kavel," Sally said, and bowed stiffly. "I'm Sally."

The goblin chuffed. "Beg sorry. I mean, why you are holding a ka-shovel?"

"Oh, this?" She propped the shovel onto her shoulder. "Yeah, well, um, the truth is that I was pla—"

Ji's heart clenched: she was going to say, *I was planning to club goblins with it.* "She loves to dig!" he blurted. "She's a massive fan of diggery. Tunnels, burrows, lairs, dens. There's nothing Sally loves more than a hole in the ground. And that's why we came, to see your digging. Nobody digs better than, uh, Kultultul, right?"

"Kultultul," the goblin agreed.

"Sally is eager to see what you've done," Roz told it. "Isn't that so, Sally?"

Sally frowned, unwilling to lie. "Well, that's not the main reason—"

"You want to get inside, though, right?" Ji interrupted.

"That's true!" Sally said. "I do want to get inside."

The one-eyed goblin turned to the others and chuffed in Goblish. After a few final woofles, the other goblins waved their belly-arms toward the entrance to the fake ruined temple, inviting Ji, Roz, and Sally to enter. A bubble of triumph expanded in Ji's chest: they'd done it! They were heading into the bone crypts!

Then the bubble popped.

They were heading into the *bone crypts*. That was a terrible idea!

But Sally was already marching into the temple, her shoulders square and her chin high. Stupid bravery. And Roz strolled along behind her, skirt swishing, saying "please" and "thank you" a hundred times.

ON THE INSIDE, the "ruined temple" didn't look at all temple-y. Instead, the stone walls enclosed one big room with a dirt floor and a scattering of fire pits.

A single bonfire flickered, casting a feeble glow on rough-hewn statues of three-beaked birds and knotted pythons. A dozen square nooks were carved into the walls: one contained a heap of eggshells, another overflowed with moss, and a third displayed a single clothespin.

Ji's fear faded into curiosity. Why display a clothespin? Roz was right. This *was* fascinating. In a nonhuman way that brought prickles of unease to his skin.

"Good evening." Roz curtsied to the goblins squatting around the bonfire. "What a lovely blaze. So bright, so cheery!"

The goblins watched her with narrowed, beady eyes.

"And we're very pleased to meet you," Roz said, a hitch in her voice. "Such a treat. Isn't that right, Ji?"

"Very pleased." Ji looked away from a nook packed with butterfly wings. "A very, um, pleasant pleasure to meet you."

"What's that?" Sally nodded toward an earthen ramp that disappeared underground at the far end of the room. "The entrance to the crypts?"

"Bone ka-rypts," one of the goblins said.

"Precisely!" Roz said, with a wavering smile. "And those, um, displays in the walls? Are they shrines?"

"Shrines," another goblin said, with a beaver-faced nod.

"Well, I must say," Roz told the goblins, "they are quite entirely beautiful. . . ."

As she complimented the goblins, Ji tried to think of clever ways to get into the bone crypts. The right combination of lying and bowing might work. Or maybe—

Sally pulled a torch from the wall. "Let's do this."

Two goblins hunched in alarm and gnashed their over-sized teeth. "Humans ka-eep out," one said. "Not go in ka-rypts."

"We don't have a choice," Sally told them. "Follow me, Roz. C'mon, Ji."

Five more goblins crept between Sally and the ramp. She tightened her grip on the shovel, and Ji's heart shriveled in fear.

Roz smiled weakly at the goblins. "We'd be so grateful

if you'd let us explore just a tiny bit."

The five goblins shifted, clenching their digging claws . . . then the one-eyed goblin barked what sounded like a command. The other goblins hesitated, their shoulder-arms tense and their beady eyes narrow.

"The baron told us to go into the crypts," Ji told them. "He's the reason we're here. He even said 'please.'"

The one-eyed goblin spread all four arms and woofled in urgent Goblish, like it was trying to convince the others not to fight.

Ji didn't know if his lies were helping, but he kept lying, just in case. "The baron even said 'pretty please,' now that I think about it, with a Primstone on top. . . ."

The one-eyed goblin gestured to a smaller goblin, who turned and ran outside. Ji had no idea why. But a moment later the other goblins lowered their arms and unclenched their claws.

"Let's go," Sally said, striding onto the ramp.

The goblins grunted but didn't stop her. Ji exhaled and headed down the ramp with Roz. An upwelling of damp air brushed his face, perfumed with a sweet, sugary scent, and they left the big dirt-floored room behind.

The sugary smell grew stronger as the ramp opened into a chamber with tunnels heading in five directions. The yellow flicker of Sally's torch shone on scrape marks— from teeth or claws—that swooped across the walls and ceiling. Most of the marks were packed with dried flowers and grasses, which created colorful swirling patterns.

It was wild and beautiful and strange. Part of Ji wanted to decorate the chimney the same way, but another part kept thinking, *Goblin teeth are strong enough to carve rock—imagine what they'd do to human flesh.*

Roz nodded toward the second largest of the five tunnels. "The mausoleum is that way."

"How can you tell?" Sally asked.

"It's the right size for humans."

Sally pointed her torch toward a tunnel with dizzying flower-and-grass-filled grooves. "What about this big one?"

"Not with all the . . . decoration," Roz said. "I doubt that priests appreciate goblin art."

A faint *scritch-scritch-scritch* sounded from one of the tunnels.

"W-what is that?" Ji stammered.

"Probably nothing," Roz said, pressing her hand to her throat.

"It doesn't sound like nothing," he said. "It sounds like claws."

"Knights always face their enemies head-on," Sally said, and stalked into the second-largest tunnel with her torch in one hand and her shovel in the other.

"You're not a knight!" Ji said. "You're not even a squire."

"C'mon!" she called, over her shoulder. "We have to stick together."

"Yeah, like a shish kebab," Ji muttered. "So they can eat us all once."

"Is that worse than being eaten separately?" Roz asked, and took Ji's hand. "I don't think they'll eat us. It'd be quite rude, now that they know our names."

The tunnel angled down into the gloom, past jade torch holders fixed to thick wooden beams. The sugary scent faded as the air grew damper, and Ji tried to make himself take slow, calming breaths.

When that didn't work, he tried to make himself stop imagining the ceiling caving in.

That didn't work, either.

The tunnel ended at a flight of stone stairs that plunged into pitch-blackness. "I—I wonder how deep this goes," Sally said.

"Miles," Roz said, her voice thin. "Lightless miles underground."

A wave of fear made Ji dizzy. He tried to gather his courage, but the chill air seeping from the stairwell raised goose bumps on his aching arms. What if they died down here? What if goblins thought humans tasted better *with* names? What if someone caught them and they hanged?

Then he exhaled. Forget brave. Brave didn't matter. He knew what mattered.

"If we turn back," he said, "we'll never see Chibo again."

For a dozen heartbeats, nobody spoke. The light from Sally's torch brushed the stone stairs with a feeble glow—then faded into shadows.

"For Chibo," Sally said.

"For Chibo," Roz repeated, and her musical voice lightened the gloom.

Sally swallowed a few times, then tromped down the stairs.

Ji followed a little less briskly. His breath sounded harsh in his ears and his sandals scraped the steps. For Chibo. To buy his freedom, to save his life. And because if Ji didn't do this, he'd end up like his oldest brother, Tomás, disappearing without a trace. Like the tiny bluebats that swarmed and swirled and died in a single week.

The stairs finally ended in a circular room with a stone table and rows of glass bottles. Racks of ceramic jars stood in the shadows against one wall, and spiky tools lined a polished marble rack.

Ji grabbed a torch from the corner. "What is this place?"

"It's where they prepare bodies for burial," Roz whispered.

"Why are you whispering?" Sally whispered.

"I don't know," Roz whispered.

"Well, it's freaking me out," Ji whispered, lighting his torch from Sally's.

"After a noble is buried, the priests bring an urn to the mausoleum, to represent the person's memory." Roz pointed toward a second flight of stairs, on the other side of the circular room. "Up there. For souls to rise as high as possible, the bodies are buried as low as possible. That's how it works."

"How what works?" Sally asked.

"Magic," Roz said.

Ji started toward the second flight of stairs. He didn't care about magic; he just wanted to kill the lotus flower and return to his chimney before the goblins slathered him with salsa and started chewing.

"Magic always balances out," Roz explained, as Ji climbed the steps.

Sally's voice drifted up behind him. "Like scales?"

"Yes," Roz said. "If you strengthen one person, you weaken another. If you become more alive, someone else becomes less alive."

"There's no such thing as 'less alive,'" Sally said. "There's just dead."

"If you brighten the path ahead," Roz continued, "you darken the one behind." Her breath grew ragged as she climbed. "And if the bodies are buried deep, the souls rise high."

Ji climbed until his legs burned. The ever-present ache between his shoulders throbbed with his heartbeat. He heard nothing but the rasp of his breath, saw nothing but the glow of his torch.

Then he caught a whiff of fresh air. Almost to the top!

When he reached a wide landing with a jade-studded door, he sprawled to the floor. He gasped for breath until

Sally and Roz flopped down beside him, then forced himself to his feet.

"The mausoleum's through here?" he asked, staggering to the door.

Roz nodded, too winded to speak.

"Then watch out, lotus blossom," Ji said. "Because here I come."

The door swung open, and Ji blinked into the moonslit mausoleum. A jasmine-scented breeze wafted through the holes in the jade wall, which looked like black lace in the gloom. Dozens of urns hung from chains, while others rested on pedestals—all of them twined in desert lotus vine.

Ji shivered in the fresh air, listening to night birds sing. He suddenly felt wrong. Like he shouldn't have come. Like he was trespassing on sacred ground.

"Stay there," he told Sally and Roz, his voice low. "We shouldn't *all* get cursed."

10

WHEN JI CREPT forward, the leaves carpeting the floor crunched underfoot. The braided stems of desert lotus curled around the urns and shivered in the faint breeze. A dozen flowers bloomed, each of them bringing—according to the baroness—a different blessing. Roz said it was just superstition, because the blossoms looked like dragon heads, but that didn't exactly calm Ji's nerves.

He slipped between two urns and found the blossom that the baroness said had bloomed when Brace came to the manor . . . and the night birds fell silent.

Like they'd heard something.

Ji's blood turned to ice. Was someone there? Was something watching? He stared into the darkness beyond the jade wall. The only sound was the chirp of a cricket. After a moment, he put his hand on the lotus blossom.

The vine trembled, and Ji whispered, "Sorry."

He plucked the petals and let them fall to the ground. He checked that he hadn't missed any . . . and heard voices from the courtyard beyond the jade wall.

A goblin was saying, ". . . is a child in the ka-rypts. It ka-ame to the pen, yes, very polite."

It was the small goblin that the one-eyed goblin had sent away! A noose of fear tightened around Ji's neck. *Why?* Why would the goblins tell on them? And who would they tell? Clumsy with dread, he backed into an urn and almost fainted at the *clink-scrape* as it shifted.

"Which child, you filthy gob?" Butler's voice snapped.

With his heart thrashing like a mermaid's tail, Ji scrambled through the shadows toward the jade-studded door.

"A human child," the goblin said. "All loo-ka the same."

The glow of lanterns seeped through the jade wall. Dropping to his hands and knees, Ji crawled toward the door, his vision narrowing into a terrified tunnel.

"If he got this far," Butler said, "he'll hang for desecrating the dead."

"Dese-ka-rating," the goblin agreed.

The light grew brighter, and Ji lunged through the jade-studded door.

"What hap—" Sally started.

"Shhh!" Ji hissed, closing the door. "Butler's here. The goblins told on us."

"That little one that ran off?" Sally snarled.

Ji nodded, and Roz pressed her hand to her chest. "Did he see you?"

"I don't think so."

"Thank summer," she breathed.

Sally frowned. "Is the flower dead?"

"Yeah." Ji brushed past her. "And if Butler catches us, so are we."

He raced down the stairs, his heart galloping and his sandals slapping. Behind him, Sally urged Roz to move faster, but he didn't wait for them. If he reached the goblin pen first, he'd trick Butler or distract him. Heck, he'd make ghost noises if he had to.

He ran across the circular burial preparation chamber. He dashed up the first few steps that led back toward the pen. He trotted up the next few steps. Then he trudged painfully higher, his lungs burning and his thighs aching.

Finally, he dragged himself to the top of the stairs and stumbled to the chamber with the five tunnels. He staggered to the ramp that led into the "ruined temple"—and a hand grabbed his arm.

"Ai!" he squawked, his fear of goblin claws sharpening into panic. "No!"

"Yes," Butler said, standing over him.

"Oh! Um! Butler! Hi?"

Butler shook him fiercely. "You're in trouble now, boy."

The ache in Ji's shoulders turned into a burn. Tears

sprang to his eyes. "I—I'm not—I'm only exploring! I didn't do anything!"

"And the lotus flower?" Butler's nostrils flared. "The one that bloomed when Master Brace arrived just happened to die tonight?"

"The—the what? Did what?"

Butler dragged Ji up the ramp toward the temple. "Where's the stable girl?"

"I'm alone!" Ji shouted, loud enough to warn Sally and Roz. "There's nobody else! I'm sorry, Butler! I didn't do anything, I promise—"

"You entered the mausoleum."

"I stopped at the stairs." Ji swallowed a lump in his throat. "I got scared and came back."

"You'll hang for this, boot boy."

"I didn't do anything," he sniffled, trying to make himself sound even more pathetic than he felt.

"You're lying to me."

"It's the truth," Ji lied. "I swear."

Butler shoved him across the big room with the bonfire. Ji fell on the dirt floor, and pebbles stung his palms. He blinked his wet eyes toward the goblins shuffling against the rough-hewn walls. They woofled nervously and looked at the ground, like they were afraid of Butler. Ji knew exactly how they felt.

"You lying peasant," Butler said, and kicked him in the side.

"Please!" Ji curled into a ball on the ground. "Please, don't tell anyone! Don't turn me in!"

"You insulted the Primstone family."

"I didn't mean to—"

Butler kicked him again. "You dragged your filthy self onto sacred ground."

"I—I only went to the stairs. I never—"

Butler drew back his foot to kick Ji again, and Sally shouted, "Get away from him!"

Ji groaned. Why hadn't Sally stayed hidden? Now that Butler knew Ji lied about being alone, he wouldn't believe *anything.*

Sally climbed into the big room, brandishing her shovel. "You should be ashamed! Kicking him while he's down."

Ji appreciated that, though he didn't see what was better about being kicked while he was up, to tell the truth.

"You're still standing, stable girl," Butler said, his thin lips drawing downward. "Maybe I'll kick *you* instead."

"Just—" She raised her shovel, her eyes wild. "Leave us alone."

"You're a shiftless little vandal like your mothers."

With a howl, Sally swung the shovel at Butler—but his bony arm swept out and slapped it from her hands. The shovel blade hit the ground with a ringing clang, and Butler boxed Sally's ears. She reeled. He knocked her around a little, but Ji didn't watch. He was too busy staring at a faint pink dress barely visible at the top of the ramp, mouthing "No!" and shaking his head fiercely.

The last thing he needed was for Butler to discover Roz, too. Then he and Sally would be in even worse trouble—if that was possible—for corrupting the morals of a young lady. When the pink dress disappeared back down the ramp, Ji almost sighed in relief.

Except Butler was still shaking Sally and saying, "You'll both dangle from the gallows. We'll bring a picnic and watch you hang."

Ji pushed to his knees. "Butler, sir! I need to tell you—"

"What?" Butler snapped, turning to him. "More lies?"

"Sally didn't do anything. I did what you said, but Sally didn't do anything wrong."

Butler's nostrils flared again. "She didn't, did she?"

"No, sir."

"Other than try to hit me with a shovel."

"Well, yeah. Other'n that." Ji rose painfully to his feet. "She just came along because I was scared of the crypt. She didn't go where she's not allowed."

"So you admit that *you* went into the mausoleum?"

Ji swallowed. "Yes, sir."

"So you're the only one who needs hanging," Butler said.

"Yes, sir," Ji repeated.

"Ji!" Sally peeked at him from between her arms, which she'd raised to protect her face from Butler's blows. "Shut your ricehole!"

"No, I have to tell him the whole truth this time," Ji told Sally, trying to calculate exactly how little truth he needed to admit.

He'd claim that Brace gave him permission to sneak through the crypts and inspect the flower, to check how healthy it looked. But he found it dead and ran away in a panic. Yeah, that way he might get off with just a whipping.

As long as Brace backed him up. Which he would. They'd spent months together, playing with toy soldiers, reenacting battles, and killing ogres. They were almost friends. Brace definitely wouldn't let him hang for this. Well, probably not. Well, *maybe* not. . . .

Still, it was his only hope. So Ji took a breath and told Butler, "The truth is, um, that I snuck in to look at the flower. But I didn't touch it! And I had permission."

"You did, did you?" Butler asked, his nostrils narrowing angrily.

Before Ji could answer, a figure stepped inside the pen. The bonfire flared, and the goblins dropped to their knees, belly-arms folded and heads bowed.

The figure peered toward Ji. "Is that the young gentleman?"

11

BEADS OF NERVOUS sweat trickled down Ji's forehead. He looked toward the figure—and saw a familiar pair of walking boots, crafted by An-Hank Cordwainer. Oh, boy. What was Proctor doing here? Had things just gone from bad to worse? Or from completely terrible to unspeakably awful?

Proctor considered Ji, his eyes twinkling. "Surely this is not Master Brace."

"This?" Butler cuffed Ji's head. "This isn't anyone, my lord."

"There I must disagree with you," Proctor told him. "Without our boot boys, the entire realm would find itself sadly unpolished. However, I was expecting Master Brace."

"Here? I beg your pardon, my lord . . . I'm afraid I don't understand."

Proctor stroked his bushy beard and looked toward the wall shrines above the kneeling goblins, who watched with frightened eyes. He chuckled and strolled closer. Nobody spoke. Nobody moved. A silence fell, broken only by the crackle of the fire.

Oh, and the terrified pounding of Ji's heart, which was beating loudly enough to make a scarecrow wet his pants.

When Proctor plucked the clothespin from its nook, the goblins chuffed mournfully, shoulders drooping. Probably horrified by his rudeness. For all Ji knew, clothespins were sacred to them, and they worshipped laundry lines.

"And why," Proctor asked Butler, "are you here?"

"I heard that a servant was trespassing in the bone crypts, m'lord. We take violations very seriously at Primstone Manor."

"As well you should." Proctor gestured toward Ji and Sally. "And what are the names of our two miscreants?"

"This one is Jiyong," Butler said, cuffing Ji's head again. "He admits that he entered the mausoleum."

"And is he aware of the punishment?"

"He is," Butler said.

Proctor ambled closer and inspected Ji with a razor intensity.

The blood rushed to Ji's cheeks. He couldn't remember why he'd ever thought that Proctor looked friendly. Roz was right about his eyes: black and icy. Ji looked down, biting the inside of his cheek. The stitchery on Proctor's boots was neat, and the toe cap was embossed with a delicate design.

Finally, the boots moved away and Proctor asked, "And the girl with the . . . enthusiastic hair?"

"She's the daughter of petty criminals," Butler told him. "Dishonest servants who fled upon discovery of their crime."

Uh-oh. Sally didn't react well when people talked about her mothers like that. Ji raised his head to stare at Sally, like his gaze could keep her from vanquishing Butler directly in the nose bone. But she didn't notice, because she was too busy glaring.

"And what dark crime was that?" Proctor asked Butler.

"They stole valuables from the manor."

"They took an old tablecloth," Sally snapped.

"They purloined linen," Butler said.

Sally's eyes narrowed. "To make diapers!"

"Stolen from the charity bin," Butler said. "Which her ladyship had very generously set aside for the deserving poor."

"You were going to hang them," Sally said. "For a worn tablecloth."

"Not for a cloth," Butler said. "For a crime."

"*Quiet*," Proctor snapped, and quiet loped into the pen and sat at his feet like a loyal hound. The goblins stopped woofling, and even the fire settled down. After a moment, Proctor turned to Ji. "You are a boot boy. You clean, you stitch, you scrub."

"Yes, m'lord," Ji said.

"And you were in the corridor when I spoke with the baroness."

Ji hesitated for a heartbeat. "Yes, m'lord."

"You overheard us talking."

"Yes, m'lord."

"Curious as a monkey. What happened next? You told Master Brace that he couldn't study with me if the lotus blossom still bloomed?"

"Yes, m'lord."

"So you tiptoed into the mausoleum to pluck it for him." Proctor scratched his beard with the clothespin he'd taken from the goblin shrine. "Why didn't he come himself?"

"I—" Ji swallowed. "I don't know."

"Is he a coward?" Proctor asked, his eyes twinkling dangerously.

"No! No, my lord. Um, Master Brace wouldn't disobey the baroness, that's all. He's too honest. And honorable. So I came instead. As his, um, y'know . . ."

"Squire," Sally said.

"Servant," Ji said.

"Is that so?" Proctor pointed the clothespin toward the ramp. "And who, pray tell, is the other girl?"

"What other girl?" Ji asked, keeping his eyes on Proctor

and not even *thinking* about Roz. "Other girl? There's no other girl. Where? Girl?"

"The one lurking in the dark like a timid shadow." Proctor turned toward the ramp. "Come out, my child! Show yourself!"

For a second, nothing happened. Then a pink shape appeared from the darkness . . . and Roz stepped into the light of the bonfire, her cheeks flushed but her back straight.

"I believe you are a guest at Primstone Manor?" she asked Proctor, her voice barely trembling. "I am Miss Rozario Songarza, and while I regret that I haven't yet—"

"Very polite," one goblin woofled. "Eka-cellent manners."

"While I regret," she repeated, crossing toward Proctor, "not having been introduced before this awkward encounter, I am pleased to finally make your acquaintance."

Proctor eyed her with amusement; then his merry gaze flicked to Ji. "You dishonest little dissembler! You claimed there *was* no other girl."

"Yes, m'lord, sir, you see, um . . ." Ji cleared his throat. "There isn't."

"You gormless idiot," Butler muttered.

"Miss Roz isn't a girl," Ji explained to Proctor. "She's a young lady."

Proctor's laughter echoed in the big dirt-floored room. "Oh, you're a fine young liar!" He turned to Roz. "I'm pleased to meet you as well, Miss Roz."

"Thank you, m'lord," she said, with a quick curtsy. "I wonder if—"

"And now"—Proctor drew a dagger from a sheath hidden in his sleeve—"to business."

"M-m'lord?" Butler stammered, eyeing the blade.

Proctor whittled a strip of wood off the clothespin. It fell to the ground, a skinny curl on the dirt. "The boot boy eavesdropped on my conversation," he told Butler, "when I was speaking about the desert lotus."

"That was wrong of him, my lord."

"Then he repeated it to Master Brace."

"And he will be punished."

"The boy did precisely as I intended," Proctor said.

Butler's mouth opened and closed like a trout that had just stubbed the toes it didn't know it had.

Ji knew how he felt. Proctor had *wanted* him to tell Brace about the flower? At least that would explain the wink.

"And Master Brace took decisive action," Proctor continued. "Knowing that he needed to destroy the flower if he wished to train with me, he did not hesitate."

"I—I see, my lord," Butler said.

"He chose to destroy the only obstacle between himself and his goal. However, in an excess of loyalty, the boot boy decided to act in Master Brace's place." Proctor chuckled merrily and looked to Ji. "Do you understand me, lad?

You came here to destroy the flower, as a service to Brace. Is that correct?"

Agreeing with nobles was usually safest, so Ji said, "Yes, m'lord."

"To ensure that Master Brace could join me in the city, yes? Because you are a good and loyal servant?"

"Yes, my lord."

With a flourish, Proctor whittled another strip of wood from the clothespin. "And that is why you destroyed the lotus flower."

"Yes, m'lord."

"Except you didn't."

Ji cocked his head. "I didn't?"

"Absolutely not," Proctor told him.

"Oh, uh . . ." Ji frowned. Did Proctor *want* him to lie? "Huh?"

"I am going to ask you a question, boot boy, and I expect you to answer with utter scrupulousness."

"Er," Ji said.

"Honesty," Roz said. "He means *honesty*."

"Oh! Right. Yes, m'lord."

"I want nothing less than the truth, Jiyong," Proctor said. "Raise your right hand and tell me, once and for all, did you kill that desert lotus blossom?"

Ji raised his right hand. "No, my lord. I did not."

12

SALLY DREW AN alarmed breath at the lie, and Roz pressed her hand to her chest.

"In fact, my lord," Ji continued, "I've never even set foot inside the goblin pen."

Of course, he was standing inside the goblin pen as he said those words. But he was betting that Proctor *wanted* him to lie, because Proctor wanted Brace to visit the city. Which meant he wanted the lotus blossom killed—as long as the baron and baroness never learned that it hadn't died of natural causes.

"You worthless mutt!" Butler hissed, grabbing Ji's arm again. "How dare you? How dare you trespass on holy ground and despoil—"

The clothespin bounced off Butler's forehead, and for

an instant he glared at Proctor. Then the polite, subservient expression returned to his face.

"The boy didn't pluck the flower," Proctor told Butler. "The boy was never here."

Butler released Ji roughly. "I, um . . ."

"None of us were. The lotus flower shriveled and died by itself."

"But my lord—"

"This is a sign," Proctor told him. "Do you understand? The death of the lotus blossom indicates that Brace must accompany me to the city, to train for the Diadem Rite."

"Except, my lord . . ." Butler shifted nervously. "The boot boy trespassed in the mausoleum. He must be punished."

Proctor sighed sadly. "And if I say that these children were never here?"

"I'm sorry, my lord," Butler said. "I cannot tell an untruth to the baron and baroness."

"If the baroness learns what happened, she'll raise a fuss," Proctor said. "And I've been instructed to handle this quietly."

"I cannot betray the trust of my employers, my lord."

Proctor smiled warmly at Butler. "You are a brave and loyal servant and should be rewarded with great riches and with much praise."

"Thank you, my lord."

"However, instead you'll be rewarded with"—Proctor

flicked his wrist, and his dagger flashed through the firelight and thunked hilt-deep in Butler's chest—"the afterlife."

Without a sound, without a gurgle, Butler collapsed to the dirt floor.

Unmoving. Unbreathing.

Dead.

Roz gave a shriek and Ji swayed, looking at the wilted heap of Butler's body on the ground. He'd always hated Butler, but he'd never wanted *this*. Not dead in an eyeblink. Not lying pathetically on the dirt floor inside a goblin pen, his face slack and his arms outstretched.

Darkness rushed toward Ji, and he almost fainted.

Sally grabbed his arm. "Ji!"

"He—" Ji stared in horror at Proctor. "He killed him."

"Long as he doesn't kill *us*," she whispered.

Proctor pulled his dagger from Butler's chest and told the goblins, "Bury this unfortunate man in the deepest chambers."

Three big goblins turned toward the one-eyed goblin, who barked at them in Goblish, gesturing with both belly-arms.

"Ka," one of the big goblins coughed. "Yes, my lord."

"As you ka-mmand," another said, hunching toward Butler's body.

"J-just like that," Ji stammered. "Alive. Dead."

The goblins dragged the body down the ramp into the

bone crypts. Butler's leather shoes jounced on the dirt floor, and Ji felt tears on his cheeks.

"Surely you don't mourn him," Proctor said, wiping his dagger with a handkerchief. "He intended to see you hanged."

"One cannot—" Roz's voice trembled. "One cannot simple *kill* people. They matter. They're not nothing. You cannot simply kill them!"

"Sadly, I had no choice," Proctor told her. "However, I'd much rather not kill you and your friends as well. I never sleep well afterward."

Sally raised her trembling fists. "G-get away! Get away from us!"

Ji made himself breathe, he made himself think. He made himself stand there instead of running away. "We w-won't tell," he promised Proctor. "We won't tell anyone."

Proctor slid his dagger back into its sheath. "I am sure that you won't."

"Nobody would believe us, anyway," Ji said.

"They wouldn't believe you or the stable girl." Proctor's twinkling gaze drifted toward Roz. "But the young miss is a different matter."

"If you l-lay a hand on her," Ji said, feeling dizzy again, "I swear by the crown I'll, I'll . . ."

Proctor raised his bushy eyebrows. "Yes?"

"I'll *something*," Ji finished.

"And when he's done with that," Sally said, "I'll crack

your head open like a boiled melon."

Proctor raised his hands and smiled like a nonmurderer. "There's no need for threats. Let's think this through in a calm, measured manner."

"C-calm?" Sally sputtered. "You just killed Butler!"

"You should thank me. I saved your lives."

Sally scowled. "Only because you want the baroness to think the lotus died by itself."

"There's only one good option now, I'm afraid," Proctor said.

Ji's vision shrank into a pinprick. He wanted to sink into the ground, but if Proctor reached for his dagger, Ji promised himself that he'd jump him. He'd grab his legs and never let go. No matter how scared he felt or—

"I'll take you to the city with me," Proctor finished. "Along with Master Brace. Now that the flower is dead, there's no reason to delay."

"What?" Sally blurted, while Ji gaped. "Us?"

"Every last one of you," Proctor said with a low chuckle. "Master Brace will need servants, after all."

"The wha—? The where?" Ji shook his head. "You'll what?"

"The city?" Sally asked, lowering her fists.

"Yes." Proctor stroked his beard. "That's the most elegant solution."

"You'll claim that you hired Butler away from Primstone Manor," Roz said, smoothing her dress nervously.

"And that you sent him ahead, to prepare for your arrival. To explain his . . . disappearance."

"Is that what I'll do?" Proctor asked.

"Then nobody will know you killed him! And you'll get everything you wanted."

"What a bright young lady," Proctor told Roz. "I'll do precisely as you suggest. Thank you, Miss Rozario."

"You're welc—" She stopped herself. "That is, I beg your pardon, but you should be ashamed of yourself."

"I feel no shame," he told her. "Only duty. And my duty is to keep you away from the manor, so you won't tell tales. Plus I know exactly how to use you."

"H-how?" Ji asked, frowning at Proctor's boots, too sickened by the murder to feel relief at the news.

"Now I won't need to arrange other servants for Master Brace," Proctor said, not quite answering the question. "You'll do quite nicely. We'll leave tomorrow for my town house in the city. I can't trust you at the manor, so you'll spend the night in the goblin pen."

"You can't lock us in here!" Sally said.

Proctor chuckled again. "For the greater good, there is nothing I cannot do."

13

Ji STOOD WITH Sally and Roz in the entrance of the ruined temple and watched the goblins pull the gate shut with a slam, closing them inside the pen.

Outside the fence, Proctor tugged a chain onto an iron hook. The clink of the metal chilled Ji's blood. Locked in with goblins and the dead.

"If the children escape before I return," Proctor told the goblins through the fence, "you will pay with your lives."

The one-eyed goblin said, "We will ka-eep them in the pen."

"And one more thing, if it's not too much to ask?"

The goblin's belly-arms waved aimlessly. "Yes, my lord?"

"Try not to eat them," Proctor said merrily, before strolling into the evening.

The goblins chuffed, and one stared at Ji—maybe hungrily, maybe sympathetically. Ji turned away, looking toward the horizon. A few stars twinkled cheerily, and Ji hated them. It was easy to twinkle if you were safe in the sky. He sat on a log and closed his eyes. Then he opened them. Because every time he closed his eyes, he saw Butler's body jouncing down the ramp.

He grabbed a handful of pebbles and tossed one at the fence.

"Everything kind of worked out, didn't it?" Sally said, plopping down beside him.

"Not for Butler," Roz said, tugging at the strap of her handbag.

Sally gave a shudder. "Yeah. But I mean . . . now we're going to the city."

"We're going to the city *without our stuff*," Ji told her. "Proctor won't let us into the manor."

"Oh," she said.

"Yeah," Ji said. "Oh."

"So we can't pay for Chibo?"

"Not unless you have a ruby in your pocket."

Worry lines appeared between Sally's eyebrows. "The tapestry weavers won't sell Chibo for nothing."

"Really? You think? Of course they won't. That's the reason we did all of this. That's the entire—" Ji hurled a pebble against the wall of the ruined temple. "Aaargh!"

"O-o-oh," Sally said slowly. "I guess that part didn't work out, huh?"

"Yeah," he told her. "And neither did the part where Proctor is a grinning maniac who'd cut our throats just to check if his dagger's sharp."

Sally tugged at her bracelet. "I'm pretty sure it's sharp."

A breeze rattled through the bamboo garden, and the goblins chuffed and chewed at the trough. A knot of dread tightened in Ji's stomach. How were they going to save Chibo? How were they going to save *themselves*?

"Have you a plan?" Roz asked, moving to sit on Ji's other side.

Ji frowned. "You mean, do I have a plan?"

"That's what I asked."

"No, you said, 'Have you a plan?'"

Roz flushed. "It's the same thing."

"Maybe for nobles."

"Don't be a jerk," Sally told Ji.

He tossed a pebble at the ground. "We have to get into the chimney tomorrow, before we leave."

"How?" Sally asked.

"How would I know?" Ji snapped. "I just— We risked everything to get that loot, and now it's worthless."

They sat in silence for a while, until the one-eyed goblin brought them blankets. Roz thanked it politely, but Ji muttered, "Yeah, thanks for sending that little goblin to tell on us."

"Is that why one of 'em ran out?" Sally asked.

"I'm pretty sure," Ji told her.

The one-eyed goblin hunched closer. It raised its belly-arms and started barking and woofling, but Ji didn't even try to decipher the words between all the *ka-ka-ka*'s. "Sorry," he said. "I don't speak Goblish."

"That's not Goblish," Roz told him. "Don't be rude. Our goblin friend is saying that at first they worried they'd get in trouble if they let us in. Then they worried they'd get in trouble if they fought to keep us out. Then they worried they'd get in trouble if they didn't tell on us. And they are *extremely* frightened of getting in trouble."

"Humans po-kaing around in burrow?" The one-eyed goblin shook its head. "Very bad. But everything is aka-ceptable now. Only *you* are in trouble."

"Yeah," Ji said. "Everything's great."

After the goblin hunched away, Ji and the others sat around for a while longer. Then Sally headed inside while Ji and Roz stayed on the log, throwing pebbles at a tree stump. Roz hit the target every time, which was pretty annoying.

A night heron flew past, and the sweet scent from the bone crypt made Ji's stomach rumble. He knew he should apologize to Roz for making fun of how she talked—and for getting her into this—but he didn't want to.

When the breeze turned cold, they went inside. Three bonfires now burned in the big dirt-floored room, and Sally crouched beside one in a corner.

"Maybe we should sleep in shifts," she said. "In case they get hungry."

"They're not going to eat us," Roz told her.

"They might nibble."

Ji rubbed his aching shoulder. "Let's get some sleep. We'll find a way to grab the loot in the morning."

"If that doesn't work," Sally said, squinting into the fire, "maybe I can win the money in a tournament. Like archery or jousting or something."

"You've never shot an arrow in your life—and you've never even *seen* a joust."

"How hard can it be?" she asked. "I can ride. I can hold a lance."

"I suspect," Roz said, "that one might need training. And armor. And a horse."

"Like I keep telling you," Ji said, "you're not a knight. You're not even a squire."

"I'll wear a disguise," Sally told him.

Ji glanced at Roz, then said, "That'll be our backup plan."

"Cool," Sally said.

The sweet scent rose again, and Ji's mouth watered. Maybe goblins preferred to eat humans dipped in jam. He pulled his blanket to his chin and closed his eyes, but he couldn't stop thinking about that dagger thunking into Butler's chest.

"Will you read to us?" he asked Roz.

"Oh!" Sally said. "You have that book!"

"I always have a book," Roz said. "For precisely this situation."

Ji laughed. "Being locked in a goblin pen by a doolally proctor?"

"Exactly." Roz rummaged in her beaded handbag for her book. "This is a collection of Ti-Lin-Su's zozology essays. There are sections on ogres and hobgoblins and—"

"Aren't hobgoblins just little goblins?" Sally asked.

"No, they're not even related. Only the names are similar, like . . . 'eggs' and 'eggplants.'"

"Or butts and buttons," Ji said. "I thought hobgoblins were just goblins with more . . . hob."

Roz shot him a governess-y look. "Here's something Ti-Lin-Su wrote about her 'outstanding question.'"

"I remember that," Sally said. "Why do dragons gather gems?"

"Almost exactly," Roz said, and started reading a poem about a dragon brooding over a treasure hoard.

Ji watched the fire flicker as he listened. Roz's voice soothed the fear from his heart. The words of the poem tumbled around him. He closed his eyes again, and that time he saw a wingless dragon curled around a heap of jewels, flames blazing from her eyes as knights approached. . . .

A *scritch-scritch* scraped across Ji's reverie. He woke with a start and realized that he'd been dreaming.

More scritching came from deeper inside the bone crypt.

Ji peered through half-closed eyes and saw four goblins squatting at the top of the ramp beside a totem pole, while three others woofled farther down. The rest of the goblins stood in rows beneath the shrines. None of them moved. They just stood there perfectly still, like statues. It was so creepy that goose bumps rose on Ji's arms.

And that was *before* the totem pole turned and looked at him.

Panic clawed at Ji's mind, and terror chewed his heart. That was not a totem pole! That was not a totem! That was not a pole!

That was an ogre.

An actual ogre stood twenty feet away, as tall as a grown woman, with bull-like shoulders and hefty arms. A dull purple cloak was draped across the creature's chest, and the firelight glowed on its shiny red face and bright yellow hair.

White horns sprouted from its wrinkled red forehead, and its mouth was so full of fangs that they seemed to be jostling for room on its gums.

Dull yellow eyes fixed on Ji. He didn't yelp. He didn't twitch. His heart quit beating and his lungs withered into a couple of raisins.

The ogre prowled toward him, its red calves and leathery feet stomping closer. Its toes were tipped with talons. Ji watched through his eyelashes, pretending he was asleep.

"Never peeked a human this close," it growled, peering down at Ji. Its voice sounded like a boulder rolling across a tombstone. "So sleepylittle."

"Ka-eep quiet!" one of the goblins urged. "Don't wake him!"

Don't wake me, Ji prayed. *Don't wake me, don't wake me. Don't look at me. Don't touch me. I'm not even here.*

"But it's just"—a red hand stretched toward Ji, and another grinding noise sounded—"a doorbell! It's the cutemost thing I ever peeked!"

"Humans are not ka-utemost," the goblin said. "They are ka-illers."

"Ka-illers," another goblin agreed.

"Look at that prettysweet face!" the ogre crooned, and reached to touch Ji's cheek. "Buttersoft and toothless!"

Darkness swirled in Ji's vision, and he felt himself on the verge of fainting.

"Nin." A rough voice sounded from the ramp, so deep that Ji felt reverberations in his bones. "Come."

The ogre turned from Ji. "Have you peekseen? It's a doorbell!"

"Stay away from them, Nin," the deep voice said. "Stay hidden. Until the time comes."

The ogre looked at Ji with its terrible fanged face. Ji looked back through his eyelashes, dizzy with terror. And then, quick as a snake, the ogre touched Ji's cheek with a claw. Its leathery red fist snuffed every light in the world.

When Ji's eyes sprang open, the ogre was gone. He'd been dreaming. He exhaled in relief. It had just been a nightmare, a terrible nightmare.

Roz and Sally slept peacefully beside him in the warmth of the bonfire. Four goblins squatted at the ramp, with three more farther down, and there was no totem pole in sight.

Meanwhile, the rest of the goblins stood in neat rows. Completely still. For once even their belly-arms were motionless. Which was pretty creepy unless they were standing at attention or—

"Oh," Ji whispered. They were *sleeping*.

Goblins slept standing up. Weird. And in straight rows, too. Three rows, with three goblins in each row. No, one row was longer, with four goblins. As the memory of his nightmare faded, he started to drift off—then a realization hit him like a ton of boots.

Three rows of three goblins, plus one extra . . .

That made ten goblins.

Plus four squatted at the ramp, with three farther down.

Seventeen goblins.

And the *scritch-scritch* in the bone crypt sounded like more than one goblin digging. It sounded like a *dozen*, but what did Ji know about scritches? Still, he knew that there were at least eighteen goblins in the pen—and Roz said there were only twelve total at Primstone Manor.

So where had the other six come from? What were they doing?

Ji pulled the blanket to his chin. Who cared about all that? Forget the weird dream, forget those weird goblins. He needed to focus on sneaking into the manor and grabbing the loot. He couldn't buy Chibo's freedom without the stuff from the chimney. So he'd get the stuff from the chimney—whatever it took.

14

JI WOKE TO the sound of the chain rattling at the fence.

"Hey." Sally kicked Ji's sandal. "Get up."

"Muh," Ji told her, and pulled his blanket higher.

"Proctor's outside with a carriage," Roz said. "It's morning. Well, it's dawn. It's almost morning. You're a deep sleeper."

"Not usually," Sally said.

"Did you wake in the night?" Roz asked.

A scary red mask flashed into Ji's mind, but the image slipped away. He yawned and said, "Yeah, I had a nightmare."

"And couldn't get back to sleep?"

"Well, I tried counting goblins, but it didn't help."

"Use sheep next time," Sally said.

"I stopped at eighteen," he told them.

For a moment, Roz just peered at him—then her eyes widened. "Wait, are you saying . . . Eighteen? You counted eighteen goblins?"

"Yup."

"Actual, genuine goblins?"

"Well they weren't *fake*, Roz! Yeah, there are at least eighteen goblins in here, and probably more. They dig all night."

"How can there be more than twelve?" Roz shot a nervous glance toward the ramp. "Where did they come from? What are they digging?"

"I don't know," Ji said, "and I don't care. Goblins don't matter. The only thing that matters is our loot. Nothing else. We need to clean out the chimney before we leave."

"How?" Roz asked. "Proctor won't let us near the manor."

"I spent all night thinking of a plan."

"Oh, thank summer!" she said. "What shall we do?"

"Beg," he said.

"Great plan," Sally said. "What happens if he says no?"

"Then when we get close to the manor, I'll distract Proctor and you'll run to the chimney and stuff everything in a sack."

"What shall I do?" Roz asked.

"Convince Proctor not to stab me for distracting him."

Roz's forehead furrowed. "Ah."

"That's not much better than begging," Sally said.

"It's short and simple," Ji told her. "Like you."

Sally didn't have a chance to bonk Ji with her shovel, because three figures suddenly entered the pen: Lady Nosey, Lord Pickle, and Proctor's valet, a bald guy the size of a well-fed mountain range.

"Your burro awaits," Pickle told Roz.

"Poor animal," Nosey muttered.

"I b-beg your pardon?" Roz asked Pickle.

"Your burro," Pickle told her.

The valet dragged Ji outside, and he blinked in the dawn light. A coach waited just past the gate, painted red with gold trim, drawn by a team of four horses. A coachman sat in the box seat while Proctor leaned against a door, through which Brace was peeking.

"We'll arrive at the city in two days if we don't dillydally," Proctor announced heartily. "Come, my children! Lord Nichol, Lady Posey, join Master Brace inside the coach. Miss Roz, you shall ride upon this noble steed." He gestured to a saddled burro standing behind the coach. "And the servants will lead you."

Roz narrowed her eyes at Proctor. "You're making them *walk* to the city?"

Proctor didn't bother answering her. He merely chuckled and opened the coach door for Nosey and Pickle while the bald valet lifted Roz onto the burro's saddle and gave Sally the lead.

"Just our luck," Sally muttered. "We're stuck with Gong-ong."

"Is Gongong the burro or the valet?" Ji asked.

The valet lifted a hand to whack Ji. "My name is Mr. Ioso, guttersnipe."

"Mysterioso?" Ji asked. He almost said *Mysterioso Guttersnipe*, which was an awesome name, but he didn't want to push it.

"Mr. Ioso," the bald valet said, and for some reason didn't actually whack Ji.

Instead, he grabbed a strap and stepped onto a running board. He stood there, clinging to the outside of the coach, keeping a wary eye on Ji and the others.

"What's wrong with Gongong?" Roz asked, nervously stroking the burro's neck.

"Just don't laugh," Sally told her.

"Um, Mr. Ioso?" Ji asked. "Can I run to the manor to grab my buttons and thread?"

"No," Mr. Ioso said.

"I'll serve Master Brace better," Ji said, "if I have all my stuff."

"There's thread in the city," Mr. Ioso said.

"Please?" Ji asked. "You won't even know I'm gone."

"Ask one more time," Mr. Ioso said, "and I'll pop your head off like a cork."

The coach jerked forward, creaking and swaying.

Sally clicked her tongue and followed with Gongong the burro. Ji trotted quickly to her side. He didn't know much about burros, but he knew enough to stay away from the kicky end.

"Okay, new plan," he told Roz under his breath, as the coach rumbled loudly twenty feet in front of them.

She gripped the saddle horn with both hands. "I'm going to be sick."

"Exactly!" he said. "But not yet!"

"What? What are you talking about?"

"You're going to fall off the donkey."

"Very possibly, if you keep talking to me!" She took a shaky breath. "Give me a few moments to acclimate to the motion."

"She's not a bad girl, Gongong," Sally said. "As long as you don't laugh. Burros aren't stubborn, you know. They're just deep thinkers. They like to ponder."

"I mean on purpose," Ji told Roz. "You're going to fall off on purpose."

"I am?" Roz asked.

"When we pass the manor, you'll fall off and make a racket. That's a good time to be sick if you want. Then Sally and I will run for the chimney and grab the stuff before Mr. Ioso pops both our heads off."

"He'll pop one head for sure," Sally said.

"That's the downside of my plan. But I can't think of a better one."

"Okay," she said.

"Sound good?" he asked Roz. "You can do that?"

Roz tightened her grip on the saddle horn. "Of course. It's as easy as"—she showed Ji a wavering smile—"falling off a log."

"Good," he said. "I'll tell you when."

The goblin pen disappeared behind them. The orange rays of dawn brushed the fir trees, and a flock of golden wagtails hopped around a lawn.

"Roz isn't like you and me," Sally told Ji, as the coach swayed along the path. "She was born for better than falling off a donkey."

"I know that," he said, and saw Roz stiffen. She didn't say anything, though Ji knew that she didn't like being coddled."But she's tough, and she's our friend."

Roz unstiffened, and maybe a glimmer of gratitude showed in her face. Ji didn't know. He didn't look. He just kept walking . . . and felt a little more hopeful, for some reason.

The coach wheels rattled across the stone bridge. Then Ji drifted to the other side of the burro, to be closer to the manor. That way, he'd have a head start when Roz started making a distraction.

Except the coach suddenly veered off the carriage path, away from the manor. The horses clip-clopped onto a little-used trail that joined the main road a mile past the manor. They were taking a shortcut, and Ji was losing his chance to run for the chimney.

"Oh, no," he groaned. "No, no."

"Shall I fall off now?" Roz asked. "I'll fall now if you'd like."

Ji shook his head. "We're too far! C'mon, Ji. Think, think, you gormless buttonhead . . ."

He rubbed his neck as the coach led them away from the manor. He couldn't lose all those beads and baubles, all that silver and silk! He'd spent months stealing his loot, and Chibo was lost without it. But what could he do? Lead the burro under the coach wheels? Tell Sally to bite Mr. Ioso's face?

"There's no way," he finally said, his throat tight and his eyes swollen. He'd failed. He'd done everything he could, and he'd still failed.

"All that stealing for nothing," Sally said.

"Yeah."

"That's another reason we shouldn't act dishonorably. Because it might not help."

Ji wiped his face with his palm. "Well, *not* stealing wouldn't have helped, either."

"What shall we do now?" Roz asked.

"Raise money in the city," Ji said. "I guess."

"Plan B?" Sally asked, perking up.

"Yeah," he said. "I mean, no! Not jousting, that's plan C."

"Then how?"

"Maybe cheating, maybe stealing." He shrugged,

swallowing the lump in his throat. "I don't know yet."

"You'll figure something out," Roz told him, and sounded like she believed it.

15

THE COUNTRYSIDE CHANGED, becoming flatter and greener around Summer River, which flowed the length of the valley. As noon approached, rice paddies stretched across flooded fields instead of stepping down hillside terraces. The sun was reflected in the shallow water and rippled around teams of oxen pulling plows.

Despite the blue sky, the day felt cloudy and grim to Ji. He'd lost everything, every bauble and bead. Months of work, months of hope . . . all gone.

The coach rolled onward, far ahead. He thought about running away, except why bother? Where would he go? What would he do? He still needed to get to the city to save Chibo. Without a single copper coin to his name.

"I'm hungry," Sally said.

"Drink more water," Ji told her.

She kicked a dirt clod. "I bet there's a whole feast in the coach, with tamales and noodles."

"And dumplings," Ji said.

"And sausages." Sally sighed. "I'm *starving*."

"Do you want to ride for a while?" Roz asked.

Sally frowned. "The burro's for you."

"I don't mind walking."

"It's not right. You're almost a proper lady. You've got a surname and everything."

"We should call you Miss Songarza," Ji said.

Roz ignored him. "I could use a break. Gongong isn't exactly cushiony, and my bottom's about to fall off."

Sally started to answer when sunlight flashed from the road ahead. Ji squinted downhill, shielding his eyes with one hand. "What's that?"

"Mirror Lake," Roz said. "The largest in the realm."

When it came fully into view, Ji felt himself smile. The lake looked peaceful and grand at the same time, with villages and towns built snugly on the shore. A few fishing boats drifted across the still surface, and birds swooped and dived and splashed.

"Makes me want to jump in," he said.

"Do you know how to swim?" Sally asked.

"Nah," he said. "But it's got to be easier than jousting."

"For one thing," Roz said, with a laugh, "you don't need armor or—"

A horrible bray shattered the peace. Gongong the burro laid her ears flat on her head and lashed out with her rear legs, bucking wildly.

Roz shrieked and started tilting off the saddle. She windmilled one arm and Sally snatched at her leg to keep her mounted while Ji grabbed for her wrist. She whacked him in the ear before he caught her, and Gongong bucked twice more.

An instant later, it was over. Gongong stood there, placid and peaceable, like nothing had happened.

Roz slid from the saddle, her eyes huge and her breathing fast. "Oh my! My-oh-my! Oh! My!"

"Sorry," Sally told her, stroking the burro's nose. "But I warned you not to laugh. When you do, Gongong bucks."

"I'll never laugh again," Roz vowed.

Which made Ji want to laugh, mostly to see what happened.

"Don't you dare!" Roz told him.

"What?" he asked, trying to look innocent.

Sally climbed onto the burro, and they followed the path downhill toward a small village. The gold-and-red carriage waited outside a sturdy timber-framed inn, and two villagers watered the horses and checked their hooves.

"Hey!" Sally said, riding closer. "That's my job."

"Don't give them any ideas," Ji told her. "Or they'll make me clean their boots."

Nosey and Pickle strolled from the inn, holding

embroidered parasols. Brace followed behind, his shoulders slumped—which made Ji scowl. Even now, heading to the city to train for a fancy rite, the twins were ruining Brace's triumph.

Lady Nosey pointed her parasol across the road, and Brace slouched toward a dusty strawberry-guava bush.

"How come the stable girl is riding?" Nosey asked Roz, when they neared. "Shall we have Mr. Ioso whip her?"

"I chose to walk," Roz said, though Sally slid from the saddle just in case. "Thank you very much."

"I don't even know why you're tagging along," Pickle told her. "We don't need a governess, much less her little sister."

"Although she's not exactly a 'little' anything," Nosey said, stroking a strand of her gold-painted hair.

"I was surprised to see you along, too," Roz told Pickle.

"Our mother insisted that Proctor escort us to the city for training," Lord Pickle said. "And introduce us to the Summer Queen. She even sent Butler ahead, to help make Proctor's town house comfortable for us."

"Is that right?" Roz said, faintly. "How very . . ."

"Killed," Ji muttered.

"Speak up, boot boy!" Nosey snapped.

"How very *kind*, m'lady," Ji said.

"Of course she's kind. Our mother is . . ." She trailed off at the sound of hoofbeats. "Oh! How tiresome."

She and Pickle stepped beneath the awning of the

timber-framed inn, while Sally tugged Gongong behind the coach with Ji and Roz.

Five riders thundered toward them from the direction of the city, wearing the Summer Queen's armor, with swords and shields and jaguar-hide boots. Ten more rode past, then ten more after them. Dust clouded the air, and Ji barely heard Sally's gleeful shouts above the clomp of hooves.

He watched her, though. Her hair danced and her eyes shone. She shoved Gongong's lead into Ji's hand and peeked around the coach. Another few soldiers rode past, and then a great armored warhorse heaved to a halt, all rolling eyes and flaring nostrils.

Ji backed away along the side of the inn. Slowly. Carefully. Not because he was scared of a massive snorting warhorse or anything. Just to protect Gongong.

"You like horses, girl?" the soldier on the warhorse called to Sally.

"I love 'em!" Sally told the soldier. "And swords, too—is that chain mail you're wearing? Does it get hot? Where's your helmet? Do you know how to *joust*?"

The soldier smiled. "I've never used a lance," she told Sally, wiping a strand of brown hair from her sweaty face. "I'm a common soldier, not an officer."

"I'd totally use a lance!" Sally announced. "Where are you heading? Is there a war? Am I missing out?"

"We're riding to the mountains," the soldier said. "And

it's not war—not yet. But the ogres are restless."

"*Ogres*," Sally said, her eyes shining. "Awesome."

"They might invade."

"An invasion! Double awesome! Are you going to vanquish them?"

The soldier smiled again. She looked like she might laugh, so Ji tugged Gongong even farther away. The burro snorted along the timber-framed inn, past a row of bushes bursting with yellow daisies. Ji stopped beneath a window as more riders thundered along the road. When the brown-haired soldier galloped away, Sally turned to Roz, waving her arms in excitement, probably explaining how she'd win an invading contest.

Ji tugged the lead, but the stupid burro refused to budge. So he pushed from the side. Gongong still didn't move. She just nibbled his shirt. He bonked her nose and she gave him a cross-eyed stare, then chewed on an overgrown daisy bush.

"Move your stupid face," he muttered.

"My concern," Proctor said, from inside the open window, "is that we're running out of time."

Ji fell silent. Well, he didn't just fall silent. He plunged silent. He plummeted silent. He careened through the bottom of silent and tumbled—silently—out the other side.

"That's the cavalry riding past, m'lord," Mr. Ioso said. "Which means Her Majesty is defending our borders

115

against the ogres. Of course the beasts are too weak to attack before the rite, but . . ."

"She's pushing them deeper into the mountains, just in case?" Proctor asked.

"I believe so, my lord. And the goblins are restless."

"The goblins are worthless."

"They're weak alone," Mr. Ioso said. "But if they join forces with the ogres . . ."

Footsteps sounded as Proctor paced inside the inn room. "The realm is at risk until the Diadem Rite chooses an heir. I hope you're right that this is the correct child."

"Nothing is certain in matters of magic, my lord," Mr. Ioso said.

A meaningless chuckle sounded through the window; Ji hoped Gongong didn't hear it. "So you keep telling me."

"And all of my castings pointed to Primstone Manor."

"Brace's bloodline is impeccable," Proctor said, a satisfied edge in his hearty voice. "However, if this rite doesn't select an heir, the next one may be too late. How is the queen's strength?"

"Her Majesty is mighty."

"And ancient," Proctor said. "Check on her."

After a pause, Mr. Ioso said, "Yes, my lord."

A metallic clink sounded from inside, then a splash. Ji glanced warily at the open window and chewed on his lower lip. C'mon, Ji, just creep away. *Clink-clink! Glug-glug-splash.* No spying, no peeping. *Clink-splash.* Get out of here, you chuckle-knuckle! Don't even think about peeking in the window!

Ji peeked in the window.

Sturdy wooden chairs surrounded a square table. A bouquet of sunflowers rose from a vase, and Proctor stood behind one chair while Mr. Ioso sat in another, pouring water into a polished copper bowl on the table. As he poured, he spun the bowl. The water inside sloshed and . . . glowed.

White light shone on Mr. Ioso's face, and outside the window Ji swayed, flushed and dizzy. Magic. *Magic.* Mr. Ioso was a mage. One of the handful of people who the Summer Queen lent a tiny bit of her power to. The stories said that they had to eat the heart of a mermaid to prove themselves worthy of wielding the royal magic, but Ji didn't really believe that. At least, he didn't *think* he really believed it.

His grip tightened on the burro's lead until his hand throbbed. But throbbing was nothing; Mr. Ioso's hand *glowed.* White light swirled around his fingers and rose like steam from the copper bowl.

The sunflowers in the vase twisted and twined. Buds formed on the sides, then grew into tiny ears of corn. Ji gawped in amazement. That must've been a side effect of Mr. Ioso's magic! The sunflowers were turning into cornstalks, or at least into a twisted combination of sunflower and cornstalk.

When Mr. Ioso gestured, a sheet of water rose above the bowl and hung there, unmoving. "The queen's power flows like water, my lord," he told Proctor. "Can you read the ripples? She is as strong as a hunting eagle, while we're just blue-bats."

"And how long will she remain strong?"

"There's only—" Mr. Ioso stopped suddenly when the sheet of water inflated into a round globe.

Except not a globe: a head.

A woman's head, five times life-size, with a wide mouth and square chin and short black hair—and a golden crown. Hovering above the copper bowl, made of water but looking like flesh and blood.

"Your Majesty!" Proctor cried, and dropped to his knees.

Mr. Ioso bowed from the waist but stayed in his chair, focusing on his magic. When his hands brightened, the sunflower-cornstalks wilted and drooped.

"Art thou inquiring into my fitness to rule?" the queen asked Proctor, her voice somehow both soft and loud.

Ji stared at her in breathless awe.

"Never, Your Majesty," Proctor said. "I am merely worrying over your remaining strength, like a mother hen with a nervous disposition."

The queen's laughter sounded like the bubbling of a spring, and Ji gripped the reins tighter. If Gongong bucked, Proctor would notice them! But apparently the bubbling-gurgle didn't sound like real laughter, because the burro just stamped a few times.

"Thou art forever insolent!" the queen said, her voice amused. "Explain thyself."

"Your Majesty is no longer a young lady in her tenth or eleventh decade," Proctor said. "For the past five years, every Diadem Rite has failed to find an heir. Now time is running out. Your Majesty wields *all* human magic." His gaze flicked toward Mr. Ioso. "Even the mages simply borrow scraps of your power. And after a successful rite, the new prince or princess will still need training. We must find an heir soon or face catastrophe."

"Thou servest my realm truly, in spite of thine unmannerly words," the queen said, her dark eyes twinkling in the water. "Thou art correct; this rite must appoint an heir. And so it shall."

"There will be a new heir?"

"Verily, for I have felt it," the queen said, and the sunflower-cornstalks blackened and shriveled.

Ji gaped at the dead flowers. That was the "balance" that Roz had mentioned in the bone crypt: magic always had a cost. A chattering water-head spell was incredible, but it warped the sunflowers into bizarre hybrids . . . then sucked the life from them.

Proctor bowed again, and sorrow sounded in his usually merry voice. "I pray that I won't live to see the end of your reign. I pray that even after Lord Brace becomes your heir, he will not take the crown until long after I'm gone."

For a second, Ji didn't understand. Then he realized that Proctor was saying he hoped the queen would live for so long after the rite that Proctor died before she did.

The queen's liquid head inclined gracefully. "Thou art certain that this young gentleman is the strongest candidate?"

"I merely hope," Proctor said.

The queen closed her eyes, and the water shimmered. Rivulets trickled and ripples spread. As the queen's face melted, she said, "Yes, yes. I sense a child near thee. One who is fit to wear the crown and protect the realm. My true heir . . ."

The globe of water splashed into the copper bowl. The glow faded from Mr. Ioso's hands and the sunflower-cornstalks crumbled to ash.

Ji ducked out of sight, his heart pounding like a six-legged horse galloping across a field of drums. The world tilted and shook, and his mind reeled. The queen. The actual Summer Queen, in a bubble of water, saying that Brace might end up king!

He leaned against the wall beside the dead cactus, waiting for the world to stop spinning, and—

Wait. The *dead cactus*?

Ji blinked. Whoa. What had happened to the daisy bush? The green stems and yellow flowers had turned into gray stalks and cracked needles. Mr. Ioso's magic must've transformed that too, just like the sunflowers.

When Proctor voice sounded from inside the window, Ji started crawling away, tugging at the burro's lead. Gong-ong actually followed that time. Probably because there weren't any more daisies to eat.

". . . happy news," Proctor was saying. "The queen herself feels Brace's potential."

"Yes, my lord," Mr. Ioso said.

"We'll beat him into shape like a blacksmith beats a blade. We'll forge him into a prince—and then a king."

"And the others?"

"What of them?" Proctor said. "One cannot attain power without paying the price."

16

WHEN THEY LEFT the village, Ji told Roz and Sally what he'd seen—four times. Then he told them twice more that night. The next morning, he added some details to improve the story. Like that Gongong had gobbled the cornstalk and Proctor turned into a frog-man and snapped at blue-bats with his tongue.

He didn't make up any lies about the queen, though. She was too majestic.

By lunchtime, he'd stopped making up lies about anyone. He just trudged beside the burro, past fields and haciendas and villages.

"All these manors," he finally said. "One after another. It's weird."

"What is?" Sally asked.

"They're all exactly like Primstone, but totally different. Like there's a boot boy in each one, another version of me, and grooms just like you."

"Well," Sally said. "Not *just* like me."

"Yeah," he said. "But a hundred versions of us and the twins, and the Folly, and the bone crypts, and . . . I don't know."

"The butlers?" Roz asked.

"Yeah." Ji rubbed his aching arm. "The butlers."

Nobody spoke for a moment. Then Sally said, "It's like a molehill."

"What is?" Ji asked.

"The goblin tunnels. I wonder if they ever dig into each other by accident." She patted Gongong. "I'd bet they'd freak out. I bet even goblins are scared of goblins."

"The haciendas are too far apart for the tunnels to meet," Roz said. "At least, with only a few goblins at each one."

"What if there are extra goblins, like I saw at Primstone?" Ji asked.

"I've no idea." Roz fiddled with her handbag strap. "Though it's true that goblins are rather larger than moles."

"And rather freakier," Sally said, then tugged the burro out of the way as a grain cart jostled past them.

The villages grew larger as they neared the city, and the fields shrank. Soldiers marched and vendors called and nobles cantered on fancy horses.

Ji ducked his head when nobles passed, and wanted to steal their boot baubles. Because how else could he save Chibo? There was only one way. If he didn't succeed as a thief, he'd have to try more serious crimes. Like sneaking into the tapestry factory and kidnapping Chibo.

Ji spent another night sleeping beneath the coach and another morning trudging beside the burro. Roz and Sally switched places every hour or so, but after riding Gongong for twenty minutes, Ji decided to keep walking. Riding a burro felt like wearing cactus underpants.

Finally, Roz said, "There, look."

When Ji raised his head, he caught sight of the city ahead.

Summer City was built on a mountain that loomed above the coast, with the Forbidden Palace rising at the very top. Although it was called a palace, Roz said that it was actually dozens of buildings: pavilions, barracks, galleries, gardens, courtyards, temples, and halls. And of course the tower where the Summer Queen lived. Below the palace, fancy mansions and estates encircled the mountain. Then came normal neighborhoods, linked with stairs and ramps and zigzagging streets. Waterfalls and canals cascaded past houses and shops packed together around flights of stairs and precarious walkways.

"Chibo's in there somewhere," Sally said. "Working his fingers bloody . . ."

"Not for long," Ji said.

"We don't even know where he is!"

"We'll find him," Roz promised.

Hours later, they entered the city proper. The cobbled streets overflowed with traffic and noise. The air smelled of cinnamon and roasting chicken, of pigsty and pastry shop. They followed the coach higher on the mountain until Brace leaned from a window and bought a bunch of lychee fruit from a vendor.

When he noticed Ji, he gave a wave and said something to the coachman. A moment later, the coach stopped and he stepped onto the road.

"Hey, Ji," Brace called before nodding politely to Roz. "Miss Roz." He didn't seem to notice Sally.

"Master Brace," Ji said, bowing his head. "We're finally here, huh? Bet you can't wait till Proctor starts training you."

"He already started," Brace said. "In the carriage."

"He's giving you lessons?" Roz leaned forward on the burro. "About art? Politics? I'm terribly jealous, my lord. Are there *textbooks*?"

"Just conversation so far. No art yet. But plenty of military history and strategy."

"Your favorite," Ji said.

"The only thing I'm good at." Brace sidestepped a couple of pigs being herded across the road. "Uh, are you hungry?"

Sally glared meaningfully at Ji, so he said, "Starving, m'lord."

"Here." Brace gave him the lychee fruit, then gazed toward the top of the mountain. "Do you know why Her Majesty needs an heir?"

"Because even queens get old?"

Brace frowned. "Because the ogres and goblins can't beat us while the crown is worn by the rightful monarch." He pointed across the street, toward three statues of soldiers. "You see those?"

Ji looked at the red-brown statues, with jaguar helmets and tomahawks. "Sure."

"They're terra-cotta warriors. There are hundreds of them around the city. If we're attacked by monsters, the queen will use her magic to ring the black-glazed bells that are hanging in towers around the city. The sound will wake the warriors, and they'll fight for her."

Ji whistled. "No way!"

"Yeah, like the nursery rhyme."

"What nursery rhyme?"

"You know." Brace thought for a second. "'Bells ring once in the city of summer, to wake the soldiers from their slumber.'"

Ji shook his head. "I've never heard it."

"*Everyone* knows that!"

"Surely you've heard it, Ji," Roz said. "'Bells ring once in the city of summer, to wake the soldiers from their slumber. Ring the bells twice after blood's been shed, and tuck them back in like a sleepyhead.'"

"A *sleepyhead*?" Ji asked.

"Well, it is a nursery rhyme, after all," Roz told him.

"I heard something close," Sally said. "Um. 'Ring the bells once to call the clay, ring them twice to send it away.'"

"What if you ring them three times?" Ji asked.

"In *any* case," Brace said, "that's just one power of the Summer Crown. Waking the terra-cotta warriors. Almost makes you wish we *would* be attacked."

"Totally," Sally said.

"Not me," Ji said. "Though I heard the ogres are restless."

"The queen will protect us," Brace said. "She's the heart of the realm, Ji. I pray that she'll rule forever."

"Me too! I totally pray for that! I—"

Roz took a sharp breath. "My goodness!"

A stone's throw from them, six goblins shuffled across the road. Belly-arms folded, knees bending in three different directions, collars gleaming around scrawny necks. Two women in green hats strode beside them, ushering them toward a dark underpass.

"There are gobs in the city?" Sally asked.

"Of course," Brace said. "They dig tunnels and repair canals."

"Weird to see them just . . . walking around."

"If you can call that walking," Ji said.

The goblins disappeared into the underpass, and then Proctor called Brace into the carriage and Sally grabbed the lychee fruit from Ji's hands.

As the zigzagging road climbed higher on the mountain, the houses sprouted steeples and gardens, and tree-lined canals burbled beneath ivy-covered bridges. Then the coach rattled through a pretty square with a high white tower.

Three soldiers lounged on the tower stairs, and conversation spilled from the open doors of a nearby tavern. A squad of terra-cotta warriors stood in a fountain, tomahawks raised. They looked fierce until a few pigeons landed on their jaguar helmets, squawking and strutting.

Ji would've laughed, except he was afraid of making Gongong freak out. Instead, he nodded toward the tavern. "I bet they make lots of money."

"We're not robbing a tavern!" Sally said.

"Fine," Ji said. "We'll rob a jewelry store."

"That's not what I meant!"

"Stop teasing Sally," Roz told Ji. "We're not robbing anything."

"We might have to. If we—" Ji stopped, catching sight of a banner hanging from the white tower, which showed the Summer Queen standing over weird half-human beasts. "What's that?"

Roz shaded her eyes. "It's a watchtower."

"Oh," Ji said, and didn't mention that he'd meant the banner.

"There's a black bell at the top," Sally said.

"Then I suppose it's a bell tower," Roz told her.

"The bells are just for trolls and stuff, right?" Sally asked.

"Yes, I believe they only sound if the city is attacked by nonhumans."

"What if they ring while we're here? Do we get to fight?"

"There's no chance of that." Roz swayed on the saddle. "The bells haven't rung in centuries."

"There's *some* chance," Sally said. "The ogres are restless, after all."

Ji kicked a cobblestone. "I guess nobody rings a bell for kids dying in tapestry factories."

"No," Roz said. "I suppose not."

"Stupid nursery rhymes."

A glum silence fell as they left the square behind. Then Sally asked Ji, "You really think we might have to rob something?"

"One way or another," Ji said, "I know we will."

"What does that mean?" Roz asked.

"Either we steal stuff from houses," he said, "or we steal Chibo from the weavers."

17

Two servants opened a gate on a pretty cobbled street and the coach rumbled through, disappearing behind high walls. Ji and the others followed, walking beside a canal that reflected the branches of cherry trees. Parrots chattered and swooped across blossom-strewn walkways.

Inside the gate, Proctor's elegant town house rose in front of them, with creamy stone walls and square windows. A low stable stood to the left, while the servants' quarters sprawled beside the wall to the right.

With a hearty cry of "Come, my noble children!" Proctor escorted Brace, Nosey, and Pickle up the front stairs. "This way—watch your step." He paused at the door and looked over his shoulder. "We must find you a room inside the main house as well, Miss Roz."

She shot a quick, desperate look to Ji, but curtsied and said, "Yes, my lord."

After the door closed behind them, Mr. Ioso told Sally, "Settle the burro, then help the coachmen with the horses."

"Are there any *war*horses?" she asked.

"It's a town house, not a barracks."

"Is it a town house with warhorses?" she asked hopefully.

"Get moving!" Mr. Ioso barked, then turned to Ji. "Bring the luggage inside. The servants' door is around the corner. You are to remove the travel-soiled clothing and help the laundress clean it."

So Ji spent the next five hours in the laundry hut. Apparently in the city, they did the nobles' laundry every day, just in case the queen summoned them. By the time he finished, he stank of sweat. He slouched into the servants' quarters, and the cook gave him a steamed bun. He shoved the whole thing into his mouth and was still chewing when Mr. Ioso ducked through the door.

"This isn't a vacation, boy," Mr. Ioso said. "There are a dozen pairs of shoes that need fixing."

Ji swallowed the rest of the bun. "Yes, sir."

That night, he collapsed onto a pallet in a corner of the kitchen. He didn't know where Sally and Roz were sleeping, and he was too tired to wonder.

He didn't get a break for three days. Not one free

moment to search for Chibo.

He cleaned walking boots, dancing boots, formal boots, and for the first time, *court* boots: fancy boots that were encrusted with jewels. Ji eyed the topaz and garnets greedily. He could sell them for enough to buy Chibo from the tapestry weavers . . . except if he stole anything that expensive, someone would notice.

During the days, he sharpened knives and polished silver and scrubbed dishes. At night, he handled his boot boy duties. He heard that Brace and the twins visited the Forbidden Palace for an audience with the Summer Queen, but didn't see them. He caught a few glimpses of Sally mucking out the stables, but didn't even lay eyes on Roz until the fourth day.

That was when he decided to demand Brace's help. Brace wouldn't even be in the city if not for Ji and Sally and Roz sneaking through the bone crypt. He'd still be at Primstone Manor, probably locked naked on the roof.

So Ji crept to the second floor of the town house, slunk to Brace's room, and knocked.

No answer.

Hm. If nobody was around, maybe he could snaffle a few little things. He didn't really like the idea of stealing from Brace, though. So he took a breath and crept to Lady Posey's room. He scratched softly, just in case. No answer. Good. Nosey probably had a chest full of coins and trinkets under her mattress.

Except the door was locked.

He was trying Lord Nichol's door when a girl's voice said, "Hey!"

Ji's heart burst out the top of his head, smashed through the roof, and shot into the sky. Then he realized that the girl wasn't Nosey; it was Roz, carrying three books in her arms.

"I'm so glad to see you!" she said. "What are you doing? Have you seen Sally? Have you seen the *library*?"

After Ji's heart fell from the sky, dropped through the hole in the ceiling, and lodged back in his chest, he said, "You almost killed me! I'm, uh, looking for Brace."

"Oh! He's in the courtyard."

"What are *you* doing?"

The light faded from Roz's eyes and she said, "Nothing. Chibo is slaving away, Proctor is a murderer, and I'm . . . reading." She showed him the books in her arms. "I'm bringing them to my room. I didn't know what else to do."

"Are you shoveling facts and poems into your head?"

She swallowed. "I—I suppose so."

"I'm glad to hear it," he said. "Because your job is being smart. Figuring out how to get Chibo is my job."

"Have you thought of anything?"

"Only that we need Brace's help." He reached for the book on the top of the pile. "What are these?"

"Don't touch!" she said, stepping back. "Your hands are . . . bootish!"

He looked at his callused, scraped, dye-stained hands. "Oh."

"These are rare." She gingerly opened one. "And illustrated. Look."

She tilted the book toward him, and the page showed a horrible red mask with horns and tusks and yellow eyes. For an instant, a memory sparked in Ji's mind, like he'd seen that picture before.

"That's an ogre?"

"A young one," Roz told him. "Just a cub."

"I'd hate to see him all grown up."

"It's not a he, it's an ogre child. They say 'cub' for the children instead of 'he' and 'she' and 'him' and 'her.'"

"What? No way."

She nodded. "They're not male or female until they're fully grown. For example, if you were an ogre, Sally would say, 'Did you see Ji in the hallway?' Then I'd say, 'Oh, yes, I saw *cub* talking with *cub's* friend Roz and—'"

"Wait a second." Ji frowned at the book. "These are rare?"

"Quite rare."

"So they're valuable."

"I suppose they're worth a fair amount, if you—" She stopped suddenly, her eyes narrowing. "Oh, no. Don't you *dare*! Don't you even think about it, Jiyong!"

"What?" he asked, spreading his bootish hands innocently.

"You're not"—she lowered her voice—"stealing books!"

"Why not? I bet we could sell each illustration separately."

Roz flushed in anger, and it looked like the only reason she wasn't smashing Ji's head in with the books was because she didn't want him to bleed on the covers.

"Fine," he grumbled. "I won't touch the stupid books. Where's your room?"

"In the attic. The old servants' quarters."

A thought occurred to him. "Are you the only one there? Is there room for me and Sally? Because I can't sneak out at night if I'm sleeping in the kitchen."

"There's plenty of room," she said. "I'll show you."

Roz led him higher in the town house. On a wide landing, Ji paused at a window to gaze over the fence that surrounded the town house. He hadn't seen the city since they'd arrived. He eyed the mansions lining the canal—then caught motion inside the gate and saw a frizzy head emerge from the stables.

"Oh," he said, tapping at the glass. "There's Sally!"

Roz unlatched the window. "Sally!" she called softly.

Sally didn't notice. She just dragged a bucket across the yard.

When Ji tapped harder, Sally raised her head. She peered at the house, and Ji and Roz waved wildly until Sally saw the motion. She flashed a toothy smile and raised her bucket in greeting. Ji felt his own smile widen, and they just stood there for a bit, grinning like idiots.

Then Sally stuck her tongue out and disappeared under the eaves, and Roz closed the window. She led Ji to a stairway so steep that it was almost more of a ladder than stairs.

A wide attic squatted under the angled roof, with four doors in the walls. When Roz opened the nearest one, sunlight flooded into the central room. Ji blinked and followed her into a bedroom with a ceiling that slanted to the floor. A strip of window, not quite as high as his knees, ran the length of the wall.

There was a bed and a writing desk and a bench piled with books.

"Are the other rooms like this?" Ji asked, looking around.

"I took the largest." Roz blushed. "And the best furniture. And the one with the most light. Which was very wrong of me."

"You're the only one here, Roz. You can take the best room."

"It still feels greedy," she said. "I'd offer you tea biscuits, except I haven't any."

"So you've just been sitting up here by yourself, reading?"

"I should have done more!" She turned toward the window. "I know I should have. I've been checking maps for the tapestry factory, but I haven't found it yet and I—I'm sorry."

"Roz, all I've been doing is scrubbing pots and boots."

"But it's not fair. I . . . I've been enjoying myself, reading all these books." She turned back, her eyes shiny with unshed tears. "Well, except Proctor sends for me at mealtime."

"The twins are mean to you, huh?"

A fragile smile rose on her face. "I cannot accuse them of being overly polite."

"How's Brace holding up?"

"He's studying hard. Books, strategy games—" Roz shook her head. "He dislikes when I call them games. Strategy *scenarios*, I should say. And of course he's studying swordplay, as well."

"No way! How's he doing?"

"See for yourself," she said, and gestured to the window.

Ji rubbed his aching forearm. "Huh?"

"Just look."

So Ji crouched and peered through the window into a multilevel courtyard paved with flat rocks. Flowering fruit trees rose here and there, and stone benches sat beside gleaming urns and leafy shrubs. And Brace crouched beside one of the benches, gripping a wooden broadsword.

Lady Nosey slashed at him with a blunted rapier and Lord Pickle circled, holding two padded daggers. Brace jerked away from the slash and swung wildly at Nosey.

She ducked and his broadsword swept over her head.

Nosey lunged and her rapier caught Brace in the shoulder. Pickle darted closer, but Brace kept turning with the force of his swing and his broadsword smashed Pickle in the arm.

"Go, Brace!" Ji whispered. "C'mon, beat him like a borrowed egg!"

Nosey thrust again, and Brace spun, raising his sword to fend her off. She stayed behind him, gliding sideways with catlike grace. Brace dodged wildly but she jabbed him three times between the shoulder blades.

Stepping into sight, Proctor lifted a hand to stop the mock fight. But Pickle didn't care. He grabbed Brace from behind, and Nosey used the edge of her rapier like a whip, whacking at Brace's head as he cringed.

Proctor lowered his hand and watched, his expression curious.

"Hey!" Ji shouted at the window. "Stop them!"

"Jiyong," Roz said, touching his shoulder. "Hush."

"They're ganging up on Brace!" Ji felt his jaw clench. "It's not fair!"

"Proctor encourages them to bully him," Roz said. "I suspect that's why he's learning so fast."

"If bullying made him stronger," Ji grumbled, "he'd already be unbeatable."

"Why are you looking for him?"

Ji stood from the window, rubbing his neck. "To tell him to send me on errands in the city."

"So you can look for valuables?"

"And for Chibo, too. Except maybe it's better if Brace asks Proctor to move me and Sally into the attic with you. That way I can sneak out at night."

Roz wrinkled her nose thoughtfully. "And you won't waste time on errands. I think that's wise. Though perhaps I should speak with Brace?"

"Yeah, good idea."

Sally slipped through the door. "I've got a better one."

"Sally!" Roz gasped, pressing her hand to her chest. "You startled me!"

"You invited me. Didn't you? Through the window? I thought you were waving at me."

"Of course we were," Ji told her. "What's your idea?"

"Well—" Sally stopped and gazed around the room. "Look at this! It's basically a palace."

"It's basically an attic," Ji said.

"It *is* an attic," Roz said.

"That's what I just said," Ji told her. "Sheesh. For someone who's so smart—"

"My idea is this," Sally interrupted, flopping onto the bed. "If you're already asking for permission to sleep here . . . also ask about Chibo."

Roz fiddled with her dress. "Ask Brace to buy Chibo from the tapestry weavers?"

"Yeah."

"I know Brace," Ji said. "If you ask him, he'll just ask

Proctor. And we can't trust Proctor."

"Well, he is personally acquainted with the queen," Roz said slowly. "That's a rare and wondrous thing."

"You know who trusted him?" Ji asked. "Butler. And since we got here, has Proctor even mentioned him once? Has anyone?"

Roz frowned and Sally shook her head.

"He's dead and forgotten, like my brother." Ji looked to Roz. "Proctor's a killer. Ask Brace about the attic, that's all. Nothing else."

"Are you sure?" Sally asked.

"Proctor could save Chibo by lifting a finger," Roz added.

"The last time he lifted a finger, he threw a dagger," Ji said. "We can't trust him, not for a second."

Sally and Roz exchanged a glance. Then Sally nodded. "When it comes to liars, you know best."

"Good," Ji said. "Once we're sleeping here, I'll sneak out every night. I promise you, Sally, I won't stop till Chibo's free."

18

THE NEXT DAY, Ji cleaned encrusted pots and greasy pans until lunchtime. He was elbow deep in a casserole dish when the kitchen maid curtsied, and Brace stepped inside.

He seemed different, though Ji couldn't figure out exactly how. Maybe he looked a little taller, or older? His eyes were still blue, though, his face was still long, his shoulders were still bony. Maybe he was just standing straighter.

Ji bowed his head. "My lord."

"Miss Roz told me that you'd like to sleep in the attic."

"Me and Sally," Ji said.

"I discussed your request with Proctor." Brace strolled closer, running a gloved finger along a countertop. "He told me to decide, and I chose to allow it."

"Did Roz, uh, ask about anything else?" Ji said, wondering if she'd mentioned Chibo. "My lord?"

"Is that all you have to say?" Brace asked.

Ji dried his hands on a cloth. "Yeah. I think so."

"Truly?" Brace cocked an eyebrow just like Baroness Primstone. "Nothing else?"

"Well, I've got plenty of other questions, if that's what you mean. Like, for example, are ant lions actually part lion? Why is it called Mirror Lake? And what—"

"I meant," Brace cut in, "is there anything you have to say, considering that I'm allowing you and Sally to sleep in the attic?"

Ji scratched his cheek and pretended to think. He knew what Brace wanted: his groveling thanks. And maybe he should just grovel . . . except he liked Brace too much to kiss his butt. So instead he said, "Nah, I don't care which room I get."

"I'm not talking about rooms! A servant with better manners might *thank* me, you know."

Ji bowed his head deeply. "Yes, my lord. I am so very grateful for your kindness, my lord. You are as caring and wise as Baroness Primstone, my lord."

Brace scowled. "What's that supposed to mean?"

"Nothing, my lord," Ji said innocently. He needed Brace to help him, but he also wanted to help Brace—to remind him that he wasn't like Nosey and Pickle. He was better than them.

After a tense moment, Brace's scowl turned to a thoughtful frown. He glanced at the kitchen maid, then murmured to Ji, "Let's go outside."

Ji tossed the cloth into the sink and followed Brace into the kitchen garden, a patch of earth where Cook grew ginger and cilantro and chilies. A handful of edible flower bushes bloomed on the border, and bees buzzed from blossom to blossom.

"I guess I'm a little worn out," Brace said, plucking a leaf from a passionflower trellis.

"You're working hard," Ji said.

"Yeah, all this studying and sparring is backbreaking. . . ." Brace grinned, looking more like his old self. "But amazing. I'm learning things I'd never even imagined. It's exhausting, though, and it never stops."

You're probably working almost as hard as a servant, Ji didn't say. "Long hours, m'lord?"

"Late nights, early mornings . . . and I never, uh, got a chance to thank you." Brace tossed the leaf into the garden. "For what you did. At the bone crypt."

"I'm happy to serve, my lord," Ji said.

"You should be!" Brace nudged Ji with his shoulder. "Anyway, thanks."

Ji didn't push his luck by saying *you're welcome,* but he liked that Brace had thanked him. Most nobles wouldn't have even thought of thanking a servant. And they never would've nudged him like that—like a friend. So even after he'd been studying with Proctor, there was still a lot of *Brace* left.

A bee buzzed past, and Ji smiled, remembering the afternoon he and Brace had spent eating honey bread and arguing about the big questions. Like, who'd win in a fight, a spearman or a swordsman? Which was stronger, an ogre or a bugbear?

"So Proctor's teaching you to fight, huh?" he asked.

Brace nodded, his eyes dancing with eagerness. "It's better than I ever dreamed! And swordplay's only a tiny part of it. Proctor's amazing. He knows everything about politics, tactics, and power."

"Yeah?"

"Power is a tool, Ji, like an anvil or a loom or a, a—" Brace looked around the garden. "A watering can! Just having it isn't enough. You need to be trained in its use."

You didn't actually need to be trained in the use of a watering can, but Ji decided not to mention that. "I bet he's good with a throwing dagger, too."

Brace frowned. "What?"

"Er, nothing." Ji tried not to think about Butler. "Thanks for letting us sleep in the attic."

"Happy to help!" Brace said, with a chuckle he'd obviously copied from Proctor. "Oh, and Roz did say something about Sally's brother. Um, apparently he's not happy with his job?"

"He's spending twelve hours a day at a loom. I bet he's a tiny bit gloomy."

"Well, Proctor says that the finest tapestries are worth any sacrifice. They bind the realm together, you know. Have you ever seen a true tapestry?"

"A magic one, with pictures that move?" Ji shook his head. "Nah."

"In the Forbidden Palace, there are dozens of them," Brace said, his blue eyes glinting. "They show the rise of the first queen, and when the terra-cotta warriors slaughtered the ogre nation. Then there's the enslavement of the goblins. . . ."

Ji nodded along without listening. Tonight was the night. He'd climb the wall and sneak through the streets. He'd slip into windows and creep through mansions, dodging servants and guards. His heart pounded with excitement—and fear.

That evening, after scrubbing dueling boots and riding boots and walking boots, Ji headed to the attic instead of his pallet, rubbing a painful knot in his shoulder. He'd never cleaned dueling boots before, and the laces took an hour. He hoped that nobles would choose a wiser, kinder method of resolving arguments in the future.

Or that they'd start dueling barefoot.

Two lanterns glowed in the attic's main room, and a bouquet of scraggly flowers tilted in a mug on a table. Sticks of incense sprouted from a copper burner, and Roz curled in a chair with a book, wearing a cheerful yellow frock.

"What do you think?" Sally asked Ji, grabbing a bottle of rice milk from a bench. "Better than the stables!"

Ji smiled. "It's better than the kitchen, too."

"It's almost a barracks," Sally said. "If you kind of squint."

"There is no way in which this looks like a barracks," Roz said, gently closing the book. "There are no bunks, there is no armory. There isn't a single soldier."

"There would be if someone gave me a sword," Sally said.

"You're not a soldier," Ji told her.

"You're not even a little drummer girl," Roz said.

"And it's more like a picnic than a barracks," Ji said.

Roz blinked at him. "A *picnic*? Did a load of boots fall on your head?"

"Nope, but I stole these!" Ji pulled a stack of tortillas from under his shirt. "Instant picnic."

"Tortillas!" Sally grabbed one from his hand. "They're still warm."

"Of course they're warm," Roz said, with a shudder. "Did you not see where he was carrying them? In his actual armpit."

"Soldiers can't be choosers," Sally told her, and tore into the tortilla.

Roz read a few pages of Ti-Lin-Su's sonnets while they ate. Ji didn't understand a single line, but that didn't matter; he liked Roz's voice, and the way she read the words. When they finished dinner, she looked at Ji and said, "When are you leaving?"

"Middle of the night. And while I'm stealing stuff, you find out where the tapestry factory is."

"How? The maps aren't helping."

"I don't know," he told her. "Use that big brain of yours."

"What about me?" Sally asked.

"Use your less-big brain."

"Jerk." She threw a cushion at him. "I mean, how can I help? You want me to come along tonight?"

"You can't steal things, Sal."

"I could for Chibo."

"And if the guards catch you, you'll confess. It's easier if it's just me."

Sally frowned at him, her gaze thoughtful. "What aren't you telling me?" She looked to Roz. "What isn't he saying?"

"That if he gets caught," Roz said, "he wants you to stay free, to help Chibo."

"Oh."

"I wasn't thinking that," Ji lied. "I was thinking that I need to do this. I need to prove that I'm not worthless."

"Sally and I already know that," Roz told him. "So who, exactly, are you trying to convince?"

"Oh, shut up," he grumbled. "And read another sonnet."

Three crescent moons were shining when Ji crept to the stables for a length of rope. He wished he could leave through the front gate, but the coachman lived in the carriage house and he'd investigate any suspicious sounds.

Ji crossed to the kitchen garden. He climbed a passionflower trellis beside the spike-studded stone wall that surrounded Proctor's property. A grassy scent rose when his sandals crushed the vines. He tied the rope to the top of the trellis, then clambered onto the wall. He almost fell but caught himself with a lunge, scraping his shin. He checked for blood, then lowered himself down the rope on the other side of the wall.

He stepped on a steep slope—and slipped on the wet grass.

His yelp echoed across the canal. He grabbed the rope, barely staying on his feet. Five feet below him, the water rushed past, black as an ogre's heart. When his pulse stopped pounding, he sidled carefully along the slope to a narrow footbridge.

He climbed the railing and looked toward the glowing lanterns outside Proctor's town house. He'd made it!

He slouched away, past ornate gates and lavish lawns, and beneath a gargoyle in a flapping purple cloak that seemed to watch him from a rooftop.

On the next block, two gentlemen strolled along, swinging canes. Then came a lady wearing a pointy hat, followed by two maids wearing shorter versions of the same hat. If Ji had been twice as big, he would've mugged them. Sure, and if he pooped diamonds, he wouldn't have needed to.

He strolled past mansions and shrines, memorizing

landmarks and scanning for open windows. That was why he spotted the gargoyle in the flapping cloak again. Except it wasn't a gargoyle: it was a *person*, running across the rooftops.

"Either someone really hates sidewalks, or . . ." Ji swallowed. "Or that's a thief."

Craning his neck, Ji followed the fluttering cloak around a corner. Because he needed a thief. Maybe this rooftop bandit would help him steal stuff . . . or lead him to a stash of loot.

He jogged along a canal, tracking the flashes of movement above. He stopped eight blocks later, panting, outside a town house with hibiscus flower banners. He didn't see anything on the roofs other than chimneys. He'd lost the thief.

"Stupid sidewalk hater," he grumbled.

He climbed a flight of stairs and crossed a park . . . and a crew of goblins loped across the street in front of him. They woofled and hunched, their knees bending the wrong direction. Ji's stomach twisted. They looked so *wrong*. Nonhuman and beaver faced. He ignored them, until one goblin pointed at him with a belly-arm.

Ji's nerve broke. He raced away and didn't stop until he reached the attic.

Maybe slinking around at night wasn't the best idea. Everything was locked and the streets were quiet—plus the idea of breaking a window or squeezing under a gate terrified him. Almost as much as goblins.

Except he'd promised Sally that he'd save Chibo. And he needed to replace all the loot he'd lost at Primstone. So he kept climbing the wall . . . until the night the city guard caught him.

19

FOR THE NEXT three nights, Ji poked into alleyways and peered through shop windows, prowling the dark streets, looking for something to steal. Once he almost snuck into a town house, but a guard dog barked at the last second.

Then Roz learned that the tapestry factory was in the Oilpress, a neighborhood crisscrossed with canals and waterwheels. So Ji headed for the fancy cobblestone terraces, which offered a panoramic view of the lower city, to memorize the way to the Oilpress.

When he arrived, lanterns and torches illuminated the nighttime streets far below. He crossed a terrace for a better view, walking beside a canal that stopped at a sheer cliff face. The water kept going, though, gushing from the canal and plunging into a pool a hundred yards below.

Three statues rose from the canal. Except these statues

weren't terra-cotta warriors. They had long, seaweedy hair and angular faces. And from the waist down, they were covered in thick fish scales. The current splashed and bubbled across their stony fins, which poked up from the shallows.

"Mermaids," he said, and felt himself smile.

Ji touched the scaly arm of the statue closest to him. Her scales were slick with mist and glimmered in the moons-light. He rubbed one and—

"There!" a man's voice barked. "There he is!"

Boots slammed across the terrace and Ji spun, his throat clenching. They'd found him! They knew what he was planning. They were closing in.

"At the mermaids!" a woman's voice called. "Spread out."

Four guards jogged toward him from a canal-side path. The moons-light glinted on steel-banded boots and bronze helmets. Three of the guards held swords while the fourth carried a *woldo*, a long pole with a curved blade at the end.

Frantic with fear, Ji scanned the terrace. He saw only one way out: he could jump into the canal and let the current sweep him down the waterfall. Except he couldn't dive. Or swim. And that was a loooooong way down.

Sally would've been brave enough to try, but Ji just raised his hands and shouted, "I didn't do it! It wasn't me!"

"It's just a kid," the guard with the *woldo* said, stalking closer.

"What're you doing here, this time of night?" a bearded guard asked.

"I'm a boot boy!" Ji blurted. "I mean, I'm just walking around, looking at the city." He pointed at the streets below the terrace. "Look! The city!"

A light-skinned guard sheathed her sword. "Well, he's not Red Mask, we know that."

"You seen anything unusual tonight?" the bearded one asked Ji.

"Red Mask?" Ji asked.

"A guy wearing a purple cloak," the one with the *woldo* said.

"A gal," the light-skinned one said.

"A guy," the one with the *woldo* said. "In a red mask that looks like an ogre face."

"N-no, ma'am," Ji stammered to her. "I—I don't think so."

The bearded guard's eyes narrowed in suspicion. "You don't *think*?"

"I saw a picture once! A picture of an ogre." Ji frowned, half remembering a red face and yellow hair. "It gave me nightmares."

"This mask doesn't look that realistic," the light-skinned guard told him. "How about the cloak?"

Ji thought about the sidewalk-hating "gargoyle" in the purple cloak and said, "No, ma'am, I haven't seen anything like—"

"I'm telling you," the bearded guard interrupted, "I saw

the Mask two minutes ago. She jumped across the canal."

"You saw a boot boy standing at a mermaid statue," the guard with the *woldo* scoffed. "I'm not sure there *is* a Red Mask."

"Well, someone is lurking in these neighborhoods at night. Climbing walls, peering in windows."

Ji gulped. That was *him*! They thought he was this ogre-masked bandit. "Wow, that's . . . um . . . Can I go now and—get out of your way?"

The light-skinned guard smacked his shoulder. "Go on then."

"If we catch you wandering around at night again," the guard with the *woldo* said, "we'll throw you off the mountain. That clear?"

"Yes, ma'am!" Ji said.

He scurried from the terraces and trotted toward the town house, half terrified and half relieved. He couldn't wander the midnight streets anymore, not with guards searching for a bandit. That was too dangerous. So there was only one thing to do: break into the tapestry factory and kidnap Chibo.

Sure, *that* wasn't dangerous at all.

Ji scrubbed boots, scoured laundry, and waited for his chance to sneak away before sunset. Then he'd make his way to the Oilpress, find the tapestry factory, and save Chibo. Somehow.

Two days after the guards caught him, Ji watched Brace spar with the twins, then made a break for the front gate—but the coachman was lurking in the drive. The day after that, he saw Brace playing a strategy game against Mr. Ioso and slunk toward the garden to hop the fence— but Cook was gathering herbs.

Sally didn't say anything to rush him, though he sometimes caught her eyeing him impatiently. And then late one afternoon in the attic, she attacked Ji with a broom— using the moves she'd memorized watching Brace—while he defended himself with a cushion.

Sally whacked Ji's shin. "Die, troll!"

"Ow!" He hopped a few times. "Ow! Ow!"

"She's here!" Roz burst into the room. "I can't believe it! She's in the city!"

"Who?" Ji asked, while Sally said, "Huh?"

"Ti-Lin-Su!" Roz said, flapping her hands with excitement. "She lives in the city!"

"That writer you like?" Sally asked.

Ji rubbed his shin. "She's still writing?"

"She must be!" Roz beamed. "She's probably at her desk right now, in her water garden. Mulling over her outstanding question, about dragons hoarding treasure."

"It's way cooler that they shoot flames out of their eyes," Sally said.

"Yeah," Ji said. "What does she care that they hoard treasure?"

"Because she's a scholar!" Roz said. "She answers the unanswered questions."

"You should visit her," Sally said.

Roz blushed. "I could *never.*"

"Sure you could," Sally said. "You're almost a proper lady, and you're smart as a cactus kitten."

At least, that was what Ji thought she said. He wasn't listening, because he'd heard the rattle of coach wheels in the drive, followed by the squeak of the gate opening. The coach was leaving. And if he trailed behind it, maybe he could sneak through the gate! Roughly two seconds later, he burst through the side door of the town house. He heard the wheels crunching in the drive and raced around the corner. There! The carriage was halfway to the front gate. He sprinted after it, arms pumping, sandals slapping the drive.

He lunged forward, grabbed a strap . . . and scrambled onto the running board!

Yes! Victory! Then he spotted Nosey and Pickle watching him from a window in the town house. *No! Defeat!* They'd caught him sneaking out. His stomach dropped . . . but this time he didn't turn back. Instead, he gave a big fake wave and a quick bow of his head, like he was supposed to be there.

The twins muttered to each other and Ji smiled wider and faker while the carriage rumbled through the gate and turned onto the street.

Ha! Forget the twins—he'd done it! Maybe he couldn't steal stuff with guards patrolling the nighttime streets, but now he didn't need to. Now he just needed to find the Oilpress neighborhood with the tapestry factory and free Chibo.

Of course, he didn't have the faintest clue how he was going to do that. Still, he'd cross that bridge when he came to it, and hope there weren't too many trolls lurking underneath.

20

LOWER ON THE mountain, the avenues narrowed into streets and the mansions shrank into houses. The carriage clattered through an intersection with two terra-cotta warriors. Then the horses' harnesses jangled around a steep corner, and Ji caught sight of a tile-roofed building he recognized from his nighttime prowling.

He hopped off the running board and jogged downhill to a marketplace overlooking the Oilpress neighborhood. A dozen canals reflected the sunset, and hundreds of waterwheels rose between brick buildings.

Ji asked a woman selling kimchi buns where to find the tapestry weavers. She pointed the way, telling him to look for the columns and the yellow doors.

Ten minutes later, a maze of gray walls rose around Ji.

The road was rutted with tracks and lumped with horse poop. Ji hopped over a fresh pile, dodged a wagon, and caught a glimpse of two square columns.

He trotted closer and saw a few words on a brass plaque. He guessed that one of them was "Tapestry"— but it might've been "Guttersnipe" or "Tuba" for all he knew.

He peeked into a factory yard. A pair of broad yellow doors led into a big building with grand windows. Four smaller yellow doors on the same wall reminded Ji of goslings waddling behind a goose. A pair of chattering clerks stepped from one door, then disappeared into another. Grooms and drivers bustled outside an open stable with five fancy carriages and a dozen horses. One of them— the horses, not the grooms—nickered disdainfully at Ji and flicked flies with her tail.

Ji wrinkled his nose at her. Stupid horses.

He retreated into the street and followed the high wall of the weaving factory. The evening darkened as he checked doors and windows, trying to find a way in. Everything was locked tight. He paused at the last door and said a silent prayer.

Then he grabbed the doorknob . . . and it didn't budge. Great. He swore under his breath—and a cloaked man drifted from behind a stack of crates.

"Yi!" Ji jerked backward. "I mean, hi. Hello! Hi there! I, um, was just looking for . . ."

He trailed off when the man stepped into the light: a little taller than Ji, and as broad as a blacksmith with a fondness for potatoes. Shadows fell inside the hood of his dingy purple cloak, but Ji saw a glint of red. *Red Mask*, the bandit. Right here. Three feet away.

". . . for my brothers," Ji finished, as sweat beaded on his skin. "Who are big and mean. And armed. And nearby. And did I mention armed?"

"I peeked you from the toproof!" Red Mask said in a deep, gravelly voice. "Downbeneath, in the street."

"Downbeneath?" Ji asked, his fear warring with his confusion. "What? From the roof?"

"The toproof!"

"Wait—" Ji blinked. "You're the sidewalk-hater!"

Red Mask either giggled or swallowed a handful of gravel, it was hard to tell. "I don't hate side walkers!"

"Uhhhh, sure. Well—"

"You're not so cutemost awake," Red Mask said, and his hood seemed to duck apologetically. "Sorrylots."

"That's, um, okaybunch?" Ji said, shifting nervously. "So . . . you're Red Mask?"

"Sillybeet!" Red Mask scoffed. "I'm Nin."

"Right," Ji said, backing away farther. "Well, nice meeting you, Nin. Watch out for, y'know, guards."

"Ha!" Nin barked a laugh. "They tremblescared you at the splashroad."

"Splashroad? You mean the canal?"

"Canal, yes." Nin's laugh sounded like an amused avalanche. "Guards were hunting me, but they caught Sneakyji instead, next to the mermaids. I peeked that easyclear."

Ji stopped backing away. For some reason, this jibbering weirdo didn't feel like a threat. "You were there when the guards caught me?"

"Hidden in shadow." The deep hood nodded again. "That was third time I peeked you. First time, sleepy-little underground. Second time upmountain, Sneakyji climbing over fence around fancy house. Almost fall in splashroad!"

"I barely slipped! And what were *you* doing there?"

"I hide and watch the houses of the three candied dates for—"

"Wait, wait!" Ji interrupted. "What did you call me? Sneakyji?"

"Sneakyji."

Ji couldn't help it; he grinned. "Awesome."

"Awww," Nin said. "Aw."

"Um. What are you doing?"

"You told Nin to 'aw, some.'" Nin shrugged a cloaked shoulder. "So I aw-ed." He scratched his head with a red-gloved hand. "Some."

"Right, okay. Thanks." As Ji's fear ebbed, he realized that he'd found the perfect person to ask for help. "So, um, Nin? You're a criminal, right?"

"No!" Nin growled, which sounded like a millstone with indigestion. "Not a crim *or* an animal."

"No, no," Ji said, raising his hands. "I mean, you're a bandit. An outlaw. A thief?"

The millstone ground a laugh. "No, no! Just a spy."

"Yeah, sure," Ji said. What a weirdo. "Do you know how to pick a lock?"

"Of course I do. I'm not skullnumb."

Ji nodded toward the door in the factory wall. "Could you open that for me? As a favor? I'll owe you one."

"I can't open that," Nin said. "It's locked."

"You just said you can pick locks!"

"I can! Show me a tallstack of locks, and I'll pick the best one." Nin prodded the lock in the door. "Like this one. This one is good."

"No, you buttonhead, I didn't mean—" Ji took a breath. "Do you know how to open locks without a key?"

"Smash through."

"Quietly?"

"Oh! Yes, of course! Except . . . no. Not even a tinyspeck."

Ji rubbed his face with his palm. "Then how'm I supposed to get inside?"

"Through window," Nin said, pointing to a set of closed wooden shutters.

"They're locked, too."

"Don't be a headbutton!" Nin said.

He leaped onto the windowsill, climbed the wall, and

disappeared onto the roof of the weaving factory.

"It's 'buttonhead,'" Ji said faintly.

A minute later, the shutters swung open and Nin's hood appeared, the red of his mask glinting faintly.

"Whoa," Ji said, trotting closer. "Thanks."

"Now you owe me one!" Nin said, grabbing Ji's arm and dragging him toward the window.

"Hey!" Ji said, tugging away. "Let go!"

Nin released him. "So squirmy!"

"I'm not squirmy," Ji said, glaring. "I just don't like being grabbed by big gormless headbuttons is all."

"I'm not gormless. I have plenty of gorm."

Ji squinted at him. "What do you want in return?"

"A favor," Nin said.

"What kind of favor?"

"A valuable one. See? Not gormless."

"Just tell me what you want."

"Prick up your earflaps," Nin told him, "and listen for the right."

"For the right what?"

"The rite! The Diadem Rite! We need to know when it starts."

Ji peered into the shadows of Nin's hood dubiously. "That's all what you want? To know when the rite is happening?"

"That's not all I want. Also want pickled beets. But that's the whole favor."

"Then sure," Ji said. "If I hear about the rite, I'll tell you."

"Rock vow?"

Ji had no idea what that meant, so he said, "Rock vow."

"Some aws," Nin said happily. "Grab you now, Sneakyji?"

"No! No grabbing. Just give me your hand." A red leather gauntlet was thrust at him from the dingy purple cloak. "And how'd you know my name's Ji?"

"Been watching!" Nin pulled him onto the windowsill. "From toproofs."

"Watching *me*?"

"Not you," Nin scoffed from inside his red mask. "Peeking noble houses."

"Which houses? Why?"

"Your house, the hibiscus house, and the young warlady."

"Oh! You're watching the noble kids who are training for the rite?"

"That's what they told me to—" Nin stopped suddenly. "Hibiscus house! Sorry, Sneakyji, I have to tumble! Try not to forget!"

Nin jumped or climbed or scaled—sort of jump-climbscaled—to a warehouse roof across the street and vanished into the evening. For a guy who was shaped like a barrel of rocks, he really could move. Especially considering that his gruesome red mask must've blocked his vision.

"Don't worry," Ji told the empty street. "Nobody could

forget *that* much weird."

He slid down from the windowsill into the tapestry factory. He found himself in a cramped storage room full of burlap sacks. The faint *thum-thud-whack* coming from the left sounded like looms, so Ji headed in that direction.

He ended up at the front of the complex. Great. He'd walked in a big circle. At least the factory yard was quieter now—though the horses in the open stables still eyed him warily. He listened for the *thum-thud*, then slipped through a yellow door into a clerks' office with neat desks and tidy calligraphy brushes. The room was empty, thank summer, so he didn't have to tell any lies.

He opened a door that led farther into the main building, and a bell jingled overhead.

Ji died. No breath, no pulse, no thoughts. Just a scrawny corpse holding on to a doorknob.

When nobody shouted or kicked him in the knee bone, he came back to life. He slunk through the door, careful not to jingle the bell again, and found himself in a lemon-scented hallway lined with sliding, paper-paneled doors.

Ji heard a low moan, maybe the grind of waterwheels or the shuttling of looms. He headed toward the sound, hoping that it would lead him to Chibo—and the bell jingled again as the door opened behind him.

Someone was coming.

Ji leaped sideways, trying to shove through a sliding door. Except you can't shove through a *sliding* door. He crashed into the paper panels and slammed to the ground, caught in the wreckage of the door frame. Pain burst in his elbow and ribs, and the footsteps pattered closer.

A moment later, two figures stood over him in the broken doorway.

21

"WHAT IN THE moons are you doing?" Roz asked, peering down at Ji.

"Vanquishing doors," Sally said.

"You—here—*what*?" Ji babbled.

"We followed you on the burro," Roz told him. "I told a few untruths, and the footman didn't suspect a thing. You would've been proud."

"But—but how'd you get in?"

"The front entrance," Roz said.

"What about the grooms and clerks and stuff?"

"I stuck my nose in the air like I belonged, and Sally trotted behind me."

Ji felt himself deflate. "Oh."

"How about you?"

"A jibbering weirdo dragged me through a window."

Sally clasped Ji's hand and helped him stand. "You dragged yourself through a window?"

"Ha ha," he said. "I met a—"

"Did you find Chibo?"

"No, I—"

"Oh!" Roz pointed to the wall. "Oh! Oh-oh! Oh!"

When Ji turned his head, his breath caught. A tapestry stretched across the wall. A *true* tapestry. A magic tapestry of brilliant reds and rich greens, sweeping silvers and obsidian blacks. For a moment, that was all that Ji saw: pure beauty, gorgeous colors.

Then the image snapped into focus, and he gasped. "Oh!"

"Oh!" Sally echoed. "Oh. My."

"Whoa," he breathed.

"Yeah," she agreed.

"I mean," he explained, "*whoa.*"

"Totally," she confirmed.

"Indeed," Roz summed up.

The tapestry showed the whole Summer Valley and bits of the lands beyond. The Coral Islands dotted a blue-green sea to the west of a rocky coast that rose into rolling farmland—except for one spot where the palace-topped mountain loomed, covered in buildings. The river flowed across the tapestry, branching eastward past Mirror Lake toward the ogre mountains. To the south, the salt flats stretched to the goblin mounds, and to the north, the cloud forest touched the bright snowlands.

"The known world," Roz whispered, and spun a bronze cylinder attached to the edge of the tapestry.

"It's amazing," Ji said, his voice reverent. "It's beautiful."

"Imagine *conquering* all that," Sally said.

As the cylinder whirled, the picture shifted until the coast was in the center. With every spin of the cylinder, the image changed: the palace-topped mountain shrank and the city faded into meadows and farms. Finally, all that remained was a village with thatched roofs and muddy streets, huddled behind a palisade of sharpened logs.

"This is history," Roz said. "The tapestry is showing us the distant past. Now if I spin the cylinder in the other direction, time will move forward. . . ."

The image rippled until hundreds of tents covered the fields outside the palisade. Families in tattered clothes squatted around cook fires. Half of them wore ragged armor, and most wore slings and bandages.

"It's showing us what it must've been like hundreds of years ago," Roz said, her eyes shining. "Before the Summer Crown protected humanity from the rampaging hordes. This is what they faced. . . ."

The next time she spun the cylinder, the back of Ji's neck prickled. Because dark shapes swarmed at the humans from the edges of the tapestry: creatures out of a nightmare, with claws and hooves and fangs.

The beasts struck the human defenders like an iron boot strikes a fat bullfrog. With a splat. The images on the tapestry were so detailed, so lifelike, that Roz turned away, while Ji peeked between his fingers.

Sally flinched but didn't cover her eyes. "Spin it again, Roz! The knights will save them. They'll cut through those monsters like war-wolves through a pumpkin pie."

Ji's disgust faded slightly at Sally's words. *War-wolves through a pumpkin pie?*

"The knights didn't save us," Roz said, whirling the cylinder again. "Not that time. The Summer Queen saved us."

"She was alive back then?"

"Not our queen. The first Summer Queen."

In the center of the village, a lean woman with bronze skin and black hair stood on a platform beside a stone well. She was dressed like a forester, in leather leggings and a tightly wrapped tunic. An empty baby sling lay across her back.

Ji looked closer, but the tapestry didn't show her boots.

"What happened to her baby?" Sally asked.

"Ogres," Roz told her. "Or trolls."

"She doesn't look like a queen."

"Not yet," Roz said. "This shows her *becoming* the queen. She's gathering magic from every single human. She's absorbing enough power to defeat the beasts and save humanity."

In the tapestry, dozens of people surrounded the

woman. Soldiers held swords and spears while robed servants knelt before her, empty-handed. Roz spun the bronze cylinder, and time scrolled forward. The woman lifted her arms and—

Water rose from the well.

A river flowed upward into the air, then spread like a parasol over the woman. Her skin turned white, her hair turned silver. Then the water sprouted into a liquid tree, with a thick shimmering trunk splitting into branches.

"No way!" Ji felt himself smile. "Now that she's got the magic, she's going to make those creatures pay!"

"Holy guacamole." Sally started to laugh—then gasped. "Wait! No! She's too late!"

Monstrous faces and malformed figures appeared between the branches of the water tree. Shadows writhed, with clawed hands and horrible grimaces—and familiar robes.

"The servants!" Roz gasped. "They're changing into beasts."

"Must be ogre magic." Sally tugged her bracelet. "The queen's got to *do* something."

And she did. She gestured again, and the entire village heaved upward, the earth stretching toward the clouds.

"She's making the mountain," Ji said, his voice soft. "She's growing the mountain."

"And she's beating the beasts," Sally said.

As the coastal village rose higher, branches of the

water tree stabbed the half-human beasts, skewering first one, then two, then every single monster. Showing the moments when the first Summer Queen took all human magic into herself, then raised a mountain and destroyed the monsters. Protecting the humans, creating the realm.

When the bronze cylinder started whirling more slowly, the branches wove into a royal crown, which glinted with gold and gems. Then the tapestry stopped moving entirely, freezing on an image of the crown.

"Do it again!" Sally said, her eyes dancing. "Spin it again! Did you see the branches killing those beasts?"

Ji rubbed his shoulder. "I wonder what it's worth."

"It's priceless! It's awesome!"

"Tapestries are remarkable," Roz said. "Although we must remember how they are woven."

"By kids like Chibo," Ji said, his excitement fading.

Sally frowned. "It's woven with their blood. With their lives."

"Right," Ji said. "Let's go."

He led Sally and Roz down the hallway, following the moan of machinery. He pushed through a door and froze. Two women were strolling toward him, arguing about "threading heddles." He panicked, his mind blank and his sandals rooted to the floor. Then he ducked his head, and the women walked past without looking at him: just another invisible servant.

A moment later, the women disappeared toward the tapestry room. Ji took a shuddering breath; then Roz and Sally slipped through the door to join him. Together, they headed into a hallway where a *thum-thud-whack* drummed and the floor trembled.

"The looms are close," Ji said.

He opened the nearest door, and the stink of sheep smacked him in the face. Hundreds of bales of wool tightly packed a storeroom. He squeezed inside and peered down a narrow aisle toward the far wall.

"The noise is louder that way," he said.

Sally climbed a few wool bales blocking the aisle. "C'mon."

"I'll wait here," Roz said.

Ji followed Sally over the bales to three square iron doors at the other end of the room. When Sally tugged on one, it swung open on hinges at the bottom instead of the side. The *thum-thud-whack* burst into the room and a chute angled downward and—

Ji slammed the hatch closed, his heart pounding. "Loud."

"Yeah," Sally said.

"Sounds like the factory floor, though."

He trotted back for Roz. "Climb over—there's something on the other side."

"So I heard." Roz started to follow—then paused. "A little privacy, if you please."

"Oh! Right, sorry!"

He'd forgotten that Roz got shy about "improper behavior" that might get a governess fired—like climbing around in her dress. Ji didn't really understand, but he didn't need to understand. He looked away until Roz joined him. Then he led her to the hatches.

"I think the looms are at the other end of these," he told her. "Through the chutes."

Sally rubbed her face. "And so is Chibo."

"Possibly," Roz said.

Sally opened the hatch, and the *thum-thud-whack* thundered into the room again. "Here goes nothing," she said, and started climbing into the chute. "No fear, no retreat."

"Don't be stupid!" Ji grabbed her arm. "There's always fear—and we retreat if *I* say we retreat."

"You—" Sally eyed him. "You're coming?"

"Of course I am."

"Why?"

"Because they'll chop your head off if I don't," Ji said, "and make *me* brush the stupid horses."

"Just admit it," she said. "You like my head."

"Yeah, if only it didn't have your mouth attached."

"You'll need this," Roz yelled over the racket, pulling a length of twine from a wool bale. "To help you climb down. I'll stand watch."

Ji and Sally climbed into the hatch and slid down a chute

that ended after five feet, at a panel made of stretched cloth, vibrating with the sound of the looms. Sally opened the panel, and the two of them tumbled down another five feet and smacked into an iron grate.

When Sally slid the grate aside, silence fell. Ji's ears rang from the sudden lack of noise, which didn't make any sense. How did the looms get quieter when he got closer?

He shrugged to himself, peered through the opening, and saw the factory.

A heap of wool bales rose on the floor ten feet below him—because the grate opened high in a wall. Across the room, massive wooden frames rose and fell, each stretched with brilliantly colored thread. A thousand shuttles zipped back and forth through sheets of half-woven fabric, and tree-trunk-sized posts turned huge wheels and an enormous fan.

Oh, and the air was filled with flecks of color. Floating, swirling color flakes like a blizzard of sunsets or a shredded rainbow.

Ji gaped at the churning colors. "Is that dye? Pigment?"

"I don't know, but I think it's soaking up the noise," Sally said, because only a faint thrum sounded. "That's why it's quiet in here."

"Magic," Ji muttered. That explained how the looms were quieter when he got closer, and sounded loud again farther away.

The fan kept the colorful flecks blowing through the

room, and an eddy of them drifted through the now-opened iron grate. Ji waved his hand in front of his face, and the pigments—if that was what they were—swirled and swooped.

"Ow!" Sally said, blinking.

"What?" Ji asked. Then his eyes starting burning. "Oh! It's like getting soap in your eyes."

"Ji!" She elbowed him. "Look!"

He followed her watery gaze beneath the looms. Threads plunged down from the frames, surrounding hundreds of kids working in rows beneath the tilting, clattering machines. With their heads shaved, and dressed in identical mud-brown tunics, the kids all looked the same. And they moved the same, too—with small, endlessly repeating motions as they tied knots, applied colors, and wrapped fabric around spindles.

Ji wiped tears from his eyes. The threads never stopped falling, the kids never stopped working, and two burly overseers patrolled the rows, wearing gauzy veils to protect their eyes from the swirling flecks of color.

"There," Sally said, and pointed to a row of kids standing at spinning gears.

At first, Ji couldn't tell which one was Chibo through the color-swirling air. Then an overseer strolled closer, and a little bald kid tilted his head. It was Chibo: braiding a thread onto his gear, then another, then another and another.

"We found him," Ji said. "Now what do we do?"

"First I'm getting my brother," Sally said, sticking her leg through the opening in the wall. "Then I'm getting a sword."

22

Ji PULLED HER back into the chute. "Wait!"

"No way," Sally said. "I'm getting him right now."

"You see those guards?"

"I'll take care of them."

"With what, Sal? They're twice your size. And what about the threads?"

She wiped tears from her face. "What threads?"

"Those kids are woven in place," he said. "*Chibo* is woven in place."

"What are you talking about?" Sally looked closer . . . and her jaw tightened when she saw what he meant. "That's *evil*."

Threads were wrapped around the kids' wrists and ankles in thick knots, roping them to the looms. Every time they moved, shuttles slid and gears turned and spindles bobbed. Ji felt a simmer of anger. A hundred kids, treated worse than servants—treated more like machines than people.

Sally took a shuddering breath. "I can't leave him, Ji."

"I know."

"I'd rather be tied there beside him."

Ji rubbed the sting from his eyes. "Yeah."

"So what're we doing to do?" she asked.

Ji frowned into the color-swirling air. "I don't know. How about, um . . . okay. I'll run and untie Chibo. I'm good with knots."

"What about the guards?"

"They'll leave when you and Roz make the distraction outside."

"What distraction?"

"The big one," he told her. "The huge one. The massive, earthshaking, tooth-quaking distraction that gets the guards called away."

"Oh." She peered at him. "Maybe I should untie Chibo, and you should think of a distraction. It's dangerous down there."

"Sally, if someone whacks at us with a lance, I'm hiding behind you. If we have to arm-wrestle a goblin, you'll go first. But he's woven into place with *knots*. Those are my job."

"That's not a boot, Ji."

"Everything's a boot when you're a boot boy."

She bit her lip. "Just be careful."

"Don't you mean 'just be honorable'?"

"Shut up." Sally shoved him with her shoulder. "Jerk." She grabbed the twine and started climbing up the chute. "I'll see you outside."

"No, head to the town house," he told her bum as she scooted higher. "They probably won't notice I'm missing, but if we're all gone for too long . . ."

"Okay," she said. "See you there."

"And throw me more rope!" he called after her.

A minute later, another length of twine tumbled down the chute and draped around Ji's head. He tied it to the first length, then wiped tears from his cheeks, watched the guards, and waited for the distraction.

Ten minutes.

Twenty minutes.

Thirty minutes . . . and a striped flag flashed across the factory floor. One guard jerked in surprise. He grabbed the other guard, and they jogged from the room. Ji grinned to himself. He didn't know what Sally and Roz had done as a distraction, but it must've been pretty massive and earthshaking.

"Those two really know how to quake some teeth," Ji said.

He unraveled his double length of twine onto the factory floor, then jumped from the grate. He aimed for the heap of wool bales, which he expected to be as fluffy as a bunny rabbit made of smiles.

It wasn't.

He hit hard, then did a little groaning and rolled onto the floor.

The floor wasn't exactly soft, either.

When he caught his breath, he pushed to his feet and headed to the work floor, his side aching and his nerves jangly. The looms slammed overhead, like a thousand bear traps. He kept his gaze low, jogging through the colorful, swirling flakes. He slunk into a forest of threads, then slipped into Chibo's row.

Up close, the kids still looked almost interchangeable, with shorn scalps and skinny faces. Attached to the loom like puppets. Ji only recognized Chibo from his rosebud mouth and his dark skin, more like Ji's than Sally's.

He stepped beside Chibo and murmured, "Stay quiet. We have to get out of here before—"

"Jiyong!" Chibo yelled. "It's you! It's you!"

"Chibo," he hissed. *"Quiet!"*

"Hey, everyone, it's Ji!" Chibo announced, shouting to be heard through the color flakes. "He's here!"

"Would you shut up?"

"I told you he'd come, I *told* you!" Chibo clung tightly to Ji. "I knew you'd come, you and Sally."

"She wanted to burst in with her sword swinging," Ji told him. "But what do you mean, you knew? *We* didn't know!"

"'Cause I'm smarter'n you are," Chibo said, raising his smiling face.

The pigment in the air brought tears to Ji's eyes . . . but there weren't any tears on Chibo's cheeks. And his eyes weren't focused on Ji's, either. He was looking slightly to the side, like he saw the basic shape of Ji's face, but not the details.

"You're mixing up 'smarter' and 'shorter' again," Ji told him. "Let's get you out of here."

"Get us *all* out of here!" Chibo said.

Ji knelt to unravel the threads around Chibo's ankle—and jerked in surprise. "There's someone under here!"

A girl was sleeping in a cubby beneath Chibo's place at the loom, her arms and legs jerking gently as the threads around her wrists and ankles moved.

"That's Ximena," Chibo said. "She works this station when I sleep. Then I work when she sleeps and—"

"Done!" Ji said, unwinding the last tendril from Chibo's ankles. "Give me your hands."

"Um, if you untie me—" Loops of thread spewed crazily from the gear in front of him. "*That!* That happens."

"Who cares?" Ji said, starting on Chibo's wrists. "The guards are gone."

A bell dinged, shrill despite the colorful flecks. "Not all of them! Oh, *badness*. The overseer . . . he's coming!"

"The overseer?" Ji murmured, desperately unknotting the last snarl around Chibo's wrist while threads unspooled past his face.

"You did it!" Chibo told Ji, raising his hands. "Now do everyone else!"

"I can't!"

"You have to, Ji! Look at them!"

Ji looked at them. Dozens of skinny kids surrounded him, working the looms, heads shaved and eyes blank. As if while they wove magical visions into tapestries, they lost their own vision. When they heard Chibo's words, their faces turned toward Ji, unseeing but full of desperate hope.

"There's no time!" Ji cried. "I'm sorry. I'm so sorry—"

"We'll come back," Chibo told the other kids. "I promise, we're coming back."

Ignoring the sick feeling in his stomach, Ji dragged Chibo through the swirling air. At the end of the row, he caught sight of a burly man ambling toward them.

"Oh, no," Ji whispered.

"What's happening?" Chibo asked. "I can't see!"

The overseer took two steps closer . . . then a bunch of gears in the next row started spewing thread. The overseer spun, yelling something that Ji couldn't hear.

"The other kids," Ji said. "They're covering our escape."

The overseer stalked into the next row. Ji wiped the tears from his face, waited three seconds, then raced with Chibo to the pile of wool bales.

"Climb the rope!" he said.

"What rope?"

Ji shoved the twine into Chibo's hand. "Here. Put your

foot in my hands, then climb onto my shoulders and keep climbing!"

The bell shrilled again. Ji watched Chibo climb and waited for the overseer to spot him. When Chibo disappeared through the opening in the wall, he scrambled up the twine. Slats in the wall made perfect footholds, and a minute later he crawled into the chute beside Chibo.

He yanked the twine in with them and slid the iron grate closed.

With the color flakes on the other side of the grate, the noise of the looms started again. "You can't leave the other kids!" Chibo shouted.

"What else can I do?" Ji asked.

Chibo wrinkled his nose. "Save them."

"How?"

"You'll think of something."

"I—I'll try," Ji said, hating himself for lying. "But first we need to finish saving you."

"Okay, as long as you'll try!" Chibo squinted higher in the shadowy chute. "Where's Sally? Is she up there?"

"She's waiting for you at home," Ji told him. "She and Roz distracted the guards and had to run."

"I haven't run in *forever*!" Chibo raised one foot. "Look, no threads! Forget running, I can jump and tumble! I can hop! I can spin till I'm dizzy!"

"Hop later." Ji started to close the cloth panel overhead. "They'll be searching the streets. We'll wait here a few hours, then sneak out."

Chibo reached up to help with the panel but missed the strap by two inches. "Ow! Oops."

Ji frowned at his wide brown eyes. They looked the same but didn't seem to work so well anymore. Still, Chibo was as bubbly and enthusiastic as ever. Ji didn't know how he'd stayed so cheerful, after what he'd been through. Ji would've wanted to burn the factory down and spit on the ashes.

Actually, he *did* want to do that. He remembered the other weaver kids' hopeful faces and nearsighted eyes when Chibo promised them that he'd save them. He remembered their broken expressions when he'd said that he couldn't. All they wanted was freedom; he knew how that felt. But he couldn't help. Instead, he curled in the chute with Chibo for hours, quiet as a cheese-flavored mouse in a room of cats.

Deep in the night, Ji shook Chibo awake. They crept through the factory together and slipped into the midnight street.

23

THE FIRST HINT of dawn was touching the horizon when Ji and Chibo reached the footbridge near Proctor's town house.

"Climb over the railing," Ji said.

"Here?" Chibo asked, peering into the dim light.

"Yeah, but watch out. The grass is slippery on the other side, and there's a canal at the bottom."

"I know *that*," Chibo said. "I can see a little."

"Oh, right."

"Plus, it smells totally canal-ish."

Ji helped Chibo over the railing. As he led him across the grassy slope, a carriage rattled in the street and a frog croaked in the canal. They stopped outside the stone wall of Proctor's town house and Ji rubbed his neck.

"You'll have to stand on my shoulders and climb," he said.

"Awesome!" Chibo said. "I love climbing."

"There's spikes on top of the wall. Don't stab yourself."

"Climbing good, stabbing bad." Chibo nodded. "Got it. What happens once I'm up there? I mean, how do you get up?"

"I hid a coil of rope in the vines. Throw it down and—"

"I can see a canal, Ji. That doesn't mean I can find a rope hidden in vines in the dark."

"Oh. Well, there's always my backup plan."

"What's that?"

"Cry like a baby," Ji told him.

Chibo laughed, and a dark shape fluttered softly to the ground behind him, like a man-sized leaf falling from a tree.

"No babycrying, Sneakyji!" Nin said, his gravelly voice muffled by his weird mask.

Chibo yelped in surprise. He spun and slipped on the grass, tumbling toward the canal.

"Nin!" Ji yelped. *"Quick!"*

Nin swooped toward the canal, his cloak fluttering but his boots solid. He grabbed Chibo, tossed him across one broad shoulder, and gave a raspy giggle.

"Caught her!" he said.

"Wahoo!" Chibo yelled, raising his arms. "I'm flying!"

Ji clasped a hand to his heart. "First, you buttonhead, Chibo's a boy. Second—"

"Sillybeets!" Nin stomped up the slope toward Ji. "Boy, girl. Too young to choose."

"Okay." Ji took a breath. "Stop being weird for five frothing seconds, would you?"

"Can't stop," Nin said. "Never started."

"Very funny," Ji said. "Are you going to help us over the wall?"

"And who are you?" Chibo asked, steadying himself against Nin's cloaked head.

"This is Nin," Ji said. "A friend of mine."

Nin leaned closer to Ji's face. His gruesome mask glinted faintly in the gloom of his hood. Then he lowered one red gauntlet from Chibo's leg and made a fist in front of Ji. "Stonefriends," he said solemnly. "Sneakyji and Nin."

"You didn't even last five frothing seconds," Ji said.

Nin just stood there with his fist extended. "Stonefriends?"

"Stonefriends," Ji agreed. He didn't know what Nin meant, but he touched Nin's fist with his own.

Nin made a sound like a two boulders colliding, then cocked his head toward Chibo. "So Chibald like swoopflying?"

"I *love* swoopflying," Chibo told him.

"There's no such thing!" Ji said. "And even if there was, you've never done it! And even if you had, there isn't—"

With Chibo still on his shoulders, Nin swarmed up the stone fence, as fast as a blue-bat. When they reached the top of the fence, Chibo said, "I'm high as the treetops! I'm tall as a mountain!"

Nin hopped around and Chibo waved his arms until Ji hissed at them to shut their stupid mouths before they woke anyone.

Chibo whispered, "Sorry," and Nin ducked his head apologetically. Then they disappeared down the other side of the fence.

"I've got to keep those two apart," Ji muttered.

Nin vaulted the fence and landed beside Ji. "Grab you now?"

"Go ahead. Just—" Ji yelped when Nin carried him to the top of the fence like a bulldog carrying a rag doll. "Just remember, I don't like swoopflying."

"Sorry!" Nin said cheerfully.

"How come you're so good at climbing?"

Nin pulled his hood lower. "I'm mountainborn."

"Oh, that makes sense."

"I know! Sensemaking is my favorite thing."

"I was being sarcastic."

"Sarcastic?" Nin asked. "Like sardine and fantastic? Sarcastic means fishexcellent?"

"No, it doesn't mean 'fishexcellent.'" Ji looked toward the horizon for a moment. "So why do you want to know about the rite?"

"As a favor!" Nin said, and bounded away into the darkness.

"Weirdo," Ji called after him.

There was no answer except the babbling of the canal.

When Ji climbed down the wall into Proctor's property, he found Chibo in the garden, inhaling the scent of the flowers and herbs. Smiling softly, his eyes closed and his arms spread. *Free.*

The town house slept. Quiet on the ground floor. Quiet on the landing. Yet when Ji ushered Chibo upstairs toward the attic, he heard voices.

"We have to go back," Sally was saying. "Right now."

"We'll wait until morning," Roz said. "Then we'll ascertain precisely what—"

Sally swore. "Stop with the fancy words!"

"We'll find out what happened," Roz explained, though Ji heard a rare impatient note in her voice. "And we'll make a plan."

"What plan?"

"I don't know! Do I look like Ji? *You* make a plan."

"My plan is we run back and try things."

"That's not a plan. Racing across the city in the middle of the night—"

"—is doolally," Ji finished, climbing the last few steps.

"Jiyong!" Sally shouted, beaming like she'd burst.

"You're alive," Roz said, and swayed like she'd faint.

"I'm going to kill you!" Sally said. "We waited and waited but you never—"

Then Chibo stepped around Ji.

He was underweight and shaved bald—but when he peered blurrily at his sister, his smile was the biggest thing in the world. Sally's face flickered from amazement to delight, then stopped on a combination of awe and joy.

Ji had never seen anything better.

Sally swooped Chibo into her arms. She touched his face and stroked his arms. They laughed and sobbed and held each other like they'd never let go. Tears streamed down Roz's face, which glowed with such happiness that Ji's exhaustion vanished. He was crying, too. He didn't know why, and he didn't care.

Then Roz kissed Ji's cheek. "I'm proud of you."

His face caught fire and he grew nineteen feet. "Shut up," he mumbled. "Um, er . . . so how did you make that distraction? Outside the factory?"

"We stabled Gongong with the horses," Roz said, "then snuck outside the wall and laughed."

"We laughed and laughed," Sally said.

"So Gongong started bucking and drove the horses crazy?" Ji shook his head in admiration. "That's evil."

"Thanks," Sally said. "Then Roz threw stones over the wall and broke the windows. She could hit a toad's nose at twenty yards."

"Not that I'd do such a thing," Roz said. "I harbor no grudge against toads."

Chibo clunked the rice-milk jug onto the table. "We have to free the others."

"The other what?" Sally asked.

"The weaver kids! I'm here, but they're still *there*. Right now. Every minute, every day."

"We barely got you out," Ji told him, and boots clomped on the stairs.

Ji lunged for Chibo, to hide him in a back room—but he was too late. The twins strode into the attic, followed by Proctor and Mr. Ioso.

"There!" Lady Posey pointed at Chibo. "I *told* you we saw the boot boy sneaking out. And look what he brought back. A bald monkey."

"This is the younger brother?" Proctor stroked his beard and eyed Ji. "You kidnapped him from the weavers?"

"I can explain," Ji said, trying to think of a lie.

"Please do," Proctor said.

"Well . . ." Ji gulped. "I kidnapped him from the weavers."

"That's not an explanation." Proctor chuckled. "It's a confession."

"But I swear that I ran off without telling Roz and Sally!" Ji said, sticking to the literal truth so Sally wouldn't contradict him. "They weren't there when I untied Chibo, and they didn't—"

"Enough," Proctor said, and glanced at Mr. Ioso.

When Ji followed his gaze, a blinding white flash exploded across the attic.

24

WHEN JI WOKE, he was in his bedroom. His neck hurt and his arms hurt and his eyes hurt. He lay there for a moment, letting his memories filter into his mind. Then he lay there for a few more moments, hoping his memories would improve.

They didn't.

Eventually he rose to leave—but the door was locked.

"Huh," he said.

Locked in his room. That wasn't good. It was better than hanging, though. Unless they were planning to hang him later, in which case . . . well, it was still a little better.

"Hello?" he called, through the door.

Nobody answered. Where was everyone? Locked in

their own rooms? Had Mr. Ioso's flash of light knocked them out, too?

He called again, and nobody answered again, so he paced for a while. Then he lay on his stomach on the floor and looked out the window. Paper lanterns hung from tree branches in the courtyard, bobbing in the breeze. Leaves swirled and tumbled across the flagstones. The fountain reflected a cloudy afternoon sky.

He paced a little more. Then he worried about Roz and Sally and Chibo. Then he napped. He woke sweating from a nightmare about being woven into a massive colorful loom, surrounded by bald kids begging him for help.

Then he watched shadows lengthen in the courtyard as the sun moved across the sky. He wished he could follow it. Instead, he was trapped here, waiting for his doom. Even worse, he might've doomed Sally and Roz too. And after months of lying and stealing, all he'd done was free Chibo from the weavers . . . and brought him straight into even worse trouble.

Finally, footsteps sounded in the attic and the door opened. A menacing figure stood there, silhouetted by lamplight. He looked exactly like an executioner holding a disembodied head in a horrible sack. Then Mr. Ioso stepped inside, and the head in a sack turned out to be a load of dirty boots.

"Get to work," he said, and dropped the boots.

"Oh, thank summer," Ji said.

Mr. Ioso frowned at him. "What did you say?"

"Er, yes, sir," Ji said. "Um, and where are Roz and Sally and Chibo?"

Mr. Ioso cracked his knuckles, then stomped away. He didn't forget to lock the door behind him, though.

"Thanks," Ji muttered. "You big cuddle-bear."

He rubbed his aching shoulder and looked at the boots. Did they really expect him to clean them? What would happen if he didn't? He could hardly get into worse trouble. Except maybe he *could* get into worse trouble. So he cleaned the stupid boots, even though he hated it even more than usual.

Mr. Ioso returned the next morning. He stuffed the clean boots into a bag, then gave Ji a bowl of rice and a soggy churro.

"What's going to happen to me?" Ji asked.

"You'll help Lord Brace at the Diadem Rite."

"Help how?"

"However he tells you." Mr. Ioso eyed him the way a butcher eyes a pig. "It's a high honor, boy."

Ji gulped. "Lucky me."

"You should've served His Lordship better all these years. That's the only way a half-smart peasant like you can get ahead."

"I always treated Lord Brace nicely!" Ji said. "We . . . we're almost friends."

"Friends?" Mr. Ioso asked. "A mutt doesn't make

friends with a lion. You should've pledged your life to him. Maybe then you wouldn't . . ."

"Wouldn't what?"

Mr. Ioso hunched a massive shoulder. "Just serve His Lordship well at the rite, boy. That's all you need to know."

"Oh. Yes, sir."

Mr. Ioso peered at him. "You remind me of myself as a kid."

"Um." Ji tried to smile, to get Mr. Ioso on his side. "I do?"

"Yeah, I was a little snake, too."

Ji flinched when the door slammed behind Mr. Ioso. A snake, huh? Then maybe he should slither away. He started prying a loose board from the floor in the corner of the room. Forget about the tapestry kids, forget about Roz and Sally and Chibo, forget about the stupid Diadem Rite. Just focus on escaping; focus on four inches of wood.

He spent the day on his belly, and when he finally pulled the board from the floor, he found another board beneath it. And that one wasn't even loose.

After he finished crying, he lay on his stomach and gazed through the low window. In the evening gloom, five lanterns hanging in the cherry trees cast crazy shadows across the stone-paved levels of the courtyard. Nothing else moved—until he saw Brace vaulting a bush, his practice sword slicing the air.

"Whoa!" Ji gasped.

Halfway over the bush, Brace's sword smacked into

the staff that Pickle twirled at him from behind. Brace landed, pivoting away from Pickle, and swung his sword toward Nosey's two thrusting rapiers. She crossed her blades, caught his blow—but he kept pivoting. He hooked her ankle with his boot and tripped her into a bench.

"Ha!" Ji said. "Go, Brace!"

Down below, Brace bowed to Nosey—then whipped his sword upward. *Clank!* He blocked Pickle's staff, then ducked and lunged. Bursting forward, he punched Pickle with his sword hilt.

Pickle stumbled into a shrub, and Ji gave a low whistle. "He's kicking their bums!" he called into the main room. "Look at him go!"

Nobody answered, of course.

Instead of bowing to Pickle, Brace spun and strode down a path. He looked confident and strong, like a swordsman.

Holding his blade low, Brace prowled toward a cherry tree. Ji didn't know why . . . until Mr. Ioso slipped forward, holding a curved dagger in each hand.

"No way," Ji breathed. "You can't beat *him.*"

With his sword flicking like a snake's tongue, Brace lunged forward—and even though he couldn't hear, Ji thought that he laughed. He met Mr. Ioso in the moon shadow of the tree, with the lanterns bobbing around them. They exchanged blows too fast for Ji to follow. *Clank-clink-clink-clink-clank.* Then a flurry of *clink-clanks*, a sudden *thunk* . . . and Mr. Ioso took a step backward.

A thrill rose in Ji's chest. Maybe Mr. Ioso wasn't so tough without magic. Maybe serving Brace wouldn't be so bad.

"Get him," he whispered. "C'mon, get him!"

With a slash and a thrust, Brace drove Mr. Ioso into the branches of the tree—until Mr. Ioso smacked a paper lantern through the air at Brace's face. Brace knocked the lantern away . . . but not quickly enough. Mr. Ioso slipped inside his guard and touched a dagger to his throat.

With a wry grin, Brace surrendered. He and Mr. Ioso bowed to each other, and then Brace gestured to Mr. Ioso's daggers, like he wanted to try again. More like a young warrior than a coltish kid.

That night, Mr. Ioso brought another load of boots.

"Where is everyone?" Ji asked. "Where's Chibo?"

"None of you can be trusted with freedom."

"How would you know? We've never had any."

"When I was your age," Mr. Ioso told him, "I worked as a ditchdigger and dreamed of becoming an undergardener. Look at me now."

Ji frowned. Mr. Ioso had been a *ditchdigger*? And now he was a magic-wielding . . . whatever, working for the queen's favorite proctor?

"You pledged yourself to Proctor?" he asked. "That's how you got ahead?"

"I made myself useful. But first I decided not to *serve* at the feast of life. I chose to eat. I've seen the look in your eyes. You want the same. You want freedom."

Ji shrugged. "Maybe."

"The price of freedom is high, boy. The only way to break your bonds is to lock them to someone else."

"That's not freedom," Ji told him. "That's just holding on to the other end of the chain."

"You little—" Mr. Ioso snarled, raising his arm to backhand Ji.

Then he stopped, his teeth clenched and his eyes horrible. A white shimmer flickered across his knuckles. For three heartbeats, he didn't move . . . and Ji *couldn't*, paralyzed by fear like a bunny by a bobcat.

Finally, the shimmer faded. Then Mr. Ioso lowered his arm and left.

Ji fell onto his bed and trembled like a bunny. Except he wasn't one. Maybe he wasn't a bobcat either, but that didn't mean he was helpless. And Mr. Ioso was right about one thing: he wanted freedom. Not just for himself, but for Roz, Sally, and Chibo.

He crouched at the loose floorboard and got to work.

A tapping woke Ji in the middle of the night. He blinked at the ceiling. *Tap-tippity-tap.* Sounded like branches against the roof.

Tap! Tap-tap-tap!

"Okay," he said. "That's not branches."

He crawled across the floor and peered out the window. The whole world was inky black. Not a glimmering of light. Nothing but—

The blackness shifted, and Ji yelped. That wasn't blackness, it was a dingy purple cloak pressed against the window.

Then a hooded face appeared upside down and a gravelly voice called, "Sneakyji!"

"Nin!" Ji said. "What're you doing out there?"

"Hanging from toproof by my footclaws," Nin said. "Of course."

"I mean, why?"

"Need my favor," Nin said. "And I didn't peek you for days."

"I'm locked in here."

"You picked the wrong lock?" Nin asked, cocking his upside-down head.

"No, I didn't pick the—" Ji took a breath. "I need another favor."

"Did you hear when the rite's happening?"

"Pretty soon, I think. I'm serving at it."

"That's badnews!" A stiff wind flapped Nin's hood. "Troublebig badnews!"

"Why?" Ji yelled.

"What?" Nin yelled.

"Forget it." Ji put his face to the glass. "Nin, I need you to find my friends!"

"Find what?"

"Look around and . . . peeksee my friends? Tell me where they are, and help us get out of here and—"

The wind blew Nin's hood away from his head, revealing a red face, glossy as polished leather. *Not a mask.* Yellow hair. *Not a mask.* Yellow eyes. *Not a mask.* And fangs.

"Not a mask!" Ji jerked away, his heart pounding. "You're an ogre!"

"I am not, you headbutton!"

"I can see your face."

"No, you can't."

"Nin, I'm right here!"

"No, you aren't."

Ji took a slow breath. "What's an ogre doing in the city?"

"Um." Nin squinted at him with terrifying yellow eyes. "Spying."

"What? Why?"

"After the rite, the evilqueen is weak for a moon or three or until the new prince or princess—"

Light shone from the courtyard beneath Nin. The beam of a bull's-eye lantern swept across the window, and Ji's view changed to a swirl of purple cloak as Nin vanished. The light flashed past the window three more times, like someone thought they'd seen something on the roof but wasn't sure.

Ji crawled back to bed and pretended to sleep. He waited half an hour, but nobody came to question him. He couldn't sleep, so he started prying at the floorboard again. He'd removed four nails in the past two days. Just fourteen more, and he'd squeeze through to the floor beneath.

When the door opened the next morning, Brace stepped inside.

"Brace!" Ji said. "I mean, Master Brace!"

Brace smiled. "You mean Lord Brace."

"That's *exactly* what I mean!" Ji said. Brace had officially become "Lord Brace" after being presented to the court, though he'd been called "lord" as a courtesy before then. "How're Sally and Roz? Is Chibo still here? They didn't send him back to—"

"Check it out." Brace thrust one booted foot forward. "What do you think?"

"Those are An-Hank Cordwainer!" Ji gave a low whistle. "They're awesome."

And they were. The stingray-leather boots boasted elaborate eyelets and rows of silver-and-pearl bangles. Crimson stitches offset the turquoise inlaid in the stacked heels, and clusters of garnet, topaz, and fire opal decorated the toes.

"I mean, they're awesome, *m'lord*. Topaz and opal."

"Perfect for my big day," Brace said, smoothing the cuffs of his embroidered jacket.

"Whoa," Ji said. "You're all dressed up. But, um, what about Roz and Sal—"

"Shhh!" Brace raised a finger and strolled closer. His

skinny frame now looked sleek and wiry. "You have to start by asking for permission to speak."

"Oh, okay," Ji said, the ache in his neck throbbing. "Um . . . but do I have to ask permission to ask permission? I mean, otherwise I'm asking for permission without having permission to ask, aren't I?"

"Would you just *ask*?" Brace said. "C'mon, Ji, you know how this works."

Ji eyed him for a moment. "May I speak, m'lord?"

"Not now, no. There's no time."

So Ji dropped to his knees, then touched his forehead to the ground in front of Brace. He felt stupid, but kowtowing didn't cost anything and might get him what he needed. And also, he liked seeing the gems on Brace's new boots. They must've been worth a fortune; even Baroness Primstone didn't wear clusters of fire opals, and the garnets seemed to glow from within.

"Will you please tell me where the others are, my lord?" he asked. "And how exactly we're going to serve at this rite?"

"Just do what I tell you and you'll be fine," Brace said.

"And are the others—?"

"They're serving, too."

Mr. Ioso stomped through the doorway. "Let's go, boy. Time for the Diadem Rite."

"Now?" Ji asked, raising his head. "Now?"

Mr. Ioso grabbed the scruff of his neck. "Try 'Yes, sir.'"

"Yes, sir!" Ji squeaked, and Mr. Ioso dragged him down the stairs.

In the front yard, he was relieved to see Sally and Chibo already sitting above the rear wheels of the carriage. But where was Roz? Before Ji could ask, Mr. Ioso barked at him to plant his bony bum beside Sally, then hopped onto the running board.

Ji squeezed into place, and the carriage clattered through the gate and onto the street. They headed upward, higher on the mountain. Toward the Forbidden Palace. Toward the Diadem Rite.

25

"Where've you been?" Sally asked, putting her arm around Chibo.

"Locked in my room," Ji said. "How about you?"

"Locked in the stables."

"Where's Roz?"

Sally jerked a thumb over her shoulder. "In the carriage."

"Thank summer," Ji said, feeling a wash of relief. "Was she locked up, too?"

"I hope not. She's born for better than sleeping on a hay bale. Where are they taking us?"

"We're serving at the rite," Ji told her, then saw movement on a rooftop down the block.

Smoke curled from chimneys. A flock of parrots

swooped over treetops. And *there*, Nin's purple cloak fluttered in the morning light.

Ji pointed to the ground furiously, trying to indicate, *Now, now, it's happening now.*

Nin's cloaked head nodded, and he bounded down the roof toward Ji. Like he thought Ji was saying, *Come here now.*

Ji made a shooing motion. *No, no! Run away.*

Across the canal, Nin made a shooing motion back at Ji.

"No, you buttonhead," Ji mumbled, shooing even more shoo-ily.

Nin scrambled closer, making huge, two-armed shooing motions back toward Ji.

"Go!" Ji mouthed. "Go away!"

Nin paused, then disappeared behind a canal-side tree. Maybe he'd gotten the message and maybe he hadn't, Ji couldn't tell. Ogres were weird.

"I wonder what we're serving at the rite," Chibo said.

"Proctor and Brace, I guess," Sally said.

"No, I mean, like, tea? Or appetizers? Or—"

"I don't think we're serving a meal, Chibo," Sally said.

"Well, we can serve all sort of things." Chibo blinked happily at a silver-trimmed coach that whooshed past. "We're servants."

The carriage rattled toward the mountaintop, along tree-lined boulevards with shrines and parks. Chibo chattered nonstop, thrilled by everything he heard and smelled and almost saw. Then the buildings fell away and the carriage stopped at the outer wall of the Forbidden Palace. After soldiers spoke with Proctor, the journey continued. The road zigzagged through steep parkland with boulders and wildflowers. Ji thought he saw another flash of purple in the trees, but he wasn't sure.

"Look at that!" Sally said, pointing to a meadow.

"What are they?" Chibo asked, squinting. "Flowers?"

"Peacocks," she said.

"Ooh!" He beamed in almost the right direction. "What else? Tell me!"

Sally described bridges and prayer flags and carp ponds as the carriage rumbled higher. Finally, they rattled into the parade grounds: long plazas where the queen's troops marched and sparred. The clatter of weapons and the sound of military chants filled the air.

"There's a couple hundred soldiers," Sally told Chibo, in awe. "They're training with swords and *woldos* and atlatls."

"What's a lalala?"

"An atlatl," she said. "A dart launcher. You load one end, then fling it and— Ew!"

"'Ew,' what?" Chibo asked. "What, 'ew'?"

"Goblins," Sally said, peering to the side.

A crew of goblins hunched along a side street, bowed under the weight of buckets filled with dirt. The collars around their necks were brightly polished, but their mole-feet were bare and dirty.

"I guess the palace needs stuff dug, too," Ji said.

Sally tugged her leather bracelet. "They remind me of what happened to Butler."

"Yeah," Ji said, and a commotion rang out from behind a barracks.

First shouts, then the clang of weapons—and screams. Ji frowned toward the sound but couldn't see anything.

"I hope that's not Nin," he said.

"The cloaked lady Chibo told me about?" Sally asked. "Red Mask?"

Ji looked at Chibo. "You think Nin's a girl?"

"Sure," he said. "Don't you?"

Before Ji could answer, a shadow fell over them. The massive inner wall to the Forbidden Palace rose in front of the carriage. Guards in plumed helmets lined an open gate. On the other side, dozens of halls and temples faced the queen's tower, like servants kowtowing to a monarch.

"There are banners everywhere," Sally told Chibo after the carriage rumbled through. "And lords and ladies strolling around, and— Look! I mean, don't *look*. I mean, over there, the Royal Menagerie."

"The zoo?" Chibo bounced with excitement. "No way!"

"Yeah, there's boa constrictors and—are those raccoon dogs?"

"What I want to know," Ji said, peering toward the front of the carriage, "is what's *that*?"

A grand pavilion towered in front of them, draped in tapestries. Windmills spun in the breeze, turning bronze cylinders that sparkled and whirred. Shapes moved across the tapestries, like the spreading branches of a silver tree.

Ji gawked in amazement as the carriage stopped.

"It's like watching a thousand-year-old tree grow," Sally told Chibo, "except it's made of silver and—"

"You lot, follow me," Mr. Ioso grunted, then raised his voice. "You too, Miss Songarza."

As Proctor escorted Brace toward the front entrance of the pavilion, Roz stepped from the carriage, wearing her favorite pink dress and carrying her beaded handbag.

A knot of fear loosened in Ji's heart, and he mouthed, "Are you okay?"

"I am now," she said with a quick smile.

Mr. Ioso led them into the pavilion through a servants' entrance. The scent of forest streams filled the tented corridor, where a dozen servants waited. They looked about Ji's age, half of them wearing ponchos decorated with hibiscus flowers, and the other half wearing brown-and-blue livery.

"Who's that?" Chibo asked, peering forward.

"Servants," Ji told him.

"Oh!" Chibo smiled toward the other servants. "Hi! I'm Chibo, and that's my sister Sa—"

"Shut your ricehole," one of the livery kids snapped.

"Keep your voices down or I'll cut your throats." Mr.

Ioso listened to the sudden silence, then said, "Now follow me. Eyes down."

Roz walked beside Mr. Ioso, with Ji and the other servants trailing behind. A hush descended. Ji felt itchy with nerves. Fabric walls billowed to either side, and lanterns glowed on ornate jade stands. Deeper in the pavilion, a breeze touched Ji's face, and the soft burble of water grew louder.

Then Mr. Ioso opened a flap, and Roz stepped inside and gasped.

Ji followed her into an enormous tented hall at the center of the pavilion. The peaked ceiling rose higher than a towering tulip tree, and the cloth walls stretched as wide as a meadow. A semicircular balcony swept across the hall, and a pond bubbled in the center of the floor.

A big pond. Maybe a small lake.

Overlapping carpets covered the floor, sloping down toward the glimmering white-sand shore of the pond. At Mr. Ioso's gesture, all the servants headed for a carpet near the shore and knelt facing the water.

Ji scowled. He didn't mind kneeling, but telling *Roz* to kneel made his fists clench and his jaw tighten. She was better than the nobles, and the fact that they didn't realize it only showed how true it was.

He knelt beside Roz, just in front of Sally and Chibo, and was about to say something when he realized that the white shore wasn't *sand*. It was pearls. Thousands and thousands of tiny pearls. Whoa. A couple of handfuls of those and they'd be rich. . . .

Without moving her mouth, Roz said, "Don't even think it."

A gong sounded, and stone chimes trilled. Fancy-dressed lords and ladies promenaded onto the balcony and perched on plush benches, no doubt being rewarded for loyal service with front-row seats.

And then . . . nothing happened. The lords and ladies chattered and the servants waited. The chimes trilled. Even more nothing happened. After a while, Ji could barely hear himself think over all the nothing going on.

Then the gong sounded again, and the servant kids around Ji kowtowed. Behind him, he heard Sally telling Chibo to bow low. Ji started to do the same when he caught a glimpse of the queen taking her throne on the balcony. She was tall and slender, with a crown that rose from her hair like golden flames—and in person, she shone with presence. She seemed more *real* than anyone he'd ever seen, more *there*. Even the briefest glance made his breath catch.

He gaped at her until Roz elbowed him. Then he lowered his forehead to the carpet.

"The queen!" he whispered.

"I know," Roz said. "She's so entirely . . . *royal.*"

Priests gave speeches from the balcony, but Ji couldn't hear most of the words over the bubbling of the pond.

". . . only the crown of summer will save us from the hordes . . . ogres and hobgoblins, merfolk and . . . The ice witch and the winter snake never rest . . . pray that today, the Diadem Rite will choose an heir to the Summer Crown!"

The queen stepped to the edge of the balcony and silence fell.

Even the pond stopped bubbling. A few ripples spread across the water, and then the surface turned as smooth as glass.

"Every year for the past five," the Summer Queen said, her voice as pure and strong as a blizzard, "the Diadem Rite hath tested possible heirs. None yet have passed. However, this day shows rare promise. Three young people strive for greatness. Three souls reach for the diadem, three hearts beat with the blood of nobles . . . yet only one shall be declared the true heir."

She gestured to the floor below the balcony, where Brace stood with two other noble kids. One was a crabby-looking girl in a military-style brown-and-blue jacket and an awesome pair of combat boots. The other was a younger boy wearing a silken hibiscus-decorated poncho, with silken breeches and jewel-encrusted silk slippers.

The queen introduced all three possible heirs, but Ji forgot the other two kids' names immediately.

"They just look like Crabgirl and Silkyboy to me," he muttered.

"Hush," Roz whispered.

The queen spoke for a few more minutes, too softly for Ji to hear. He kept staring at her, though, unable to look away. Then she lifted her arms—

A geyser rose from the middle of the pond. A pillar of clear water stretched toward the ceiling, as wide around as the trunk of an ancient oak.

26

JI YELPED AND flinched backward. So did all the other servants, except for Sally and Chibo. Chibo stared toward the geyser, his nearsighted eyes wide with curiosity, and Sally flinched *forward*.

Ropy streams of water braided around the trunk of the geyser, then rose higher. They branched again and again until a tree of water loomed overhead, almost reaching the ceiling. The tree rippled and flowed but somehow stayed in place.

"Behold." The queen twirled her wrist and a circle formed among the branches, like a watery headband. "Only the true heir can survive the diadem's touch."

"Huh?" Chibo whispered behind Ji. "The die-uh-what?"

"There's a minicrown in the middle of the tree," Sally told him.

"I *thought* that was a tree! I didn't see it there a minute ago."

"It wasn't there a minute ago," Sally whispered. "It rose up from the pond."

"So the first kid to grab the minicrown becomes the heir?" Chibo said. "This is awesome."

"It's history," Roz whispered.

"It's holy," Sally whispered.

"It's making me nervous," Ji whispered.

"Whoever wears the diadem," the queen told Brace, Crabgirl, and Silkyboy, "shall one day take the throne. To rule and to protect our realm, the last best haven of humankind."

She clapped, and the water tree wove together around the diadem, hiding it inside a snarl of branches.

"Whoa," Ji murmured.

"Extremely whoa," Roz agreed.

The gong sounded again, and Silkyboy stepped onto the pond. Instead of sloshing around his ankles, the water supported his weight. He peered at the liquid "branches" of the watery tree, then turned to his servants in the hibiscus ponchos.

"Come along!" he called to them. "Chop-chop!"

The kids trotted forward . . . and hesitated at the edge of the pond.

"Come *here*!" Silkyboy stomped one foot, then pointed a brawny kid toward a low watery branch. "You! Hold that one down."

"Just grab it, m'lord?"

"Of course, you cud-lipped commoner!"

The brawny kid stepped onto the pond and reached out with trembling hands. His fingers wrapped around the branch like it was solid. When he pulled down, the tree reacted: the watery limbs flowed into new shapes, like a brook streaming around a boulder.

The servant kids murmured, and Ji felt his heart thumping his ribs.

"What happened?" Chibo peered forward. "What's going on?"

"When you move one branch, the whole tree randomly changes shape," Sally told him.

"Not randomly," Roz murmured. "There are laws that govern the motion of fluids. . . ."

When Silkyboy yapped orders and insults at his servants, they nervously climbed the trunk. New branches sprouted and old ones flowed as Silkyboy clumsily followed. After a minute, he reached the tangled snarl that wrapped the diadem. His servants tugged on the branches, making the tree writhe.

"They're pulling the branches apart," Sally whispered to Chibo. "So his little lordship can reach inside for the crown."

"Is it working?" Chibo asked.

"Kind of," Ji told him. "Every time they unwind one branch, another wraps around— Oh! They opened a slit."

"Wider!" Silkyboy demanded, balancing on a limb.

"One, two . . . three!" He reached inside the slit. "Almost there! Two more inches—"

The tree *heaved* and the branches whipped.

Silkyboy shrieked and flew through the air. A lashing branch caught him in the ribs, and Ji heard bones snap. His servants crashed to the solid pond and lay there moaning.

"We have to help them," Ji said, and started to rise.

Roz touched his arm. "Look at the queen."

On the balcony, the queen swept her hand sideways, and a wave crashed across the pond and through the tree, washing Silkyboy and his servants toward the far shore, where medics waited with stretchers.

The water tree shimmered and flowed into a new shape. Roz made a soft *huh* as the pond stilled, calm and motionless. Quiet fell except for the weeping of the injured kids as they were carried away.

Then the gong sounded again. It was Crabgirl's turn.

"Move in!" she barked at her servants, the livery kids. "You two, anchor the branches, there and there!"

The biggest livery kids dragged two branches downward. A narrow limb unfurled, and Crabgirl sprang forward, planted one foot on a servant's back, and leaped onto the branch. Balancing like a cat, she raced toward the trunk. She dived through a thicket of flowing twigs and landed on a wider branch.

"No way," Ji breathed.

"I bet *she* can joust," Sally said.

"I can't see!" Chibo said. "What's happening?"

"The lady's in the tree above the diadem," Sally told Chibo in an awed hush. "Her servants are hacking at the knotted branches with hatchets."

Splinters of solidified water spat at the livery kids as they chopped. Shards jabbed their skin and tangled in their clothing before melting back into the tree. The kids grunted and muttered, but they kept clearing a path toward the diadem. The branches writhed, and one of the servants shrieked and almost fell.

Then Crabgirl leaped forward, slashing with her sword like a warrior cutting down enemies.

"She's doing it," Sally said. "She's opening a hole. . . ."

Crabgirl stabbed her blade deeply between two branches. She tugged mightily and then, with a piercing war cry, she reached into the snarl—

The tree buckled and spat her out.

She hurtled through the air, arms and legs flailing wildly. She crashed to the pond and lay there moaning. Her servants smashed down around her, gasping and groaning until the queen sent another wave rolling across the pond.

"You know what this means?" Ji muttered. "We're next."

"Awesome!" Chibo said.

"*Not* awesome, you beetlehead!" Sally said. "Did you see what happened to the others?"

"Not really."

"Well, you heard the screams." Sally looked to Ji. "So what's the plan?"

Ji took an unsteady breath. "Serve Brace, like Mr. Ioso said. And pray that he knows what he's doing."

The gong sounded, a deep throbbing note in the pavilion hall, and Brace stepped onto the pond. The water rippled beneath his bejeweled court boots, and he prowled around the tree. He looked strong and confident. Maybe serving him wouldn't be so bad. Plus, if Ji helped snaffle the diadem—like Roz accused him of snaffling books at Primstone—Brace would owe him. Heck, maybe *King* Brace would owe him.

Brace circled the tree three more times before beckoning to Ji and the others. Sally trotted down the slope. The pearls crunched under her boots, but she didn't even pause at the water's edge; she just stepped onto the pond.

Ji paused, though. He'd rather clean swan poop than climb into a sloshing tree and get clubbed by waterbranches.

"Here's one more for you, Lord Brace," Mr. Ioso called, and gestured toward a side entrance.

Chains clinked as three soldiers dragged someone into the pond room. A bruised, battered, shackled someone with bright yellow hair and dull yellow eyes. With white horns and white fangs. And a grotesque red face that Ji recognized.

"Nin," he breathed.

Scrapes covered Nin's face, black bruises marred his

red arms. A chain was wound so tightly around his wrists that he bled. Ji forgot his aches and stiffness. He forgot his fear and worry. He waited until Nin's teary yellow eyes met his own, then gave a tiny nod. It wasn't much, but it was all he could do.

"I say!" a nobleman called, from the balcony. "That's an ogre!"

"Only a juvenile." Mr. Ioso dragged Nin toward the pond. "Here's your anchor, Lord Brace. Tell me where you want it."

Brace frowned. "An ogre, so far from the mountains? What's it doing here?"

"We asked it that very question, my lord," Mr. Ioso said. "But it doesn't speak human."

Ji glanced at Chibo. They both knew that Nin didn't speak *normal*, but he certainly spoke *human*.

"Give me a moment," Brace said, and strode around the water tree once more.

Despite the failures of Silkyboy and Crabgirl, Brace seemed confident and commanding. He frowned at the highest branches, he touched the lowest twigs, he watched the current flow inside the tree's watery bark.

Finally, he circled toward Ji and murmured, "All those years of strategy games finally pay off."

Ji bowed his head—he was angry about Nin, but that wasn't Brace's fault. "Just tell me where you want me, my lord."

"You see that branch there?" Brace pointed to the

center of the tree. "Climb up and attach the ogre's chain to the end."

When Ji took the chain from Mr. Ioso, he gulped at the sight of Nin. Up close, he—or *cub*—looked even more monstrous and nonhuman. An actual ogre. With white fangs and glossy red skin and a gleam of hope in cub's yellow eyes.

"Stonefriend," Ji whispered, without moving his lips.

Nin bowed cub's head, then shuffled toward the tree, which loomed high and smooth as a glass statue.

"Stable girl," Brace said to Sally, "climb between those limbs. And you, Chimpo?"

"I'm Chibo, m'lord!" Chibo said. "I used to live at Primstone! You once gave me a toy soldier that you—"

"You're the lightest. Climb to that fork at the top."

"Chibo doesn't see well, Lord Brace," Roz said.

"Then direct him," Brace told her. "The first part of the puzzle is placing my servants correctly."

Watery limbs stretched above Ji like crooked icicles. He draped Nin's chain around his neck and grabbed the lowest branch. It felt like a polished marble snake. He heaved himself into the tree, then climbed higher, tensing every time the tree shifted, waiting for the branches to thrash him into a pulp.

The chain rattled and clinked. Ji straddled the right branch, then scooted to the end. Smaller branches sprouted everywhere as he looped the chain into place.

"Tighter!" Brace called from below.

Ji looped the chain tighter, which tugged Nin's shackled wrists higher. Ji mouthed, "Sorry," but Nin didn't see.

"Now climb to the heart of the tree, where the diadem is hidden," Brace called. "Sally, push those branches apart. Yes, good!" The tree shifted and shimmered as Brace called orders and corrections and praise. Then he said, "Roz, climb onto this branch here."

Ji stopped beside the central snarl and frowned downward.

"I—I'm not entirely dressed for climbing, my lord," Roz said, smoothing her pink dress.

"I need your weight."

Roz flushed with embarrassment. "Is it proper for a—"

"Now, Roz!"

"A little privacy might—"

"You're an upper servant," he snapped, "but still just a servant. Never forget that."

"No, my lord," she said, and reached for the lowest branch.

The anger that had simmered inside Ji when he saw Nin's face—the anger that had simmered inside him for months and years—started to boil over. *You're just a servant.* Roz was better than Brace in every way that mattered. What gave him the right to talk to her like that?

Nothing.

Just a servant? Ji had wanted to help Brace, he'd

wanted to serve. Mostly because he wanted Brace to owe him, but still—now he'd show him exactly what a servant could do. A snarl of stupid watery twigs was nothing to a boot boy.

Ji yanked on one branch, unwove two more, and felt the tree shifting around him.

"Stop!" Brace yelled from below. "Ji, stop that!"

Ji tugged at the snarl. "I'm getting you the diadem, my lord."

"You're just a servant!" Brace repeated, climbing into the tree. "It'll burn you like fire."

"Just a servant," Ji muttered, as a new branch sprouted into the knot. "Roz! How do I keep this knot from reknotting?"

"I don't know!" she called. "How would *I* know?"

"Because it's a puzzle. You *rule* puzzles!"

"But I rule you!" Brace yelled, climbing closer. "And I order you to stop!"

"You want the crown? I'll give you the crown. You want a servant? I'll serve."

"Stop or I'll—I'll cut you down!"

"Sally, stay where you are!" Roz called from beneath Ji. "Chibo, kick the branch behind you! If I push against the trunk here . . ."

When Ji untangled another water-branch, it stayed untangled. Ha! He *knew* Roz was smarter than Brace. He yanked and twisted . . . and the snarl loosened.

The diadem glinted through the thicket of branches. Just a few more seconds . . .

"Brace is drawing his sword!" Sally shouted.

"And I'm getting him his crown," Ji muttered, yanking on another branch. They couldn't escape, or lie or steal or cheat. But they could show Brace—show everyone—that they weren't *just* servants. "I'm almost done."

"He's almost there!" Sally called.

"I *am* here," Brace said, climbing beside Ji.

A roar sounded from below. Then Nin bellowed, "So am I!"

Brace gaped down at Nin, who strained against the chains, bright red muscles bulging. "The ogre! It talks!"

"It rarely shuts up," Ji said, untangling the last two branches.

"I'm coming, Sneakyji!" Nin hollered. "I'm fishexcellent!"

"Ji, duck!" Sally yelled.

Ji ducked, and Brace's sword flashed overhead. The flat of the blade whacked the watery tree trunk. Chips of water stung Ji's face, as hard as diamonds.

He lunged forward and grabbed the diadem.

27

THE CIRCLE OF water felt icy in Ji's palm.

A shock of frostbite ran up his arm and into his chest. When the numbness reached his head, the world turned bright and still, like sunlight shining on snow. He couldn't see, he couldn't move. Nothing remained but the crackle of ice in his ears.

Ji felt the tree around him, he felt the tree *inside* him. His watery roots plunged into the earth, flowing through the mountain and across the entire valley.

Feeding the crops, filling the wells.

Protecting the realm.

Defending humanity against the hordes. Against the creatures, the beasts. Against the twisted nonhuman monsters that threatened everything.

And with a frozen clarity, Ji knew that he needed to

seize the power of the tree. The queen had created the tree not just with her magic, but with her goals and needs and vows. And with those of every king and queen who came before her. That was what Ji felt now, the urgent commands of every royal who'd ever ruled.

He needed to accept the diadem. He needed to wear the crown and destroy the enemies of humankind. Every last one, until no ogre lurked in the mountains and no goblin dug in the earth. Until no mermaid swam, no sprite flew, and no troll bellowed.

He'd pay any price to defend his fellow humans. Like Mr. Ioso said, the cost of freedom was high—but that didn't matter. Ji needed to protect his realm. He'd rule the humans wisely, safely, powerfully. He'd never bow again, he'd never serve again.

Instead, they'd serve *him*.

And in return, he'd do anything to protect them. He'd do *everything* to protect them. He'd enslave the goblins and wipe out the ogres, he'd weave children into tapestry looms and—

"No!" Ji shouted into the silence. "I won't!"

The snowy brightness turned clear as a mirror, and the queen's face appeared in his mind. Larger than life and more commanding.

"Thou must wear the diadem," she said, her voice echoing in the snowy white blankness. "Inherit the throne, and protect the people."

"I'm not—" He swallowed. "I'm just a boot boy."

"Wear the crown, and become a king."

"I can't," he said, in a small voice.

"A mighty and unyielding monarch," the queen continued. "An unconquerable shield against the monsters."

Ji's heart thrilled at her words. He longed to take the crown, to wield the power, to prove that he mattered. But he made himself say, "I can't. I won't. I won't kill them. I won't enslave them."

"Selfish child! Thinking only of thyself." The queen's eyes darkened and her voice boomed in his mind. "The people need protection."

"Is there anything you *wouldn't* do, to protect them?"

"Nay," the queen said. "Nothing."

"If there's nothing you won't do," Ji asked, "then what are you?"

"A monarch."

"A monster," he said. "Worse than any ogre, worse than any—"

"Thou must rule! Wear the diadem, and complete the rite!"

"Never," Ji said, and the queen's face vanished.

His senses returned in a jagged burst: the water tree swayed, the lords and ladies gasped, and the diadem burned his fingers. Agony throbbed down his arm. When he tried to hurl the circle of water away, it stuck to him. He screamed and shook his hand until the diadem tore a strip of skin off his palm and sailed between the branches of the tree.

And through teary eyes, he watched Brace snatch it from the air.

"Brace, don't!" Ji sobbed. "You don't know what it'll do to you!"

Brace lifted the diadem in triumph. "I told you it burned commoners."

Then he jammed it onto his head. The water flowed through his hair onto his skull, like the diadem was bonding to him, and in two heartbeats he seemed more real, more present, more *powerful* and—

The tree heaved.

Ji watched in horror as a branch stabbed Sally in the heart. Three more branches thrust toward Roz and Chibo and Nin. He opened his mouth to scream, but the tree speared his own chest. He didn't feel pain, he didn't feel cold. He didn't feel anything as the world turned black.

28

STICKY DARKNESS SWIRLED around Ji. A thousand blue-bats buzzed in his ears, and the world stank of wet fur and old manure.

Which wasn't great news, in terms of an afterlife. Maybe he shouldn't have lied quite so much.

Then the buzzing turned into words: "Ji, wake up!"

He moaned and shifted on a cold stone floor.

"C'mon, you beetlebrain," Sally called, her voice gruff. "*Jiyong!* I know you can hear me!"

He groaned. "I can't see anything."

"Your eyes are closed," she growled. "You chuckle-knuckle."

When Ji tried to open his eyes, they stayed shut—and he panicked. His eyelids were glued closed! He couldn't open them, he couldn't see! His eyes burned and throbbed . . . then sprang open.

Ji shivered in relief as the darkness wavered into a lighter gloom. He rubbed his stinging eyes—until a tightness in his fingers stopped him. A ropy burn mark crossed his palm, shiny with scar tissue. A wound from grabbing the diadem. But how had a scar formed already? How long had he been out? Where *was* he?

He peered through the gloom at rows of cage bars. "We—we're in the zoo?"

"Yeah, welcome to the Royal Menagerie," Sally growled at him from the darkness beyond the bars. "You're in the tusk deer cage. At least they moved the animals before they locked us in."

Ji moaned and looked around. Leaves scattered on the dirt floor of his cage. Two boulders sat beneath a narrow tree, and a spring lapped at a muddy bank covered in hoofprints.

"What happened?" he asked.

"We passed out after the ice tree stabbed us," Sally growled. "At least, that's what I think."

Ji touched his uninjured chest. "Are you hurt? If we got stabbed, how come we're not hurt?"

"Because magic."

"I guess." He scanned the darkness. "Where are you? Why are you talking so weird?"

"Don't freak out," she yipped.

"Then stop talking like that!"

She growled. "Just promise you won't freak out."

"I'm not going to freak out."

"You're totally going to freak."

"I'm not!"

"I'm in the crocodile cage to your left," she growled. "Twenty feet away."

When Ji pushed to his feet, his knees felt shaky and his throat tight. He crossed toward Sally, his feet squelching in the mud around the burbling watering hole.

"Where's Roz?" He peered into the gloom of Sally's cage. "Is everyone okay?"

"She's in the mountain goat enclosure. Just promise you won't panic."

"I told you, I'm not going to panic." He grabbed the bars and peered at the flat rocks and swampy bog in Sally's cage. "How can you even see me? Where *are* you?"

"Hiding from you."

"Why?"

"So you don't freak out."

"I'm not going to freak out!" he repeated.

"Okay." She didn't speak for a moment. "Look at your hands, Ji."

"What?" He glanced at them. "They're dirty, so what?"

"That's not dirt."

When he looked closer, he frowned. Faint scales covered the backs of his hands and disappeared under his shirtsleeves, like a snakeskin tattoo. He rubbed at the markings, but they didn't blur, they didn't fade. Sally was right. They weren't dirt. *They weren't dirt.*

"Oh, no," he whimpered. "No, no. Th-there are f-f-fish scales on my arms."

"You got off easy," Sally growled, and stepped to the bars of her cage.

The evening light brushed against her furry face and stubby snout. It shone on her tufted ears. She looked like herself, except crossed with a fuzzy, big-eyed fox. And when she smiled reassuringly, her pointy teeth glinted.

Ji freaked out.

After his babbling terror faded, Ji stood from behind a boulder in his cage. He wiped leaves from his pants and said, "Sorry."

"That's okay," Sally growled. "I did the same thing."

"You did not."

"Well," she said, "I didn't jibber like a monkey and wave my arms around."

"I didn't jibber like a monkey."

"What did you jibber like?"

Ji scuffed back to the bars of his cage. "Shut up."

"I freaked a little, though," she told him. "I woke up first, you know? I saw my reflection in the water and . . . yikes."

"You're actually kind of cute."

She scowled adorably. "I am not."

"You are." He tried to smile. "You're totally cute, Sally."

"Shut up."

"Is that a *tail*?"

"No," she yipped, and swished her bushy tail out of sight behind her. She looked like a walking, talking stuffed animal. Her fur was redder than a fox's, with black stripes like a chipmunk. And she'd shrunk to about four feet tall: she'd abandoned her trousers and belted her shirt around her waist. It fell to her furry knees like a baggy dress.

"You're shorter," he said.

"At least *I'm* not a mermaid."

Ji frowned at the fishy-looking scales on his arms—then groaned. He opened his shirt and groaned again. Sally was right! He was a mermaid. Only a few faint scales spread across his arms and shoulders, almost like tattoos, but from his chest downward they grew deeper and thicker. And when he yanked up his pant leg he saw heavy, overlapping scales covering his calf.

The rite had changed him into a half mermaid.

Only one more thing to look at. He took a breath and peered fearfully at his feet. They weren't fins! That was the good news. The bad news was that they were three inches longer, covered in scales, and tipped with short claws instead of nails.

"Do you have gills?" Sally asked, when Ji finished groaning.

He patted his neck. "I don't think so. At least I've still got both legs."

"And your fingers aren't even webbed."

"Lucky me. Um. So what are *you*?"

"Roz says I'm part hobgoblin. She says the rite must've gone wrong when you grabbed the diadem. Brace got the power and we got . . . turned into beasts."

"She's changed, too? And Chibo?"

"He's still in his sack, but she's over there." Sally flicked her tail to indicate the next cage. "In the cave. She won't come out."

"His *sack*?" Ji asked. "What are you talking about?"

Sally's tufted ears flattened against her head. "I don't know! He's wrapped in *something*. I don't know what's going on! Just—" She took a breath. "Just talk to Roz, okay?"

"Yeah." He started to turn away, then turned back "Are *you* okay?"

"I'm scared out of my skin," Sally admitted. "Or my fur, I guess."

"Your pelt?"

"Thanks, fishfeet," she said. "That's a big help."

At least she still teased him like Sally. And she still *was* Sally. A furry snout and a bushy tail didn't change her essential Sallitude.

"Nothing wrong with being scared," he told her. "Being scared just makes you extra determined, remember?"

Her fuzzy face tilted adorably. "It does?"

"You told me that once."

"I did?" Her ears pricked up. "Really?"

"Yep," he said. "And you never lie."

"It must be true, then." When she nodded, she looked like a tiger cub licking a saucer of milk. "Yeah. Yeah, who cares about scared?"

"Not you, because you're doolally."

"I'm *brave*." She held her snout higher. "Whatever's happening, I'll face it like a knight."

"An adorable knight," he said.

A pebble flew through the bars and pinged off Ji's forehead.

"Ow!"

"Go talk to Roz," she said, and shooed him toward Roz's cage.

"Evil chipmunk," Ji muttered, rubbing his head.

He crunched through fallen leaves to the other side of his cage, looking at his scaly hands in the moons-light. When he whacked his fingers against a bar, he felt a sting of pain. So apparently mermaid scales weren't armored. Just fishy.

"Roz?" he called, staring at the rocky slabs in the goat enclosure. "Are you there?"

Silence from the other cage.

"C'mon, Roz! Talk to me."

A rough voice rumbled from a shadowy crevice. "Go away."

"I'm locked in a cage, Roz. Even if I wanted to go away, I couldn't."

More silence.

"What's a tusk deer?" he asked, because he thought Roz couldn't resist sharing information.

She stayed silent.

"I bet it's a deer with a tusk."

Nothing.

"Probably two tusks," he said. "Maybe even three."

"Would you hush?" she grumbled.

"Not until you tell me about tusk deer," he said.

Silence again.

"Fine," he said. "What are *you*?"

"I—I don't know anymore. I don't even sound human. We . . . we're not human anymore."

He swallowed. Joking around was easy with Sally, but this was *Roz*. "What happened? I mean . . . *how*?"

"I'm not sure. When you grabbed the diadem, you must've affected the rite in . . . horrible ways. I'm . . . I'm part *ogre* now."

"I'm sorry," he said, his stomach hollow with regret. "I'm so sorry, Roz."

A rasping twang sounded from the darkness. Ji gazed into the shadows and realized that she was crying. A lump formed in his throat, and he stood there like an idiot, listening to her cry and trying to think of the right thing to say. He could apologize again, but Roz wouldn't care about that. So he kept his mouth shut, completely useless.

"I m-miss my sister," Roz cried into the darkness.

"Yeah," he said.

"I just—I want everything back the way it was before she left."

"Yeah," he said.

"And before they came for Chibo." Roz took a slow breath. "I didn't even realize how good things were."

"Yeah," Ji said.

"Would you please stop staying 'yeah'?"

"Okeydoke," he said.

The rasping twang turned to a sniffle of laughter. "That's hardly better."

"Yeah," he said, then added, "I'm sorry, Roz. I'm really sorry. But if I messed up the rite, they'll have to fix it, won't they? I mean, if they want to crown Brace."

"Hm," she said. "I suppose so, yes."

"Which means they have to fix *us*."

"That's possible."

"It's more than possible!" he said, trying to sound hopeful. "It's a sure thing. Say that the Diadem Rite is like, um . . . cooking a stew! Well, I opened the lid too soon, that's all. That's why we're half-cooked."

"Not you," Sally growled from the crocodile cage. "You're half-baked."

Ji ignored her and told Roz, "Once they simmer things for another few hours, we'll go back to normal."

"I dearly hope that you're right."

"Of course I'm right! I'm always right! Now would you come out where I can see you?"

"I'm horrible," she said, her raspy voice tearful again.

"No, you're not."

"I'm a monster."

"No, Roz," he said. "You're not."

"How would you know? You can't even see me!"

"Because you're the least horrible person I've ever met. There's nobody who's less of a monster than you. Nobody. You could have a goblin face and ten arms, and you *still* wouldn't be a monster."

A low purr sounded from Sally's cage. A breeze swirled through the cages, and the water hole bubbled. In the distant parade grounds, the tromp and call of soldiers sounded through the evening.

Then a shadow shifted from the crevice, and Roz edged into the open.

29

ROZ WAS AT least a foot taller, maybe two, and much broader. Her flowing, ankle-length gown fell to her knees, and her skin looked like granite: rough and stony, a pale peach color with black specks and glittering flecks. Her chin was squarer and her nose broader. Oh, and a horn the size of a pinecone curved upward from her forehead.

Her eyes were the same, though, so Ji didn't freak. Not even a little.

"I look hideous," she whispered, tears glinting.

"You look *strong*," he told her.

"I sound like a goblin."

"Who's your favorite scholar?"

"What?"

"Just answer the question!"

"Ti-Lin-Su," Roz said. "You know that."

"And, uh, what's her 'outstanding question'?"

"Why do dragons hoard treasure?"

"You don't sound like a goblin," Ji told her. "You sound like *Roz*."

"He's right!" Sally called.

"And at least you're not a magical fish. You're part ogre, right? They're not so bad. You saw Nin. He's a—a friend."

"Cub's not a he," Roz reminded Ji. "Ogre children aren't boys or girls. They don't choose which until they grow up."

"Yeah, yeah. Well, *cub's* a friend, then. And—oh!" Ji scratched the scales on his forearm. "So, um, if you're an ogre, are you, um . . ."

"I'm still a girl!" Roz said, sounding like her old self. "Just . . . a, a monster girl."

"Least you don't have a tail," Sally growled.

"At least you haven't a *horn*," Roz told her.

Ji kicked a bar. "At least neither of you are mermaids."

"You're not a mermaid," Roz told him. "You're a mer*man*."

He snorted. "I hope Nin's okay."

"Maybe he turned into a person," Sally said.

"Yeah, but where is he?" Ji asked.

"Cub's not a he," Roz repeated.

"Who knows what cub is now?" Ji said, then told them about meeting Nin in the Oilpress, and again at the town house.

"Spying?" Roz asked.

"I guess the ogres wanted to know when the rite was happening."

"Because the queen is weak after the rite?" Sally asked.

Ji didn't want to think about that. "I suppose. So why's Chibo in a sack?"

"The same reason you're half trout."

"I mean, is he okay?"

"I think so." Sally peered with her big adorable eyes into the darkness of Chibo's cage. "At least he's breathing."

"Perhaps the sack is a cocoon," Roz rumbled.

"You think he's turning into a butterfly?" Ji asked.

Roz sighed. "I've no idea. Ti-Lin-Su would know. She's the leading authority in zozology, the study of nonhuman creatures."

"Beasts like us," Sally said, and her tail drooped.

A sad twang came from Roz's cage, and Ji ducked his head, watching the water hole burble up from some underground source. Nonhuman, beastly, monstrous. He was a creature from the depths. He picked at the fish scales on his arm. His mom had wanted him to be a footman and he'd wanted to be free. Instead, he'd become a freakish half-human merman, locked in a cage.

"Speaking of Ti-Lin-Su," Roz suddenly said. "I actually, um, did something the other day . . ."

Ji looked toward her cage. "Did what?"

"Well, erm . . ." Roz's rumbly voice thickened with

embarrassment. "Remember when you two were locked away?"

"You mean, do I remember all the way back to this morning?" Ji asked.

"Er, well, Proctor caught me trying to visit you," Roz said. "So he banished me from the house during the days. And I called on Ti-Lin-Su. I'd hoped that she would speak with me, although I know how presumptuous that sounds."

"It doesn't sound presumptuous," Ji said.

"'Presumptuous' barely sounds like a word," Sally growled, still looking toward Chibo's cage.

Roz cleared her throat. "Well, Ti-Lin-Su lives on the north side of the mountain, between a bell tower and a canal. Her home is like a fortress. It's surrounded by high walls, with big bronze-banded doors."

"That's weird," Ji said. "Why would a scholar live in a fortress?"

"If you'll listen for a moment, I'll tell you!" Roz scolded, like a trollish governess. "I arrived without an introduction, which you'd rightly say is the height of rudeness—"

"Not as bad as slipping through an open window," Ji said.

"—and Ti-Lin-Su was perfectly within the bounds of polite behavior to refuse to greet me."

"Wait, you didn't even see her?" Sally asked. "She didn't come to the door?"

Roz looked at the nighttime sky, a mournful expression

on her granite-flecked face. "A guard at the bell tower told me that she's a recluse. That's why she lives in a fortress. She doesn't see anyone, not ever. She doesn't leave the estate. She stays in her water garden."

Ji rubbed his neck. "Stupid recluse."

"She's anything but stupid, Ji."

"*You're* anything but stupid!" he said. "And what's a water garden, anyway? Just a stupid pond, I bet. Besides, it's her books that matter, not her. I mean, why *talk* to a writer? Talking to a writer is like sniffing a blacksmith or, or—"

"Singing to a potter," Sally suggested.

"Exactly!"

A faint smile spread across Roz's broad face. "I suppose you're right," she said. "I still have her books. That's all that truly matters."

"Of course I'm right," Ji told her. "Meeting An-Hank Cordwainer wouldn't make his boots more comfortable. So what happened when she didn't come to the door? You just went away?"

Roz ducked her head. "Yes."

"Hey!" Sally yipped. "Chibo's moving!"

"Thank summer!" Ji rushed to the other side of his cage. "I can't see—is he out of the sack?"

"No," she said. "But he's wriggling around."

"That's good," Ji said. "Right?"

"Definitely," Roz said. "Definitely good."

"Chibo!" Sally yelled. "Can you hear me?"

Ji held his breath, but no answer came. Sally called Chibo's name a few more times. Then her tufted ears slumped in adorable dismay. "At least we're together," she muttered. "I mean, you promised to rescue him, and you did."

"I rescued him right into a zoo," Ji said. "Into a sack."

"That's better than the tapestry weavers."

Ji swallowed. "I still think about those other kids. All the time. The ones I left behind."

"You didn't have a choice," Roz rumbled.

"I didn't even try." Ji's eyes felt swollen and hot. "And they've been there this whole time, woven into the looms. Without help. Without hope."

A breeze rustled the bushes, and then silence fell. Ji squatted beside the water hole. He splashed cool water on his prickly face, then cupped his hands and drank. The water tasted pure and fresh.

Ji inspected his reflection. At least his face looked the same as always. Except, no—a hint of overlapping scales was visible on his cheek, like he'd fallen asleep on a pair of snakeskin boots and woken with indentations on his skin. He traced the faint marks with a fingertip as the sound of soldiers marching echoed in the streets beyond the menagerie.

"You really think they'll fix us?" Sally asked.

"Sure they will," Ji said, more confidently than he felt.

"So we just wait here?"

"Yeah."

"At least I brought a book," Roz said.

Ji gave a surprised laugh. "You did not!"

She patted the beaded handbag strapped across her broad shoulders. "One never knows when one might find oneself locked in the Royal Menagerie after being transformed into a half ogre by a—"

You're not half ogre! a dozen tiny voices called out. *You sillybeet!*

"Nin!" Ji called, leaping to his feet. "Where are you? Are you okay?"

We're happy as a button in a head!

"That doesn't mean anything," Ji said. "That's not even nonsense."

We're okay now, Nin's voice said. *We didn't waste an hour weepcrying like a hundred soggy seagulls. We don't know why you think that.*

"What do you mean, *we*? Where are you?"

We're here and there, Nin's voices said. *There's more of us now, in bitty pieces. It took us longforever to find you.*

"Can you hear that, Roz?" Ji asked. "Please tell me you can hear that."

"Of course I can hear it!"

"He's talking into our heads," Sally said. "We're hearing his thoughts."

"Oh, this is all I need," Ji said. "*Nin* thinking inside my head."

We can do that now! Nin told him. *And we peek you there in the stonycage, miss—you're not half ogre, you're half troll!*

"Half troll?" Roz rumbled. "Aren't trolls simply the eldest ogres?"

No, no, not at all, Nin scoffed, possibly from behind a big ceramic urn at Ji's feet. *Though a little yes.*

Ji stared at the urn. It stood as high as his knees, and a few leafy stalks rose from the dirt—but he didn't see a hint of ogre.

But mostly no, Nin continued. *We will explain you the whole story, except first we need to tell Sneakyji something. Badnews.*

"More bad news?" Ji asked the urn.

Bad badnews! Troublebig for us, and—

"Roz! Ji!" Sally yowled from the crocodile enclosure. "The sack split! Chibo is coming out!"

Ji turned away from the urn. "Finally!"

"Hey, Chibo?" Sally called. "Chibo!"

"Can you see him?" Ji peered past Sally's cage. "Is he a butterfly?"

Troublebad bignews, Nin's voices said.

"I am *not* a butterfly!" Chibo called in a piping voice.

"Okay, Chibo," Sally growled. "Don't freak out. Things are weird right now, but—"

"I know that," Chibo said, his voice sweet and fluttery. "I heard everything! I've been awake for hours, I just couldn't talk. Let me get out of this sack and—"

BADNEWS! all of Nin's tiny voices shouted. *LISTEN TO US, SNEAKYJI!*

"Fine!" Ji said, glaring at the urn. "What? What's so important that it can't wait two seconds?"

They're coming to kill you.

30

"WHAT?" JI BLURTED. "They're coming to *what*?"

"I beg your pardon!" Roz rumbled, hunching one hefty shoulder. "To kill us?"

"Who?" Sally cracked her fuzzy knuckles. "Just point me at 'em."

"Almost free!" Chibo fluted. "Ooh, maybe I'm half goblin! Imagine how fast I could climb with four arms!"

"Nin!" Ji said. "What're you talking about?"

We heard them planning, Nin said. *They didn't see us there, listening.*

Ji squinted at the urn. "Yeah, because you're invisible."

You headbutton! We're not invisible. Just small.

"You look invisible to me."

"Ignore him, Nin," Roz said. "And please tell us what

you overheard. Er, and it's a pleasure to meet you. I'm Miss Rozario Songarza."

Happiness beamed from the not-visible Nin. *The pleasure is all ours, Missroz!*

"How are you talking inside our heads?" Ji asked. "It's impossible."

"Oh, is *that* impossible?" Sally grumbled. "Let's ask my tail what's impossible."

"Sally and Ji!" Roz thundered. "Hush this instant! Now, then, Nin—please, tell us what you heard."

We can show you, the Nin voices said. *Lord Brace was chattalking with your proctor and the magic man, like this—*

The voices suddenly stopped, and Ji saw Nin's memories instead. He didn't have time to be terrified before an image rose in his mind: a pair of familiar stingray-leather court boots, with clusters of garnet, topaz, and opals. Brace's boots. They towered above Ji, as big as houses. And even at that size, the stitching looked perfect. Wow. An-Hank Cordwainer was *good*.

When Ji's view shifted, he caught a flash of Proctor's boots, then heard voices rumbling above.

"What's wrong?" Brace asked unsteadily. "What happened? They turned into monsters."

"That filthy boot boy disrupted the rite," Proctor snarled.

"Disrupted?" Brace asked. "You mean when he touched the diadem?"

Ji's view shifted again, and he heard Mr. Ioso's voice. "The heir's servants are not meant to *survive* the rite, Prince Brace."

"What?" Brace asked with a twinge of horror. "Ji and Roz were supposed to die?"

"It is the most honorable sacrifice for a commoner," Proctor told him, from high above. "When the new heir wears the diadem, the tree impales his servants and pours their spirits into him."

"Impales? You mean stabs? It was *supposed* to stab them?"

"Yes, my prince," Mr. Ioso said. "But they weren't supposed to survive."

"How do you think our queen—or king—lives for so many lifetimes?" Proctor asked, with a low chuckle. "And harnesses such power?"

"I thought it was because they command all human magic," Brace said. "I mean, that's why nobody else has magic anymore, right?"

"All human magic flows through the king or queen," Proctor said, with a nod. "But that's merely the *source* of the power. The Diadem Rite is what allows a royal to wield it—and what gives them the strength to survive it. All that magic would kill a weaker person."

"Your servants must become less than human," Mr.

Ioso said, "so you become more than human. So you can wield that power."

"They turn beastly while you turn royal," Proctor told Brace. "They die during the rite so that you will live for centuries after it. However, that boot boy ruined everything. He interrupted the rite. Your servants degenerated into monstrosities . . . but they lived."

"So we sacrifice a few servants to save thousands of lives?" Brace asked. "To protect the Summer Realm?"

"Exactly, my prince," Mr. Ioso said. "We save far more lives than we take."

"Well, then . . . what shall we do now?"

Mr. Ioso waved his hand over a bowl of water. His palm glowed white—and somewhere in the distance, a field of flowers probably turned into shriveled eggplants.

"We wait until the full moons rise," he said, "then we finish the rite. We drag the beasts to the tree and kill them on its branches."

The vision ended, and Ji reeled, dizzy with shock. He grabbed the cage bars for support as the world tilted.

"So for a new king to soak up all the human magic," Roz rumbled in horror, "he needs to turn people into beasts?"

Ji's heart thumped like a battering ram. He took a shaky breath, trying to clear his head.

"And the reason he lives so long," Roz continued, "is

because he kills servants during a rite? He turns them into monsters, then *kills* them?"

Ji knew he should've been listening to Roz, but he couldn't get past the fact that he'd just seen a vision. An actual vision, inside his own personal head.

"How—how did you do that?" he stammered to Nin.

We don't know, Nin said. *The same way we talk to you in our minds, without mouths.*

"How do you do *that*?"

Easy, Nin told him. *Just like this.*

"Wait," Sally said. "You don't have mouths?"

"That's not the point!" Ji said. "He just sent us a vision! A vision! Um, about everyone trying to kill us. . . ."

"That's still not as weird as not having mouths," Sally muttered.

"We all heard Proctor," Roz said, her deep voice unsteady. "They need to sacrifice us on the tree to finish the Diadem Rite."

Ji chewed on one scaly knuckle for a second. "How much time do we have?"

"Not long." Roz turned her granite-hued face upward. "The moons are high."

Ji jerked at the bars of his cage, but they didn't budge. "We have to get out of here."

"At least it's not your fault," Sally told Ji. "You didn't ruin us when you grabbed the diadem. You actually saved our lives."

He considered her for a moment. "You're a little squir-relly."

"You jerk!" she yipped. "I just *complimented* you!"

"What I mean is," Ji told her, "squirrels can climb."

"Huh?" she said.

"Straight up trees and lampposts . . ."

"Oh!" Sally said, eyeing the bars of her cage.

She showed Ji a feral grin, then grabbed one bar in each paw. She flipped upside down and grabbed the bars higher up with her *rear* paws. He hadn't even seen those until now.

"Holy guacamole!" Ji said.

"Yaoooo!" Sally flipped again, higher, between two bars, then leaped away. "Hobgoblins can *move*!"

She hurtled through the air and landed on another bar. She sproinged off that one, spun around a third, then launched herself out of the top of her cage. She landed on a high crossbeam and struck a pose.

"Wow," Ji said. "I mean . . . *wow*."

"That is impressive," Roz rumbled.

Sallynx sure knows how to hob, Nin added.

"Now stop messing around!" Ji called. "And get Chibo."

"Gotcha," Sally said, and bounded across the top of her cage.

"I don't *need* getting!" Chibo said in his high, musical voice.

"Just sit tight and—"

An emerald glow shone from Chibo's cage, like a hundred lanterns gleaming through sheets of green silk.

Ji blinked at the light, then gaped at the sight of Chibo standing amid the brightness. Scraps of the sack scattered the cage floor at Chibo's feet. He was still skinny and bald, except now he had a hunchback . . . and glowing green *wings*.

"W-win-wings," Ji stammered. "You—whoa—you have wings!"

They spread to either side of Chibo, flickering and flowing in the air. Changing shape every second, but still *wings*. And as Ji stared, he realized that they weren't made of feather and bone; they were made of green light.

"A sprite," Roz said in an awed rumble. "He's half sprite."

"No way," Chibo said, as his wings stretched wider. "No way! I can fly?"

"Don't even try!" Ji snapped at him. "Not yet! What if you fall or—"

Chibo's wings swept downward and launched him into the air. He spun in a spiral toward the top of his cage, giggling as his wings left a trail of green sparkles behind him.

"Quiet down or the guards will hear!" Sally snarled, leaping toward him across the tops of the cages. "And turn that light off!"

"I don't know how!" Chibo said, and flew smack into

one of the widely spaced roof beams. "Oooh, badness," he moaned, tumbling downward. "I didn't see that. . . ."

While Sally jumped down between the roof beams to catch him, Ji turned to Roz. "Pull your bars open."

"I can't." She shambled to the edge of her cage. "They're too thick."

"Just try," Ji told her.

"They're two inches of iron."

"You're six feet of *troll*," he said. "And if you can't get out, we're all stuck here. Nobody's leaving without you."

Roz grabbed two bars with her granite hands. Her granite, *four-fingered* hands. Apparently she'd lost a couple of fingers during the rite, though Ji managed not to mention it.

She started to tug, then looked at him. "Privacy, please?"

He didn't see how pulling iron bars apart was immodest, but he turned to inspect the pool in his cage. The water bubbled from underground, maybe from a canal or a spring. He dipped a toe into the water and heard Roz grunting at her bars. Metal creaked. Then squeaked and rattled and grated.

Ji watched ripples in the water hole. *C'mon, Roz, c'mon . . .*

A squeal sounded, and then Roz grunted again. "I can't! I can't do it, Ji."

When he turned back, she was standing with her

256

shoulders slumped, like she wanted to cry. "It doesn't matter," he lied. "I have another plan."

She brightened. "You do? What is it?"

"Let me get out of here first. Then I'll show you."

"If I can't pull the bars apart," she said, "there's no way you can."

"Forget the bars," he told her. "I'm swimming out."

"How on earth are you doing that?"

"I'm half merman, remember?"

He took a breath and—before he could think twice—dived into the water hole. The cold shocked him, but instead of scrambling back to shore, he clawed deeper into the inky blackness. He thrashed in the water, more like a clumsy squid than a graceful carp, but he knew he could do this. *C'mon, fishboy, swim!*

The chilly water drained his strength. Glowing dots appeared in front of his eyes. Maybe he needed to breathe. Merfolk breathed underwater, after all. Except making yourself suck in a lungful of water was not easy. Every instinct screamed at him not to try, but he thought about Sally's courage and inhaled.

The water choked him like a noose. He couldn't breathe! He couldn't breathe water!

Mindless terror exploded behind his eyes: he needed air more than anything in the world, more than light, more than life. He thrashed wildly, trying to shove himself to the surface, but he was too far away.

He can't swim! Nin's voice shouted faintly. *Sneakyji's drowning, he's dying!*

And then Ji's lungs stopped. His eyes burned and his body shut down.

31

WHEN THE INKY darkness turned to a brilliant pink light, Ji felt nothing but a distant numbness. Not cold, not desperate. Nothing.

Now this *is a better afterlife,* he thought. *At least Roz is going to like the color.*

Then a war hammer smashed him in the back.

His body jerked and water gushed from his mouth like a fountain. He gasped and writhed, filling his lungs with beautiful pure air. The war hammer struck again, and he spewed more water and gulped more air—until his vision cleared.

He was kneeling in the tusk deer cage beside the water hole. Roz held him upright with one of her hands like a vise around both his wrists, while her other hand pounded his back.

The tears in her eyes glinted like stars.

"Stop!" he gasped. "Stop hitting me!"

"Oh, thank summer!" she rumbled with a sob of relief. "You're alive!"

"I won't be for long"—he coughed wetly—"if you hit me again."

She glowered at him. "You don't know how to swim! What were you thinking?"

"That I'd make a better merman," he grumbled. "What kind of fishboy can't even breathe underwater?"

She held him as he coughed a few more times. "I'm sure you're a fine merman."

"Whoa, Roz!" he said, seeing the ruined bars of his cage, which she'd crushed like cornstalks. "Did you crash through both cages in like two seconds?"

Once Missroz thought you were dying, Nin said, *she broke the bars in an eyeblink.*

"Wow, Roz," Ji said, with a final cough. "You really . . . wow."

Roz blushed. "Don't make a fuss."

"Can I thank you for saving my life?"

"You may."

Touching her forearm felt like touching armadillo-shell boots. "Thank you."

"Well, they heard *that,*" Sally yowled from the roof of the next cage. "There are two squads of soldiers, coming fast."

"And a few guards on horses," Chibo said, squinting

beside her. "At least, they *sound* like guards on horses."

"What shall we do?" Roz asked Ji.

He rubbed his stinging eyes. "Sally, stay on the toproofs. Find a path out of here without running into the soldiers. Chibo, climb down and—"

Chibo's vaporous wings spread from the hump on his back. They glimmered a green so dark that it was barely visible, and he swooped down and landed outside the broken bars of Ji's cage.

"And what?" he asked calmly, before doing a happy jig. "Did you see that? Did you see? I glided! I *glid*!"

"They're almost here!" Sally growled. "I can take them, Ji. Let's fight. It's the only honorable—"

"Find us a way out!" he snapped, pushing to his feet with an ease that surprised him, considering he'd almost drowned a minute earlier. "Now!"

"Fine," she growled. "Jerk."

"Nin?" he asked, looking around the destroyed cage. "Where are you?"

Here and there, like we said!

"Well, *what* are you?"

We don't know, Nin said. *We like digging and scouting and we're mostly in the urn—*

"You're mostly in the *urn*?" Ji rubbed his face with his palm. "You're some mind-talking, not-visible thing in an urn."

We're some aws! We're also in the leaves and—

"Can you lift the urn?" Ji asked Roz.

"I'm not entirely sure—" She grabbed the urn, two hundred pounds of dirt in a clay pot, then straightened. "Yes."

"Good—bring it with us." Ji looked toward the sound of hoofbeats. "Chibo, start glowing—"

"I can *glow*!" Chibo fluted.

"—and fly above the soldiers in circles around the zoo—"

"I can *fly*!"

"—and lead them away from us. Then meet us outside the palace grounds."

"How's he supposed to find us again?" Sally asked, her tail lashing. "He can barely see!"

"Right, yeah," Ji said. "Forget that, Chibo—we'll save flying for later."

"This way, fast!" Sally called, and darted across the roofs.

Roz lumbered along below her, moving fast despite her size. "Are you sure you can run?" she asked Ji in a gravelly whisper. "You almost died."

"I'm okay," he said, trotting after her. "Actually, I'm better than okay." His shoulders didn't ache, his neck didn't hurt. "For the first time ever. My eyes burn a little, but other'n that I feel kind of . . . *great*."

"Maybe mermen heal fast?" Chibo panted, trying to keep up.

"I guess." Ji grabbed Chibo's hand to help him

along—and almost pulled him off his feet. "Wah! You don't weigh anything, Chibo!"

"I weigh *something*."

"Yeah, like a sack of feathers."

"Sprites are light," Chibo informed him. "Also, we fly."

Ji dragged him after Roz. "And your eyes are green."

"No way!" Chibo blinked his unearthly emerald eyes. "Really?"

"Green as a new blade of grass," Ji said, trotting past the last cages of the Menagerie.

They followed Sally down a wide flight of stairs flanked by bugbear statues and terra-cotta warriors. At the bottom of the steps, a fancy promenade stretched in both directions, but Sally stopped halfway down.

"Follow me!" she yipped, bounding over the railing. "Quick, quick!"

When Roz hefted the urn onto the railing, a few clumps of dirt fell out—and crawled back inside. Ji did a double take but couldn't look closer because Chibo needed help over the railing. A moment later, Sally led them across the hillside and onto a wide cart path that ran between high wooden buildings inside the Forbidden Palace.

"Hide behind that caravan!" she growled. "And shut your faces—there are guards everywhere!"

Roz squeezed between the caravan and the wall, moving slowly to keep the urn from smacking the wheel. When Ji and Chibo crowded in beside her, one of Chibo's wings poked from his hump and glowed faintly.

Ji elbowed him and the wing vanished.

You all have to be molequiet, Nin announced, *but we can still talk. They can't hear us. We could tell you a story of longsince, if you want. Or how to roast sweetbeets with spicy peppers—*

"Shht," Sally hissed at the urn. "I'm trying to listen."

Silence fell. A dark cloud drifted away from the moons, and shadows loomed against the wall. Then a squad of soldiers trotted down a street on the other side of the buildings, weapons drawn and armor jangling.

Ji's breath caught. Roz grabbed his shoulder anxiously, in a painful grip, but he didn't even flinch. When the soldiers disappeared, he exhaled in relief. Chibo rubbed his bald scalp, Roz removed her hand from Ji's shoulder—

And two guards on horseback cantered into the cart path.

Plans whirled in Ji's head. Should he send Sally under the caravan to startle the guards' horses? Tell Roz to pry open the door and try to hide inside? Or close his eyes and pray that the guards didn't spot them?

Before he decided, the guards clip-clopped past. Ji took a breath . . . then managed not to shriek when Sally appeared in front of him, hanging upside down by her tail.

"We don't need to hide," she purred. "Me and Roz can kick their bums."

"Roz isn't fighting," he whispered.

"Look at her! She's a battle machine."

"I am looking," he told her. "All I see is *Roz*."

Sally shifted her big-eyed gaze toward Roz, who was prodding the big ceramic urn curiously, her expression sweet despite looking like a troll. A few papaya seedlings sprouted from the urn's dirt, and she brushed a leaf aside, her massive four-fingered hand still delicate.

"Okay, yeah." Sally's muzzle drew downward. "I guess she's not really a fighter."

"But when I look at *you*," Ji told her, "I see a battle machine."

Her huge eyes brightened. "You do?"

"The cutest battle machine in the world."

She whacked his head with a paw, then cocked her furry ears. "There aren't any soldiers nearby. What now?"

"We need—" Ji frowned. "The first thing we need is cloaks. We kind of stand out."

"You don't," Chibo fluted. "At least not much."

"Because he's half merman," Sally growled, "and mermen are already half human. So Ji's only a quarter fishy."

Roz lifted her gaze from the urn. "That is excellent arithmetic, Sally!"

"I guess three quarters of me can't breathe under water," Ji said.

And also can't swim, Nin added. *You looked like a plucked chicken throwing a tantrum in a bathtub.*

Chibo burbled a laugh, then asked Ji, "What's the second thing we need?"

"To get out of the city."

"What we really need," Sally said, "is to break the spell and turn human again."

To turn ogre *again!* Nin said.

"I couldn't agree more," Roz said. "We're not even truly a troll, hobgoblin, sprite, merman, and . . . whatever Nin is. We're twisted, we're incomplete. We cannot live this way."

"We won't live at all unless we get out of here," Ji said. "And we don't know how to break the spell."

"But we know who does," Roz said.

"Who?" Ji asked. "Brace?"

"No. Ti-Lin-Su."

"The scholar?"

"She's the world's leading zozologist," Roz said. "She knows more about creatures than anyone."

"Fine," Ji said. "But first we need to survive. Where can we find cloaks?"

"A laundry?" Chibo suggested.

"Good," Ji said. "Did you see one?"

"I can barely see *you*."

"Oh, right. Uh, did anyone see servants' quarters or anything?"

Sally pointed a fuzzy finger. "There are a few dingy buildings that way. Sort of huddled together."

"Sounds like servants to me," Ji said.

32

SALLY LED THEM in a winding path around a dozen buildings, avoiding the clink of patrolling soldiers and the nicker of horses. She made them wait behind the outhouses for five stinky minutes, then rushed them over a wall and through a rock garden full of vine-covered pagodas.

"It's on the other side of this," she said, heading toward a tile-roofed temple.

Ji rubbed his eyes, then followed her into the quiet, cool interior. Hallways extended in every direction, with sliding doors and jade lanterns. The air smelled of citrus and incense, and the carpets silenced even Roz's footsteps.

Sally prowled into a dark room in the center of the temple. Fountains burbled and splashed in the shadows. She took five steps, then stopped. "Uh-oh."

"What?" Ji asked.

Lamplight flared, and Ji saw twenty people praying in silent rows, foreheads touching the ground. And a teenager stood beside Ji, his hand on the lamp he'd just uncovered.

"Um," Ji said. "Hi?"

The teenager screamed, "Monsters!"

So Ji backpedaled . . . into an old man praying. The old man shrieked—then Sally growled and Chibo unfurled his wings.

A few more people screamed: "Help! Ogres! Help!"

Nin said, *We're ogre! We'll help!*

The rest of the people bellowed, "Guards! Monsters! Help!"

Roz rumbled, "No, no, we don't mean any harm—"

And Ji shouted, "RUN!"

So *everyone* ran: Sally, Chibo, Roz, Ji . . . and all the people. They rushed the exits, shoving and screaming—and, in Roz's case, begging everyone's pardon—then burst onto the street together, in a confused jumble.

For a moment, quiet fell.

Then a little girl pointed at Sally and said, "That monthter is cwoot!"

The screaming started again. The old man raised his cane, a shrill whistle sounded, and a stone bounced off Roz's shoulder. And hoofbeats pounded closer to them from beyond the rock garden.

"Guards!" Sally growled. "This way!"

She headed down the block. Roz hefted Nin's urn higher and followed while Ji grabbed Chibo's hand and said, "Brighter!"

Chibo unfurled his wings to their full length. The people gasped and covered their eyes against the brilliant green shimmering.

"Anyone who follows us gets sprited," Ji snarled over his shoulder.

Plus hobgobbled and merdered! Nin added, though the people couldn't hear his mind-speak. *Not* murdered! *Not like* murder. *Merdered like* merman.

Ji dragged Chibo down the block after Sally and Roz. Around a corner, Sally bounded through a pair of swinging doors. Inside, three mariachis stood on a stage, practicing a song in an empty room. A string twanged; then silence fell.

"Just passing through," Roz rumbled to them. "Lovely melody."

Sally shoved through a back door into a tangle of Forbidden Palace alleys with high, whitewashed walls. With her ears swiveling for the sound of pursuit, she led them in what felt like circles for ten minutes. Finally, she trotted along a leafy path into a hidden gap between a hedge and a stand of cedar trees.

"My goodness," Roz said. "How did you find this?"

"I can see in the dark now." Sally pointed to a low

building past the hedge. "That's a servants' quarters."

"Where are the guards?" Ji asked.

She pricked up her ears. "We lost them."

"Running . . . is stupid," Chibo panted, plopping onto a stone pile between the tree trunks. "When you can . . . fly."

"Stay here," Ji said. "I'll grab cloaks and"—he frowned at Sally's tail and Chibo's hunchback—"other stuff."

He squirmed through the hedge, then peered at the servants' quarters. Fancy banners flapped on the eaves and light pooled around ornate lampposts, but other than that, it looked like every other servants' quarters he'd ever seen. So he just marched inside the front door. Two maids and a groundskeeper glanced at him with a complete lack of interest. As long as nobody noticed his scaly "tattoos" or clawed feet, he looked exactly like was he was: just another servant.

Well, he looked like what he *used to be*.

After getting his bearings, Ji slunk into the laundry. He grabbed an oversized cloak with a hood for Roz, an empty backpack to cover Chibo's hump, and a small, striped poncho to cover Sally's tail. He tied foot wraps around his sandals to hide his scaly toes, and he was scrounging around for something to hold Nin's urn when a murmur of conversation approached.

Time to leave. He slipped down a passage, around a corner—and found himself in a boot boy's nook.

A boot *girl's* nook, actually: a scrawny girl sat at a

workbench, scrubbing mud from an elegant boot heel. She raised her head when Ji stepped inside, and she rubbed her neck. Her hair was blond and her feet were locked in a pair of twenty-pound punishment shoes.

"Cleaning dueling boots, huh?" Ji headed for the side door. "I hate those."

She frowned at her worktable. "Stupid laces."

"And they're not even An-Hank Cordwainer."

"She's my favorite," the boot girl said.

Ji stopped with his hand on the doorknob. "She's a *she*?"

"Of course she is!" The girl laughed, still rubbing her neck. "Her name is An!"

"Oh." Maybe the ogres had the right idea, and Ji should call everyone "cub," just in case. "She's my favorite too."

"What happened to your face?" the girl asked.

"Long story. What happened to your feet?"

She looked at her punishment shoes. "I tried to run away."

"Try again," he told her, and slipped outside.

When the door clicked shut behind Ji, soldiers shouted in the distance. He shuddered, then scanned the gloom until he spotted the hedge.

A minute later, he poked through the other side, and Roz raised the urn at him. "Ant lions! That's what Nin is! A colony of ant lions! Look!"

Ant lions! The queenking of insects! The littlest of bigcats.

"A whole colony?" Chibo asked. "You mean she's got

more legs than a herd of deer?"

"Nin's not a she!" Roz said. "And yes, an ant-lion colony is like a single creature, split into hundreds of tiny parts. One ant lion is simply like a . . . a finger, or an eye. Not a whole animal."

Ji peered closely into the urn for the first time. A handful of ant lions crawled on the papaya leaves, and three freshly dug anthills were mounded in the dirt. Except these ant lions were bright red, with yellow manes and fearsome stingers. And big: each one was half as long as Ji's thumb.

"May I pick one of you up, Nin?" Roz asked.

We don't feel like ant lions. We feel like tiny Nins. Uppick us all you want, Missroz!

"I'm afraid I might hurt you." She rested a big granite-flecked finger in the dirt. "Will you climb aboard?"

An ant lion tossed its mane, stroked Roz's finger with its antennae, then climbed onto her palm.

"Can you see through all your eyes?" Ji asked the ant lion. "All at once?"

We peek here, there, and everywhere!

"Amazing." Roz gazed at the ant lion on her palm. "Not even Ti-Lin-Su knows that ant lions are intelligent."

"Intelligent?" Ji tossed the striped poncho to Sally, who was straddling a low branch in a cedar tree. "This is Nin we're talking about."

"That's how we hear them!" Roz said, her deep voice

thrumming with excitement. "Ant lion colonies must use mind-speak to talk to one another!"

"Forget mind-speak. . . ." Ji watched another ant lion climb his pant leg. "Do your stingers sting?"

We haven't tried yet. Want us to buttsting someone?

"Keep your butt to yourself." Ji tossed Roz the oversized cloak. "And you, Roz, cover your horn."

Sally tugged her poncho lower. "I can't believe I have a tail."

It's a doorbell! Nin told her.

"It's more of a feather duster," Chibo said, shrugging into the backpack.

"Okay," Ji said. "Now we just have to get past the inner palace wall, then the outer palace wall, then sneak to Ti-Lin-Su's estate and pray she can help."

"*That's* your plan?" Sally asked.

"Well, yeah. What's wrong with it?"

"There are soldiers patrolling the wall, Ji. They're everywhere. There's no way out."

33

"ARE YOU SURE?" Ji asked, his stomach sinking.

"Of course I'm sure," Sally growled. "I saw them."

"So we can't get out."

Then we stay here! Nin said, as the ant lion that had crawled onto Ji's sleeve waved its antennae.

"Here is bad," Ji told Nin. "They'll find us here."

The ant lion roared faintly, like a mouse snoring. *You smell?*

Ji ignored the tiny Nin and climbed the stone pile. He didn't have time for weirdness. If they didn't escape soon, the guards would find them—and then the queen would skewer them on the water tree. He peered between the leaves and saw search beams sweeping the palace grounds from watchtowers on the inner wall.

"Don't pick on Ji just because he's a fish," Chibo told Nin.

We don't mean that! We mean do you smell an airscent, sweet like syrup?

Sally lifted her snout. "Very faint? Like boiling marmalade?"

That smell, yes! Just came on the breeze, honeyed and sugary.

"We don't need pastry," Ji said. "We need—"

"It's goblins," Sally growled at him. "It smells like the bone crypt."

Burrowdiggers, Nin agreed. *Fourarms. We can't peek-see them, but they smell nearby. And if there's goblins—*

"I could kiss you!" Ji told the ant lion on his sleeve. "You clever ogre."

"You can't kiss them," Sally said. "They don't have lips."

"What's so clever?" Chibo asked Ji.

"We can hide underground until the coast is clear."

"Hide in *goblin* tunnels?" Chibo asked, his green eyes widening. "Don't they eat people?"

"Do you have a better idea?" Ji asked him.

"Actually, yes," Chibo fluted. "You should all grow wings."

"We can't depend on goblins," Roz rumbled. "The last time we appealed to them for help, they betrayed us."

"The last time," Ji said, "we were human."

"Good point." She scratched her horn inside her hood.

"Perhaps they'll more happily come to the aid of nonhumans."

"The soldiers won't stop searching for us, though," Sally growled. "They'll know we're still inside the walls."

"She's right," Roz said. "Eventually, they'll check the goblin burrows."

Ji jumped down from the stone pile. "Not if they think we're gone."

"What are you going to do?" Sally asked.

"Cheat," he told her.

He grabbed a big round stone in both hands. He grunted with effort, waddled toward Roz, and dropped it at her feet.

She picked it up one-handed. "And what shall I do with this?"

"The nearest watchtower is a hundred yards that way." Ji pointed toward the wall. "How's your throwing arm?"

"Oh, of course!" Roz said. "Shall I aim for the searchlights?"

"Yeah, take out the lanterns," he said.

Roz stepped closer to the hedge and eyed the distant tower. She tossed the stone in her hand, took two steps backward . . . then paused. "Privacy, if you please."

"Oh, right." Ji nodded. "C'mon everyone, other side of the tree."

"I don't mind Sally and Chibo," Roz said. "Or Nin, of course."

"What?" Ji gaped at her. "Just me?"

Roz gave him a governess-y look. "Would you like me to throw rocks or not?"

"Fine," Ji grumbled, and scuffed to the other side of the tree.

He couldn't even see the watchtower from there. Stupid privacy. And why just *him*? Well, maybe because Chibo was just a kid, Sally was a girl, and Nin was an ogre. But still. He picked bark from the tree and heard Roz throw the stone. Then nothing. She must've missed. The stone pile clicked as she grabbed another rock.

"Aim this time," he told her.

"Hush," she said.

Chibo came around the tree. "I can't see anyway. But if Roz misses, I can always fly over and drop rocks onto—"

A shout erupted from the wall.

"Direct hit!" Sally growled. "One more lantern, Roz."

A trumpet sounded at the watchtower. Another trumpet answered from farther along the wall, and horses galloped in the darkness. Roz threw another rock and must've hit the second lantern, because she laughed in triumph.

"The soldiers are hopping around like fleas on a cricket," Sally purred. "They think we're attacking, or escaping, or something-ing."

"What now, Ji?" Roz asked.

"Get a few more rocks," Ji said, "and throw them over

the wall. So they'll think we're on the other side. Not yet, though."

The trumpet sounded again as the soldiers marched and shouted. After a cavalry troop passed, Roz asked, "Now?"

"Not yet."

Ji closed his eyes and imagined the guards standing in the dark, confused and nervous, scanning the shadows for strange beasts. He imagined them clasping their weapons nervously, deafened by the blare of trumpets.

"We can't stay here much longer," Roz said.

"You also can't rush a good lie." Ji waited a minute, then said, "Now! Lob one over the wall."

Roz threw a stone. "Consider it lobbed."

"Is anything happening, Sal?" Ji asked, looking into the tree overhead.

"Lots," she said from the branches. "But nothing new."

"Throw two more." He waited while Roz hurled two stones. "Now two more."

"Still nothing new," Sally reported. "They're just—" A creak sounded in the night. "They're opening the gate! They think we're outside the wall!"

And that is why they call him Sneakyji, Nin said.

"Nobody calls him Sneakyji except you," Chibo said.

"Whenever it's safe," Ji told Sally, "take us to the goblins."

She scanned for guards, then prowled into the darkness

like a tiger cub on the warpath. Ji took Chibo's elbow and followed, trying not to flinch at the soldiers shouting in the distance.

Past the hedge, Sally loped toward a stone bridge that linked the servants' quarters and the stables. Halfway there, she raised a hand—well, a paw—and stopped. A breeze rustled the trees, and Roz set the urn onto the stone path with a clunk.

"Shh!" Sally said.

"Sorry," Roz whispered.

Sally sniffed the air. "This way."

She veered off the path, slunk between red-barked bushes, then slipped into the wide arch beneath the bridge. Without the moons-light, the darkness turned inky black. A stony grinding sounded, and the syrupy scent was thick in the air.

"A little light?" Ji whispered to Chibo.

Chibo's wings slid from beneath his backpack and glowed a soft emerald. The first thing Ji saw was a wrought-iron gate, wide open in the stone wall. The second was two goblins squatting over a clay bowl, grinding the contents with their fists.

"What a lovely evening," Roz rumbled to the goblins. "We're so pleased to meet Kultultul in the city!"

The goblins bared their teeth. "We are ka-honored to meet you," one said, then peered from Roz to Sally to Chibo. "Whatever you may be."

"I, um, I am Miss Rozario Songarza."

"I'm Chibo. I have wings."

"What he means is 'pleased to meet you,'" Ji said.

"Oh, right!" Chibo said. "Very pleased!"

"We're hoping," Roz said, "that you can spare a moment to chat."

The smaller goblin took its hands from the bowl. "There is a ka-risis in the palace tonight?"

"A crisis?" Roz said. "Well, erm . . . "

"Aka-tually," Ji said, "that's why we're here. We need to hide from the ka-risis."

The other goblin hunched toward Ji. "You are not human."

"Not exactly, no," Ji agreed, and bared his teeth politely.

"The humans are hunting you," the first goblin said.

"Yeah," Ji said.

"They are ka-illers. If we help you, they will ka-ill us."

"Only if they find out," Ji said.

"We are affiliated with the—" Roz made a sound like a boulder clearing its throat. "If that helps?"

"What?" Ji blinked at her. "Huh?"

That is how you say "ogre" in Ogrish, Nin said. *It means "the People."*

The goblin chuffed and its belly-arms waved them toward the gate. "Please, step inside! Ka-reful of your horn, Miss Ka-zario."

Roz thanked the goblin and lumbered toward the

burrow, ducking her head at the entrance. "Very kind," she said. "I've always found Kultultul to be excellent hosts. . . ."

"How does Roz know the word for ogre?" Ji asked Sally, taking Chibo's arm.

"Nin told her while you were snaffling the cloaks."

Chibo squinted. "So 'goblin' means 'people' and 'ogre' also means 'people'?"

"And 'sprite,' too, I bet," Sally growled.

"No," Chibo said as they entered the burrow. "'Sprite' means '*flying* people.'"

Torches flickered on the walls of an earthen hall, illuminating nooks filled with heaps of bark and soap and beetle wings. A honeycomb glistened in one goblin shrine, and Ji caught sight of knotted bootlaces in another.

"Sheesh," Chibo said, his wings glowing brighter. "I can't see in here even more than I can't see out there."

"At least we're safe for now," Ji said.

Sally nudged him. "Except we're surrounded by goblins."

He followed her big-eyed gaze and saw a dozen goblins hunching toward them from deeper in the burrow. The light glinted on their pale, wrinkly skin, and the shovel-claws at the end of their muscular shoulder-arms looked like weapons.

Ji gulped, but Roz simply lumbered forward, spouting polite greetings and flowery compliments. Ji moved to join her—then paused. "Maybe we should let Roz handle the politeness."

"I'm totally polite!" Chibo said.

"For a bratty little brother," Sally said.

One of Chibo's wings flicked at Sally.

"Whoa!" she said, ducking beneath the shimmering green light. "You almost got me."

"I can sort of feel my way around with my wings," he said, making them shrink and grow and curve and sparkle.

The green light shone on fire pits and log benches, and Nin said, *Just like the oldgood days, Sneakyji.*

"What?"

When we thought you were the cutemost thing we ever peeked, Nin explained. *But you're not a doorbell compared to Sallynx.*

"I'm *not* a doorbell!" Sally snarled, brushing an ant lion with her tail.

The ant lion gave a tiny roar. *Prettysweet, buttersoft, and toothless!*

"Wait," Ji said, as a memory sparked. He stared at the ant lions riding on Chibo's backpack. "'Buttersoft and toothless?' I've heard that before. What do you mean, just like the olddays?"

When we first peeked you, sleepylittle above the bone crypt. In goblin pen.

Ji's breath caught. "That was real? That was *you* at Primstone? That wasn't a dream? You were *there*?"

The ant lions shook their manes in what looked like insectile amusement. *You thought we were a dream?*

"No way! What were you doing at Primstone?"

Traveling to city from mountains, of course, Nin said as the ant lions scurried higher on the backpack. *Through burrowtunnels.*

Ji rubbed his stinging eyes. "Ogres travel in goblin tunnels? Don't the goblins get mad?"

We work together, Nin said. *For years now.*

"Jiyong!" Roz rumbled, hurrying toward them. "We need to hide!"

"Hide?" Chibo asked, peering nearsightedly at her. "Why?"

"Now!" she snapped.

"Ka-wickly!" The goblins woofled, and a dozen belly-arms pointed toward a side tunnel. "Into that ka-vern!"

34

ROZ HEFTED THE urn and trotted into the shadows. Sally grabbed Chibo's hand and followed, while Ji slunk along more slowly, watching the goblins bustle toward the gate, their freaky knees bobbling. He didn't trust them. For one thing, they ate humans. And for another thing . . . well, one was enough. You couldn't trust people who found you delicious.

"Nin," he whispered to an ant lion on his shoulder, "tell everyone to get ready just in case we—"

The wrought-iron gate slammed shut with a clang. The sound echoed in the burrow and the goblins knelt, belly-arms folded and heads bowed. A chain rattled outside, and Ji caught a glimpse of human soldiers beyond the gate before he slipped into the side tunnel.

"Tell the captain we secured the gobs," a woman's voice rasped from outside.

Another soldier murmured a question.

"Nah, they won't make trouble," the raspy woman answered. "Even if they tried, we're stationed here until they catch the monsters."

In the side tunnel, Ji sagged against a cool stone wall. "We're locked in."

"Catching them isn't our job," the woman rasped. "From what I hear, the queen's working some kind of magic."

"Great," Sally growled. "Magic."

The soldiers' voices grew fainter, and Ji wanted to cry. Attacked by a water tree? Fine. Transformed into beasts? Sure. Surrounded by soldiers? Check. Hunted by the Summer Queen? Right. But now they were locked inside *another* goblin pen, all over again? It was all too much. He couldn't handle it. He was hungry and tired, and he just wanted to be left alone.

Then Chibo sniffled, and Sally said, "Don't worry. Ji will think of something."

So Ji rubbed his eyes and took a steadying breath. He peeked from the side tunnel toward the motionless goblins near the entrance. A bonfire burned outside the locked gate, which meant the soldiers were settling in for the night. Ji looked into the darkness of the side tunnel but couldn't see anything. Certainly not another way out.

"Give us some wing, Chibo," he said, and green light

brushed the tunnel walls. "Oh, that's better."

"Maybe for you," Chibo grumbled. "I still can't see."

"There are soldiers outside," Sally told him, "and the goblins are all in front of the gate. Why are they just staying there?"

"The soldiers must have ordered them to stay put," Roz said. "We need another exit."

Ji looked down the tunnel, then turned to an ant lion crawling along Sally's leather bracelet. "So ogres and goblins are friends, right? Maybe they'll show us a way out."

"Ogres and goblins are enemies," Roz told him. "At least they used to be, according to Ti-Lin-Su."

"You're the one who told them we're affiliated with ogres!"

"That was a risk," she said. "Still, I thought they might help, because at least we're not . . . human."

Goblins and ogres aren't enemies anymore. Well, we're still enemies, but working together. A few ant lions marched to the tip of a papaya leaf sprouting from the urn. *Goblins burrowed to help us get closer to the evilqueen.*

Roz's granite-flecked brow furrowed. "You mean the goblins dig tunnels for the ogres?"

"Of course!" Ji gave a low whistle when he realized what was happening. "That's why you were at Primstone Manor!"

"Who was?" Roz asked. "Nin?"

"Yeah, I saw him—cub—*them* in the goblin pen that

night. I thought it was a dream."

"So the goblins and the ogres are working together?"

"Yeah." Jin looked at the urn. "Did the goblins tunnel under every single hacienda from here to the mountains?"

The ant lions waved their antennae. *They dug one long burrow, from the mountain to the city.*

"That explains why you saw eighteen goblins at Primstone," Roz rumbled to Ji, "instead of twelve. Because the goblin burrows are all connected! But why?"

"Tell her," Ji said to the urn.

For a surprise ogre attack on the city.

"For an invasion . . ." Ji nodded to himself as everything became clear. "The extra goblins were digging extra tunnels to secretly bring the ogres to the city."

"That's why Nin wanted to know about the Rite," Roz said slowly. "Because the ogres can't invade until the queen is weak."

Have to attack after the Rite, Nin agreed. *Or the clayfighters will kill us all.*

"The clayfighters?" Chibo said. "You mean the terracotta soldiers?"

We have a few moons before the evilqueen is strong again. She can't do magic so soon after the Rite! At least, that's what we thought, but now—

"Forget about the stupid invasion!" Ji interrupted. "These tunnels crisscross the realm, right? That's perfect. We can stroll out of the city and pop up anywhere!"

"We still need Ti-Lin-Su," Roz said. "To explain how to turn human again."

"She can wait," Ji told her.

"How would you know?" Roz demanded. "What if we wait too long and this horrid transformation becomes permanent?"

We can't uppop anywhere. One of Nin's ant lions peeped at Ji from the edge of Roz's hood. *These tunnels don't reach the others.*

Ji groaned. "What do you mean? These tunnels don't lead out of the palace, farther into the city?"

Not yet! Not past the outer walls. Not ready for invasion yet. Another few weeks, and then ogres uppop inside Forbidden Palace and—

"Okay, we need another exit. Can we ask the goblins for directions?"

"That strikes me as unwise," Roz said. "At least while the guards are watching."

Ji drummed his fingers against the rough-hewn wall. Two ant lions crawled from his collar onto his neck, then tickled his cheek with their manes. He thought for a minute. And another. Then he said, "Okay. The goblins at the gate are all wearing collars, right? Can you see them, Sal?"

"Yeah," Sally growled, her tail lashing beneath her poncho. "They all have collars."

"And if there are extra goblins in the Primstone burrow,"

Ji said, "there must be extra goblins in the Forbidden Palace burrow. Right?"

"No," Roz said. "Because this burrow doesn't connect to the outside tunnels."

Burrows always have extra goblins, Nin said. *They don't tell the humans about all the gobbabies they have.*

"Good!" Ji said, exhaling in relief. "So we just have to find the extra goblins and—"

"—they'll lead us outside!" Chibo finished, his wings spreading.

"That's the plan." Ji turned to Sally. "Can you follow the sugary smell to the rest of the goblins?"

"Sure," she said, her ears flattened against her head.

"Are you okay?" he asked.

"Mm," she growled.

"Let's go!" Chibo said, and marched into the darkness, his wings flicking against the tunnel walls.

Sally leaped forward to steer him around a rock while Roz followed with the urn, her toes sticking through her torn slippers.

"Could you not walk on my face?" Ji asked Nin, following behind.

The ant lion on his cheek crawled into his hair.

"Oh, that's much better," he said.

After heading downward, Sally paused at an intersection and lifted her snout. She sniffed a few times, so Ji sniffed too. Smelled like the kitchen at Primstone when

Cook made plum jam. His stomach rumbled and he looked from one green-tinted tunnel entry to another.

Sally prowled along a new tunnel, then spun and stared at Ji like an angry chipmunk. "We have to stop this."

"What?" Ji frowned at her. "Stop what?"

"This invasion, the ogre invasion."

"No, we don't. We just have to run away and become human again."

Should help the ogrevasion and stop the evilqueen, Nin said. *Not stop the ogrevasion and help the evilqueen.*

"I am no longer entirely fond of Her Majesty," Roz said. "However, I agree with Sally. A battle will flatten the city."

Ji shrugged. "If we stick around, the queen will flatten *us*."

"We can't do nothing!" Roz said. "We can't simply watch people getting hurt."

"Then close your eyes," Ji snapped, suddenly angry. "They're trying to kill us, Roz. The Queen, Proctor, the soldiers. You think they care if *we* get hurt?"

Roz hunched her shoulders and bowed her granite-flecked face, while Sally's tufted ears drooped. For a long moment, nobody spoke. Ji heard his own breath, ragged and harsh in the narrow tunnel.

"Nobody cares about us," Ji told them, "except us. "

"Protecting the city is the honorable thing," Sally growled, more quietly than usual. "Even if they hate us."

He scowled at her. "Have I ever cared about honor?"

"Yes," she said.

"I have not."

"Innocent people will die," Roz told Ji.

No innocent people, Nin said. *Just the evilqueen. Ogres will burst from tunnels and overthrow her in an eyeblink.*

Ji flicked an ant lion from his shoulder. "You stupid ogres should've stayed in the stupid mountains."

Not stupid, Nin said, almost sulkily.

"If the ogres attack the queen," Roz told Nin's urn, "the entire realm will fight back. It won't be one raid, it will be a whole war."

"Let the realm burn," Ji said, his eyes stinging. "I don't care."

"We cannot simply—"

"I don't care!" he lied.

"But if we stop the ogres—" Sally started.

"How?" Ji interrupted. "How can we stop the ogres?"

Roz quietly told him, "You'll think of a way."

"I don't *know* a way," Ji said. "Look at us, Roz. We're monsters, we're mistakes. And worse, we're servants. We're worthless, we're nothing."

"We're better than they are," Roz said.

"*You* are!" Ji said, almost accusingly. "You're better than them! Not me. I'm not better than anyone, and I'm not letting us risk our lives for this stupid realm."

Sally's tail pouffed. "Why are *you* in charge?"

"Because I don't care about honor, Sal," he told her. "I

don't care if I'm right or wrong, I don't care if I'm good or bad. I don't about anything except *you*."

"Oh," she said.

"All of you." Ji picked up the ant lion he'd flicked. "Even Nin."

Roz shifted her grip on the urn. "There's truly no way to stop this?"

"Not that I can think of." Ji dropped the ant lion onto his shoulder. "If we ever get out of this burrow, we'll ask Ti-Lin-Su for advice. Okay?"

Sally tugged at her bracelet. "Okay."

"Will she even talk to us?" Chibo asked. "Isn't she a recluse?"

Ji almost laughed. "She studies weird creatures, Chibo. Believe me, she'll talk to *us*."

What did the wreck lose?

"'Recluse,' Nin," Roz explained. "Like a hermit."

Oh, we understand now! Nin said. *What did the hermit lose?*

While Roz rumbled softly into the urn, Sally led them along a passageway with lumpy walls. From there, she headed into a wide tunnel with swirly grooves in the walls.

She stopped in a chamber where three bamboo poles rose from dark pits. The sweet smell was almost overpowering—and delicious, like warm blackberry jam on honey bread.

Ji's mouth watered, and Chibo said, "I'm starving.

Flying takes a lot of energy."

"You haven't flown anywhere," Ji told him.

Chibo flicked a wing at Ji. "Oh, now you're an expert on sprites."

"Let's slide down the poles," Sally said.

"Um." Ji eyed the dark pits in the cave floor. "Or *not*."

"I'm not certain they'll hold me, in any case," Roz said. "And I can't carry the urn while—"

"Hai-ai!" Sally yipped, her ruff rising. "That one's moving!"

One pole swayed gently, and a scratchy clicking sounded in the pit beneath it. Faint at first, then louder. Something was climbing toward them from the darkness.

"More light." Ji hustled Chibo away from the poles. "Sally, get back!"

Sally smiled wolfishly—well, wolfpup-ishly—and prowled closer to the pits. She didn't say anything about facing danger with honor, but Ji knew she was thinking it. He stepped in front of Chibo as the bamboo pole swayed faster.

The scratchy clicking went *scratchclick scratchclick-scratchclick*.

Then a small pink hand appeared, followed by another hand—and a tiny goblin head rose into sight. Followed by the rest of the goblin, about half normal size, with bright-pink skin and no teeth. And not wearing a collar.

"A baby!" Chibo fluted. "A goblin baby! A gobbaby!"

The little goblin pointed at Sally. "Ka-ute!"

"Oh, great," Sally muttered. "Even goblins think I'm cute."

"She is highly capable, as well," Roz told the goblin, then curtsied. "It is such a pleasure to meet a young Kul-tultul."

"Very ka-ind." The goblin hopped from the pole to the cavern floor. "I beg you will pardon me, but I thin-ka you should not be here."

"Than-ka you for telling us," Ji said, remembering to bow. "We're sorry we're in your burrow, but we're lost. Um, where's the nearest exit? "

"I don't mean in our burrow!" The little goblin gestured with tiny belly-arms. "I mean *here*! In this ka-ave."

"What is this cave, anyway?" Chibo asked, inhaling deeply. "It's my favorite."

"Yeah," Ji said. "It smells delicious."

"Delectable," Roz rumbled.

The goblin cocked its pink head in confusion. "You tease? You tease me?"

"No, no," Sally purred. "This cave smells gooooood."

"Delicious?" The goblin's belly-hands wiggled in glee. "Your favorite?"

"Yeah." Sally peered into the dark pit. "What's down there?"

"Poop! Our poop! That's where we poop! You're smelling our poop!"

35

AFTER A MAD scramble away from the goblin latrine, Ji leaned against a tunnel wall and caught his breath. For a minute, nobody spoke. Then he told Roz, "I have an idea."

Roz didn't answer, her four-fingered hand still clapped over her mouth in horror.

"What?" Chibo asked Ji.

"Let's never speak of this again."

"I can still smell it," Sally moaned.

Roz lowered her hand. "Ti-Lin-Su never mentioned latrines."

"'My favorite!'" the little goblin quoted, woofling a giggle. "'Smells so gooooood.'"

Ji crouched in front of the goblin. "Now that we've made you laugh, can you show us a way out of here?"

"Of ka-ourse," it said. "Happy to help. You are ex-kallent people."

"Why, thank you," Roz said.

The little goblin nodded solemnly. "I've never met any-one so polite about poop before."

"We're special that way," Ji said.

"Follow me!" the goblin said. "This way, please!"

A long moss-carpeted tunnel widened into a series of mushroom gardens; then a winding passageway opened into a chamber packed with weird-shaped pillars. Sally and Chibo helped Roz squeeze through while Ji looked away—for her "privacy"—and then they marched into the gloom. Exhaustion weighed on Ji's shoulders. He trudged onward, one scaly foot in front of the other, his sandals scuffing along the squiggly ridges in the floor. The scent of coal smoke grew stronger, masking the syrupy smell.

Finally, the ramp opened into a cave where merry bon-fires cast a rosy glow against stalagmites and statues.

"Welcome to my home ka-vern!" the little goblin said. "A great honor to bring you."

"The pleasure is all ours," Roz said. "Such a lovely cavern."

"Where's the exit?" Ji asked. "I mean, please, if you'd kindly . . ."

He trailed off when five little goblins hunched closer, jabbering in Goblish. With their cheery pink skin and lack of beaver teeth, they looked like grinning piglets on two feet. The first goblin chattered and the newcomers chuffed happily. One gazed in awe at Roz, and the rest bowed to the tip of Sally's tail poking from under her poncho.

Chibo giggled and Ji smiled for a moment—then his blood chilled.

A dozen adult goblins watched them from the shadows deeper in the cave. Snake-shaped clubs swayed in the goblins' fists. A few wore shirts of woven pebbles, their belly-arms tucked behind the armor, and none wore collars.

"Free goblins," Ji whispered. "And I don't think they like us."

"At least the gobbabies like Sally," Chibo said.

Three warrior goblins shambled closer, pebble armor rattling, and Ji gulped. "Politeness might not work this time. Chibo, get ready to shine bright enough to blind them. Sal, when I give the word—"

The first goblin kid shuffled between Ji and the grownups, woofling in Goblish. The warriors didn't respond. The little goblin woofled more and the warriors kept not responding. Then the little goblin barked—and the warrior goblins chuffed in amusement.

"Deleka-table?" one asked.

The little goblin nodded. "That is what they said."

"The latrine?" another said. "A delicious stin-ka? They are more gracious than the politest Kultultul!"

"Thank you ever so much," Roz said faintly, giving a

curtsy. "Though nobody is more courteous than Kultultul."

Chibo swirled his wings in a shimmering bow and said, "Ka!"

The rest of the adult goblins hunched forward, suddenly welcoming after hearing the story of the sweet-smelling latrine. Apparently that's how you befriended goblins, by complimenting their poop.

"We're hoping to find an exit," Roz told them, after what seemed like nineteen hours of polite chatter. "If you'd be so kind."

The goblins woofled. Then the little goblin said, "This way, please! I'll show you. Not far."

The goblin kid took them to a narrow chamber at the top of a ramp. A statue of a bird-snake rose at the end of the chamber, and the pale light of dawn seeped around its rough-hewn stone.

Relief bubbled in Ji's heart. "Daylight!"

"Where?" Chibo asked.

"Straight ahead." He led Chibo forward. "Past the statue."

"That's a statue?" Chibo asked, his eyes narrowing.

"Fresh air." Sally inhaled deeply. "Finally."

Ji squeezed past the statue and found himself facing a high stone wall. Light glowed from a rectangular opening just above his head. An exit! He rose onto his tiptoes to peek through and saw a cobblestone path and the bottom of a wooden building.

"Where are we?" he asked.

"A ka-nal drain," the goblin kid said behind him.

"A canal drain?" Ji watched ginkgo leaves tumble along the path outside. "But where?"

"Next to a canal, you doolally trout," Sally told him, poking her furry snout around the statue.

The little goblin's pink face turned pinker. "The grounds of the palace! Between inner wall and outer wall. There is stables and ponds and shrines and hills."

"And soldiers," Ji said, when boots appeared on the cobblestones.

"They patrol all day," the goblin said. "Back and forth."

Ji groaned. Why wasn't anything ever easy? He slumped to the other side of the statue. "We're stuck here until nighttime."

"Good." Roz set the urn down. "It's safe here, and I'm exhausted."

"Me, too," Sally said.

"I'm already asleep," Chibo said.

Not us! Nin said. *We're widey wake! You want to know an old ogre recipe for pickling cabbage?*

"Hush, Nin," Roz said.

Chibo stretched out on the chamber floor, using his backpack as a pillow. "I wonder how sprites sleep."

"Try 'silently,'" Sally said.

"Maybe we sleep in the air. Gliding high above the ground."

In cloudy beds, Nin said. *Fluffysoft and white.*

"Well, I'm not dozing off underwater," Ji said, stifling a yawn. "No matter what mermen do."

"You're a terrible merman," Sally told him. "You still have legs."

"At least I don't have a tail, cuddlebunny."

"You barely look merman at all, though," Chibo said. "Just a few scales here and there."

"Plus his eyes glint red in torchlight," Sally said.

"They do?" Ji asked.

"Hush," Roz said again.

Silence fell . . . for about ten seconds. Then two goblins knee bobbled into the chamber with a pot of rice and beans and a sack of steamed buns.

Ji's stomach grumbled, but Roz politely refused the meal. She refused three more times before thanking the goblins profusely and taking a delicate nibble of a steamed bun. "It's okay now," she rumbled. "You have to say no three times to be courteous."

Roughly seven seconds later, the empty sack was draped over the empty pot. Chibo licked his fingers, lying at the base of the statue. Still chewing, Sally draped her poncho over him, then curled into a catlike ball on the floor. Roz brushed crumbs from her dress and pulled her hood over her face.

Ji hugged his knees to his chest, his belly full and his eyes aching. But he needed to stay awake, he needed to plan ahead. Once night fell, they'd sneak outside and . . . what? Find Ti-Lin-Su? What if she refused to help them? What if she couldn't? What if they were trapped in monster bodies . . . forever?

Questions swirled in Ji's mind. His eyes stung but his eyelids drooped—and the last thing he saw before falling asleep was a row of Nin's ant lions marching toward the canal drain.

36

WHEN JI WOKE, daylight glimmered from behind the bird-snake statue. He yawned and stretched, then turned to watch Sally and Chibo sleep. He smiled at the sight of Sally's face, her tufted ears twitching and her muzzle trembling with her snores.

Then he gazed at Roz. Her hood had slipped, and her horn gleamed in the light. Her skin looked like flecked granite and her face was . . . bonier, sort of. Stronger and squarer. Still, when he saw the book propped on her lap, his smile widened. He wished she were awake, so they could talk. Or at least she could read to him. It was stupid, but he sort of missed her.

The sounds of the street tumbled into the chamber from the canal drain. People talked, wheels clattered, soldiers marched. Ji listened sleepily, then drifted off again, the smile still tugging at his mouth.

The next time he woke, things weren't so peaceful.

The day had turned to early evening behind the snake-bird statue, and Chibo was stumbling around the chamber in circles, his wings outstretched, the tips brushing the walls. He staggered, caught himself, then kept going. On what felt like his twentieth circle, he bumped into Roz and knocked her book to the ground.

"Chibo," she said, "please don't—"

"Sorry!"

Chibo reached for the book and stepped on the splayed-open spine.

A *crack* sounded and Roz lost her temper. She got a little scary when someone mistreated a book. She snapped at Chibo, and maybe her glare didn't actually set the air on fire, but Ji definitely smelled smoke.

Chibo burst into tears. "I didn't *see* the book, Roz! I hate this, I hate it!"

In a heartbeat, Roz wrapped Chibo in a hug. "Shhh, it's okay. We'll find Ti-Lin-Su and she'll tell us how to break the spell."

"Not *that*," Chibo sobbed. "I don't care about that. I hate not seeing! It's not fair!"

He cried into Roz's neck, and his skinny shoulders shook. She murmured to him, her eyes shiny, until he quieted in her arms. Then she lifted her gaze to Ji, and despite her trollish face she looked strong and scared and *good*. Ji wanted to tell her how he saw her. Instead, he crossed the chamber, slipped the book into her handbag, then tucked her cloak around her shoulders to keep her warm.

"How're your eyes?" she asked. "They're a little red."

"They're fine."

"You keep rubbing them."

"They've ached since the Rite. Maybe merman eyes need salt water or something." He blinked a few times. "They're not that bad. Where's Sal?"

"Here." Sally prowled into the chamber, and one of her ears cocked at the sight of Chibo dozing in Roz's arms. "I got hungry."

"You find anything?"

She tossed Ji a ripe persimmon. "One for each of us."

"Thanks." He took a crunchy bite. "Yum."

Sally handed Roz a persimmon. "Nin, d'you want one?" She peered at the urn when Nin didn't answer. "Is Nin still gone?"

"They're off scouting, I think," Roz said.

"There's a few ant lions in the papaya plant."

"Yes, but with most of them elsewhere, Nin apparently isn't able to communicate." Roz took a delicate bite of persimmon. "They seem to require a certain minimum population. No individual ant lion is intelligent—it's the entire colony that is self-aware. The colony is a single animal, made up of hundreds of parts. As I said before,

Nin is the unified entity of—"

"O-kay," Ji said, standing. "I have to find those pits again before the sun goes down."

"The latrine pits?" Sally asked. "What for?"

"What do you think?" he said.

Ji wandered around the big cave, praising the bonfiery-ness of the bonfires until he found a goblin kid to guide him to the latrine. When he finished his pit business, the goblin complimented him—he didn't ask why—then led him through the moss-carpeted tunnel and mushroom farms to the long stone ramp.

"So you were born here?" Ji asked.

"Of ka-ourse, yes." The goblin shifted its torch from one belly-hand to the other. "Than-ka you for asking. I've never left the burrow."

"Do you want to?"

"Not onto the aboveground!" The goblin shuddered. "But I would love to tunnel into other burrows, to meet other Kultultul. "

"Oh," Ji said. "I guess you're stuck here, huh?"

"Stuc-ka here," the goblin agreed. "I dream that one day I'll wal-ka all the tunnels of the homeland."

"You mean, the goblin lands? Outside the Summer Realm?"

"Yes, please. Where Kultultul are free of everything except other Kultultul."

"What does *that* mean?"

"There is a bad worm in the homeland."

Ji scratched his cheek. Goblins were weird. "Sure, a bad worm. Anyway, at least you don't wear a collar."

The little goblin didn't speak for a moment. "I will when I'm older."

"What?" Ji shook his head. "No, the humans don't even know you're here."

"We share ka-ollars," the little goblin told him. "We all loo-ka the same to humans. So one Kultulul takes off the ka-ollar, and another wears it for a while."

Ji stopped walking. "You mean you *choose* to put a collar on? But then none of you are free!"

"None is free all of the time," the little goblin said, "but all are free some of the time."

Ji frowned into the shadows. For some reason, he thought of the tapestry kids he'd left at the looms, bound by threads instead of collars. "It's not right," he said.

The goblin's piglet face peered up at Ji. "It's the best way."

"I don't mean the *sharing* is wrong. I mean the whole thing. It's not right."

The goblin reached out a shoulder-arm shyly and took Ji's hand. "This way."

They followed the ramp downward, hand in hand. The goblin's fingers felt like leather gloves stuffed with gravel, and Ji wondered what its belly-hands felt like but thought it might be rude to ask.

After a time, the goblin tugged Ji into a side tunnel

and past an underground stream.

"This isn't the way back," Ji said.

The goblin pointed its torch. "This is another way, please."

"Oh! A shortcut?"

"Yes, a short ka-ut. Except longer."

"So a long cut?"

The little goblin chuffed. "A long ka-ut! I show you something!"

They climbed a heap of boulders into another tunnel, and the goblin stopped at a wall nook packed with broken combs: tortoiseshell combs, wooden combs, silver combs, bronze, copper, and seashell combs.

"So!" The little goblin gestured at the nook. "If you please!"

"Um," Ji said. "What are these shrines for, anyway?"

"To be pretty!" The goblin peered at Ji, a glint of hope in its beady eyes. "So?"

"Well, this one is lovely," Ji lied. "Very beautiful?"

"You truly thin-ka?"

"I do, yes," he said more firmly. "Gorgeous. The prettiest one I've seen."

The goblin's eyes narrowed. "What exaka-tly do you like-a?"

"Erm." Ji examined the nook more closely. "The colors and shapes. How the combs overlap and the torchlight shines through."

"You truly like-a?"

Ji nodded. "Definitely."

"I made it!" The goblin hopped a few times. "I made this one."

"No way!" Ji said, pretending to be surprised. "You did not!"

"I did! This is mine!" The goblin kid flushed pinker, then pressed a broken oak comb into Ji's hand. "You would honor me if you added this."

Ji looked at the comb. "Are you sure?"

"I am certain. I am ka-onvinced. Great honor for me."

"Great honor for *me*," Ji said, and placed the comb among the others.

The goblin kid took his hand again, and Ji blinked a few times. He did feel honored, for some stupid reason. He didn't know why. Who cared about a pile of broken combs in a hole in the ground?

"We should head back," he said.

"This way, please!" The little goblin tugged him away. "Humans wear ka-ombs."

"Yeah, and brush their hair with them."

"That's why they smell so tasty."

"They don't smell tasty. They're combs. They smell like heads."

The little goblin chuffed in amusement. "Human heads are tasty."

"You can't eat humans," Ji told it.

"You ka-an if they're dead," the goblin said. "And if you aska please."

"No, you can't!"

The goblin thought for a moment. "It's not polite to waste them."

"That's more polite than eating them."

"Why?" the goblin asked.

"Because they're not food!"

"They are if you eat them."

"Yeah, but . . . you can't eat humans."

"You ka-an if they're dead," the goblin repeated. "And if you aska politely."

Ji took a steadying breath. "Who do you ask, if they're dead?"

"Them," the little goblin said. "They never say no."

"Of course they don't! They're *dead*!"

The goblin chuffed happily. "Yes, thanka you! Now you understand."

Evening light seeped into the chamber from around the snake-bird statue. Ji waved good-bye to the little goblin, then told the others about their conversation. The room darkened as he spoke, and Chibo spread his glowing wings.

"They're little monsters," Ji finished.

"Hey!" Sally growled. "What's wrong with little monsters?"

"You know what Jiyong means." Roz shuddered. "Eating people."

"Yeah," Sally said. "It's pretty gross."

"They saved our lives, though," Chibo fluted. "Hiding us here."

Roz smoothed her tattered dress. "I suppose they're not all bad."

"Nobody's all bad," Ji said. "Or all good. But most of them won't eat you."

"Being eaten isn't so bad," Chibo said, "if you're already dead."

Sally grunted. "Not for you and me, but Ji would taste like shoes. And Roz was born for better than goblin barbecue."

"I'd taste great!" Ji told her. "Like fish stew!"

"The sooner we turn human again, the better." Roz moved the strap of her handbag higher on her shoulder. "I'm quite certain that Ti-Lin-Su will know how to break this spell. And that she'll hide us, if necessary."

"I guess recluses are good at hiding," Sally growled.

"Where's Nin?" Ji looked toward the canal drain. "It's almost dark enough to leave."

Sally nodded toward the ant lions clustered at the persimmon seeds on the ground. "They've been trickling in for ten minutes."

"Nin?" Ji asked. "Are you here?"

Nin didn't answer, so Ji asked again until he heard a faint *Coming, coming! We're scurrycrawling fast as we can!*

"Where've you been?" Ji asked when a few more ant lions crept around the statue.

Spying! Nin said.

"Did you hear anything?"

Important things! An ant lion climbed onto Ji's knee. *About the queen. We quietcrept into a rock garden and heard the queen's guard talking—*

"Why don't you show us?" Sally interrupted.

We'll try, Sallynx. Let's see. The whole thing started like this—

An image rose in Ji's mind of a huge, glossy beast. Red-brown splotches covered a rippling, bulging expanse of the creature's skin. Eyes bulged above a wide mouth and a mottled throat inflated horribly. The monster squirmed and—

It was a frog.

An ordinary frog, from the viewpoint of an ant lion. Three ant lions raced toward it on six legs, golden manes shimmering and stingers poised to strike. One leaped at the frog and—

Sorry! Nin said as the vision ended. *Wrong vision! That was dinner.*

"You ate a frog for dinner," Roz said.

Don't worry, Nin told her. *Still room for dessert!*

Ji gave a tiny piece of persimmon to an ant lion on his knee. "What did you hear about the queen, Nin? Just tell us what you heard."

She is weak. Very weak. The ant lion climbed onto Ji's fingertip. *The Rite always weakens queens and kings, but this time far worse.*

"Because of Ji messing around?" Chibo asked.

Yes! Terribleji! She ruins everything!

"He," Ji muttered. "*He* ruins everything."

He admits it, too! The ant lion on his finger roared faintly in laughter. *We heard the queen is weak now, and cannot ring the blackbells to wake all the clayfighters.*

"Good," Roz said.

But she is strong enough to wake a few fighters without the bells.

"Bad," Chibo said.

Then they'll hunt nonhumans and hackslash them into blood pudding.

"Even badder." Chibo shivered. "Sprites don't like being hackslashed into blood pudding."

Ji scowled at the ant lion on his fingertip. "I thought the queen couldn't wake the terra-cotta warriors without ringing the bells."

We're just tellsaying what we heard!

"Apparently she can't wake all of them," Roz said. "Only a few."

"A few is still too many," Ji said.

"What about that nursery rhyme?" Sally asked. "'Ring the bells once and wake the soldiers, ring the bells twice, they sleep like boulders.'"

"That's not entirely the rhyme," Roz said.

"Forget the stupid rhyme!" Ji lifted his finger to his face. "When is she going to wake them, Nin? Did you hear that?"

We did! We extracareful heard that. We crept close as a sideways leaf to hear that.

"So tell us!"

As soon as possible. Right now. She's weak, though. Can only wake a few on the topmountain. Is there any more persimmon?

"The topmountain?" Chibo said. "Now? Terra-cotta warriors are after us *now*?"

"I'll kick their pottery bums," Sally snarled.

"They feel no pain," Roz told her. "They're stronger than . . . well, a troll. And they can sense nonhumans."

"They sense nonhumans?" Chibo groaned. "*We're* nonhumans. And they're coming from the mountaintop? *We're* on the mountaintop!"

Ji tossed the ant lion into the urn. "Time to move. Now!"

37

THE SETTING SUN cast long shadows across the Forbidden Palace, and darkness gathered in a quiet cobblestone street between the inner and outer walls. A zither strummed, streetlamps flickered, and a raccoon dog barked.

Nothing moved . . . until a furry blur rose from a rectangular drain in the gutter. Sally scanned the street, then bounded away. A moment later, she perched atop the canal wall, her ears swiveling.

"All clear," she growled.

Beneath her, Ji strained to pull Nin's urn through the drain while Roz pushed from below. Ji rolled the urn a few feet, giving Roz privacy while she squeezed through—then Chibo soared into the street from the drain, giggling madly.

"I'm flying!" he fluted. "Wa-hoo!"

"Snuff your lights!" Ji hissed. "And shut your ricehole!"

"Sorry!" Chibo's wings darkened, and he landed beside Roz. "What now?"

Ji's neck prickled with nervous sweat. The street was quiet, but danger lurked around every corner. He frowned at the sunset, then considered the high steeple of a building in front of them.

"Sal!" he said, pointing. "You want to climb that for a better look?"

"I've got this," she growled. "C'mon!" She led them behind the steepled building and through a courtyard, then bounded onto a low roof. "Follow me from down there."

We miss the toproofs, Nin said. *We like chimneys.*

"There's a word for that," Ji said.

You mean . . . "chimneyfond"?

"No," Ji said. "I mean 'weird.'"

Sally scampered along the eaves, as quick and confident as a gecko on a lumpy wall. Then she paused and raised one paw: *stop.* At her signal, Roz halted, hugging Nin's urn while Ji squeezed Chibo's arm.

After a breathless minute, Sally lowered her paw. She leaped to the ground and loped into a park. She led them along a path past a pond covered with floating flowers. Lotus blossoms perfumed the air. Fireflies twirled and danced around three statues on a pedestal rising from the water.

"We're almost there," Sally purred, landing on the branch of a plum blossom tree. "Two hundred yards to the outer wall, then we'll hit the city streets."

"Can you find Ti-Lin-Su's house?" Ji asked Roz.

"Yes, I believe so," Roz said. "Though two hundred yards is a problem."

"Two hundred yards is nothing," Chibo said, in his piping voice. "I mean, because I can—"

"Fly?" Sally knocked him on the bald head. "Can you fly? I had no idea you could fly, because you haven't mentioned it a hundred times!"

A rocky *crrrrrrrrrt* sounded from the pond.

Ji spun toward the noise but didn't see anything alarming; just fireflies swooping and water lapping. Then another *crrrt* sounded. A shadow moved across the statues on the pedestal in the pond, and Ji's blood turned to ice.

"War-warriors!" he stammered. "There!"

"What?" Sally leaped protectively in front of him. "Where?"

"There!" he said, pointing at the statues. "Pond, *look*!"

Clay heads swiveled on clay necks with a scraping *crrrrrt*, and clay feet tore free of the pedestal. Clay arms lifted clay tomahawks, and then the three warriors turned toward the plum blossom tree.

The statues were terra-cotta warriors . . . . and they were waking up.

Shock gripped Ji's heart. Terror chained his feet to the ground. He couldn't move, he couldn't breathe, he couldn't look away.

The warriors slow-marched from the pedestal—and splashed into the pond. All three disappeared underwater. Ripples spread, and the lotus flowers shivered and twirled, closer and closer to the shore.

Then three jaguar-head helmets broke the surface.

"Run, run!" Ji yelped, backpedaling. "Chibo, into the air. Sally, get us out of here!"

The terra-cotta warriors trooped from the pond, shedding water. A lotus flower clung to one warrior's expressionless face, but that didn't make him any less scary.

"Roz!" Ji glanced over his shoulder as he raced away. "If they get too close, smash them or—"

The flower-faced warrior swiped at an avocado tree with its tomahawk, to clear a path. The trunk exploded into splinters, and the warrior didn't even pause—it just stomped slowly onward.

"Forget smashing!" Ji told Roz. "If they get too close, run faster!"

The avocado tree crashed into a lamppost. Glass shattered and oil spilled and Sally glanced over her furry shoulder. "Fire," she yowled. "They started a fire!"

Fastrun! Nin urged. *Fastrun faster!*

The thudding footsteps of the terra-cotta warriors

sounded behind them. Chibo flew closely overhead, while Ji and Roz raced after Sally—who darted suddenly into an open doorway.

"Ji!" she yelled, emerging with a spear and a sword. "Catch!"

She tossed the sword to Ji. It chopped through the air like a meat cleaver aimed at a chicken's neck.

Ji dodged sideways and yelped. "Hey!"

Roz caught the sword by the blade, a foot from Ji's face. If it hadn't been for her troll skin, she would've sliced her fingers off. She spun the sword, grabbed the hilt, and hefted Nin's urn higher on her hip with her other hand.

"What are we supposed to do with this, Sally?" she asked.

"We need weapons!" Sally called over her shoulder, loping away from the terra-cotta warriors.

"I prefer a teakettle."

"Don't be doolally! What if—" Sally's spear snagged in a bush. She tripped over the haft and tumbled onto her face. "Waaaa!"

After she scrambled back to her feet and kicked the spear, they raced from the outbuildings toward a wooded section of the Forbidden Palace. Roz tossed the sword aside, and nobody said anything about weapons again.

A quiet moons-lit meadow stretched in front of them, with prayer flags fluttering. Ji didn't see any peacocks this time—but he heard the terra-cotta warriors crashing through the trees. He and Chibo scrambled down a sage-covered hillside behind Sally, then blundered into a stony field dotted with mulberry bushes.

Where two more terra-cotta warriors marched toward them. Weapons raised, faces blank. Unblinking, unbreathing.

Roz froze. Chibo trembled. Ji gulped . . . and Sally bounded in front of the warriors.

"You've got to get through me first," she growled, raising her hackles.

She looked like an angry hamster staring down wolves, but the terra-cotta warriors didn't even glance at her. They stomped past, shedding dirt and leaves, and marched toward the hillside. Away from Sally. Away from *everyone*.

"Nobody messes with the hobgoblin!" Sally crowed, and hopped around brandishing her fists.

Oh, troublebig! Nin's voices said. *Troublebig badnews! They're not after us.*

"That's *good* news, Nin," Ji told the urn.

They sniffout nonhumans, Sneakyji. They're hunting the goblins.

"Oh, no," Chibo gasped.

Ji rubbed his face. "We don't know they're after the goblins," he said, even though they probably were. "And we're nonhuman, too. C'mon, let's go."

"The goblins helped us," Sally growled. "Abandoning them is dishonorable."

"They're not hunting goblins," Ji said, looking toward the retreating Warriors. "You know they're going to turn around any second to stomp us."

"We're only *partly* nonhuman," Roz rumbled. "Goblins are fully nonhuman. I expect the terra-cotta warriors will exterminate them first, then return for us."

"Let's not wait around to find out."

"Trouble," Sally growled, her ears swiveling toward the sage-covered hillside.

Ji peered through the dusk at the two terra-cotta warriors plodding uphill, tomahawks rising and falling. They were leaving, which was the *opposite* of trouble. Then he saw a third terra-cotta warrior—the one with flowers draped across its clay face—stomping downward, toward the stony field. Toward them.

"What's wrong with that one?" Roz asked.

"Which one?" Chibo asked. "What's happening?"

"Old flowerface is coming after us," Sally snarled. "A clayfighter from the pond."

"Why?" Chibo fluted.

"I guess he decided that we're nonhuman enough to kill."

"Either that or he wants to give us a bouquet," Ji said. "Piggyback time, Chibo."

Roz hefted the urn and Ji carried Chibo, scrambling after Sally as she prowled from the field into a stand of eucalyptus trees. A flock of parrots took flight, and Chibo raised his head and peered nearsightedly toward the sound of beating wings.

"How far is the outer wall?" Ji asked.

Sally leaped onto a branch. "Not far. And there's only a few soldiers."

"The rest are in the city," Ji told her. "Looking for us. Find a way out before flowerface catches us."

Sally peered into the night, her eyes big and her ears twitching. Ji stared toward the stony field, dreading the sudden appearance of the terra-cotta warrior. Listening for the clump of clay boots but hearing shouts of alarm from higher on the mountain, as people spotted the marching warriors and the spreading fires.

"There's a round door in the wall, covered by a grate." Sally jumped to another branch. "Flowerface is fifty yards away, but he's not moving anymore. He's just standing there."

"Perhaps he's wavering between hunting us or the goblins," Roz said.

"At least he's the only one," Sally said. "The rest of the warriors are smashing around the palace, trying to find the goblins."

"Can we do less talking," Ji said, slightly desperate, "and more escaping?"

There is no escape, Nin said. *The clayfighters will kill all the goblins.*

"We must help them," Roz said.

"We can't," Ji said.

"Jiyong, there are children."

"*Goblin* children," he said. "Who cares?"

An indrawn breath sounded from the shadows of Roz's hood. She didn't say a word, but Ji's face pricked with shame. And he wanted to help the goblins, he really did. But what if the queen caught them before they reached Ti-Lin-Su? Then Chibo would die and Sally would die and Roz would die—and for what?

For nothing. That wouldn't save the goblins.

How come Sneakyji decides what we do? Nin asked. *He says Missroz is smarter.*

"She is," Sally growled, still peering toward the stony field. "But Ji is a bigger jerk."

He is your stonefriend? Nin asked, and in his mind-speak the word thrummed with meaning: a friend as solid as a mountain.

"He saved me from the tapestry weavers," Chibo said.

"He brought me books," Roz said, "when they were my only hope."

Sally's tail lashed. "He's stone."

An ant lion marched onto Ji's wrist. *We trust you.*

"I hate you all," Ji muttered.

"Goblins are people," Roz told him.

"But they're not human!"

She touched his arm. "They're still people—like Nin. Or like us, now. They deserve better than this."

"Like your brother Tomás deserved better," Sally told Ji. "And my folks."

"And me," Chibo said.

"And all the weaver kids," Ji said. "The ones I left behind."

He thought about stealing boot beads at Primstone Manor. He thought about his mother's dream of him becoming a butler. He thought about what he'd felt when he'd touched the diadem—the urge to slaughter or enslave every nonhuman—and he thought about dozens of bald kids, living and dying beneath the looms.

"Fine," he said.

"We'll save the goblins?" Sally asked from her branch.

"They still freak me out," Ji told her. "They've got way too many knees. But you're right. You're all right. I left those weaver kids behind, and I'm not doing that again. I *can't* do that again. This isn't about goblins—this is about freedom."

Sally purred. "So how do we help them?"

"We ring the black bells twice," Ji said, "and put the warriors to sleep."

"Better do it fast," she said, jumping down from the tree. "Because flowerface is on the way!"

38

JI BURST FROM the eucalyptus trees, with Chibo's skinny arms wrapped around his neck. He ran behind Sally and Roz to a round door in the outer wall of the Forbidden Palace. A handful of sentries lurked in a nearby watchtower, but they were looking toward the fire higher on the mountain.

Roz eyed the bars crisscrossing the door, then gritted her teeth and opened them like a beaded curtain—without even asking for privacy.

On the other side of the wall, a lawn sloped to a boulevard dotted with lamplit town houses. Two horses pulled a carriage past cherry trees and fences. The clattering wheels and clip-clopping hooves covered the sound of Roz straightening the bars to slow flowerface down.

"There." Ji pointed to an alley between two houses. "Sal, check that out."

Sally loped across the boulevard, peered into the alley, then waved for them to join her. With Chibo on his back, Ji jogged down the lawn. Roz clomped beside him, hugging Nin's urn, then thundered across the boulevard.

"There they are!" a soldier shouted from the wall. "The monsters! Sound the trumpets!"

Chibo groaned. "Oh, bad. Very bad."

"Don't worry," Ji told him, sprinting into the alley. "Things are about to get much worse."

"What? Why?"

"Because we're ringing a loud bell in a city where every soldier is hunting for us."

"When you put it that way," Chibo fluted, "it doesn't sound so smart."

"We're actually ringing it twice," Ji said, trotting between adobe walls. "To stop the terra-cotta warriors."

"And attract every other kind of warrior?"

"We'll be okay as long as nobody sees us sneak into Ti-Lin-Su's place."

"There's more alleys over here!" Sally darted around a corner; then her fuzzy head reappeared. "And, um, isn't the queen the only one who can ring the bells?"

"We're about to find out," Ji told her as trumpets blared from the outer wall. "Now, does anyone know where to find a bell tower?"

Sally landed on a wooden sign outside a pastry shop. "Duck through there! There's guards ahead."

Ji dragged Chibo toward an archway, with Roz shambling behind them. Her footsteps thudded as heavily as clay. Which made him wonder if they were running out of time.

"How much longer till the terra-cotta warriors reach the goblins?" he called to Sally.

She peered into the night. "They're pretty slow, but they're pretty close. And there's more soldiers coming from the palace."

"Here we are!" Roz rumbled from the other side of the archway. "Ti-Lin-Su's estate isn't far!"

"You're sure there's a bell tower near her place?"

"Of course I'm sure!" She shifted her bulk. "I'm almost entirely certain. I'm very nearly completely positive."

She lumbered onto a wide avenue that followed a tree-lined canal. Despite the flames and chaos higher on the mountain, this neighborhood was calm and peaceful. After a few blocks, Roz crossed toward a tile wall that rose two stories overhead. Iron spikes lined the top, above elaborate mosaics depicting coral reefs, colorful fish, and flowering seaweed.

"Ti-Li-Su lives on the other side," Roz said. "The entrance is down the street."

"Pretty walls for a fortress," Sally said. "But where's the bell?"

"I'm certain I saw one nearby."

"You want me to fly around?" Chibo asked. "Because it's no problem if you do."

"There!" Ji pointed to a white tower peeking over a roof. "But, um . . . "

"What's wrong?" Sally growled.

"Once we ring this bell," he told her, jogging closer, "they'll know exactly where we are."

"*If* we ring the bell," Sally said, loping beside him. "I still say only the queen can do it."

"Roz is better than any queen," Ji said.

"That's your plan?" Sally said. "That Roz is better, so she can ring a bell?"

"I'm not stupid," Ji said, even though Sally was pretty much right. If anyone could match the queen, it was Roz. "She's strong, that's why."

"And Roz only needs to ring one bell," Chibo said. "Not all of them."

Ji took a breath. "Whatever happens after the bell sounds, we scamper like bunny rabbits into Ti-Lin-Su's estate immediately. Agreed?"

Roz nodded. "Agreed."

"I won't scamper," Sally said, looking up at the bell tower. "But I'll honorably retreat."

Bunnyscamper! Nin babbled. *Ring the bell! You are stonefriend, Sneakyji!*

Chibo spread his emerald-glowing wings. "I won't

scamper either, but I'll *fly* like a bunny rabbit!"

"Chibo!" Ji barked at him, crossing to the tower's front doors. "Wings!"

The glow dimmed. "Oops."

"Now fly to the top. Unlock any doors from the inside. Sally, keep your eyes peeled. Nin, you stay—"

"Soldiers!" Sally growled.

"How close?"

Sally pointed, and sword-wielding soldiers raced into sight from a side street. "That close. There's only four, though. I can hold them off."

"You sure?" Ji asked, scratching his arm nervously.

"I'm sure."

"Okay." He took a calming breath. "You're a hobgoblin— do some hobbing."

We stayfight too. A trail of ant lions jumped off the urn in Roz's arms. *Keep them from catching you.*

"You're tiny! What can you do?"

Buttsting! Nin's voices sang out.

"Just be careful. And if you see flowerface, run." Ji looked at the bell tower doors. "C'mon, Roz—break these down."

"I would rather not damage city property," Roz murmured primly as she demolished the doors with a single strike from her shoulder.

"Nice," Ji said.

"According to the rules of honorable combat," Sally

called to the soldiers on the avenue, "we should— *Hey! You cheater!*"

Ji glanced over his shoulder and caught a glimpse of Sally leaping over a swinging sword. Then he followed Roz into the tower and up a flight of spiral stairs. He ran higher until his lungs burned and his knees felt weak— then Roz gathered him into her arms and kept thundering upward.

"If you tell Sally that you carried me," he warned her, wrapping his arms around her neck, "I'll paint your horn white and call you a unicorn."

She sniffed. "My dress is entirely unsuitable for this sort of activity."

At the top of the stairs, Ji slid from Roz's arms and pushed through an unlocked hatch into an open chamber with a massive black-glazed bell. Fresh air swirled around him, and moons-light shimmered on the shiny blackness. When Roz followed, an emerald glow reflected in crazy patterns on the bell and Chibo landed beside them.

"Ring it, ring it!" Chibo said. "Flowerface is here! He's *here*!"

Roz punched the bell. It made a soft, disappointing *thunnn.*

"Harder!" Ji said.

She punched it harder. It made a slightly louder, equally disappointing *thonnn.*

"Roz! Flowerface is going to—" Ji gave a frightened cry

and looked toward the palace. "No!"

"What?" Roz asked, in a worried rumble. "What's wrong?"

"Keep hitting that bell!" he snapped, his voice trembling. "And I'll tell you what's wrong."

Thunnn, the bell said. *Chunnn*.

"The fire's spreading in the palace. There's flames everywhere. Do you see that, Chibo?"

"Of course *I* don't see it!" Chibo said, peering into the darkness.

Ji drew in his breath in horror. "It's a library. Those flames are *books*. There's a hundred books on fire, Roz. All those pages are turning into ash and—"

With an earsplitting roar, Roz lashed her head forward and smashed the black-glazed bell with her horn. Once, twice, and—

39

THERE ARE SOUNDS that you don't just hear, there are sounds that you *feel*. There are sounds that shake you until your teeth rattle, then hurl you to the ground and stomp on your brain with black-glazed boots.

Ji curled into a ball, his hands clapped over his ears, weeping from the deafening boom of the bell. He writhed on the floor until the shattering clamor quieted to an agonizing hum. Then Roz's half-troll face appeared in front of him, and she opened and closed her mouth like a trout.

"Stop playing around!" he said, rubbing his stinging eyes. "Where's Chibo? Is he okay?"

She pointed past him, and Ji saw Chibo swooping wildly through the evening air outside the bell chamber. Strange streaks appeared in the glow of his wings, and Ji gasped when he realized what they were.

"Darts!" he said, though he couldn't hear himself. "They're shooting darts at him with atlatls! That's why he's flying like that!"

When Roz rumbled at him, he only heard a faint whisper: ". . . wall . . . run!"

"What? Louder!"

She leaned closer and shouted. "The palace soldiers are at the outer wall! We have to run!"

"So carry me!" he said into the deafening hum. "Let's go!"

"I can't, Ji! I'm not sure I can stand."

He blinked his stinging, watery eyes at Roz. Blood trickled from her mouth and she looked even more stunned than he felt. Which made sense: *she* was the one who'd rung the bell with her face, while *he* had just flopped around like a broken shoelace.

He pushed to his knees, waited until a wave of dizziness passed, then touched one of Roz's four-fingered hands. "Lean on me."

"I'll crush you!" she said, through the finally fading hum.

"I'm stronger than I look," he said.

Which might've been true, but he still wasn't strong enough to carry a half troll down a spiral staircase. Still, they managed to stumble downstairs together, with Roz leaning against the wall, her shoulder scraping the stone.

By the time they reached the ground floor, Ji's legs felt better and his hearing worked again. Maybe merfolk had sore eyes, but they sure healed fast.

"Those poor books," Roz moaned, staggering toward the splintered front doors of the bell tower. "That poor library."

"Oh, uh . . ." Ji squinted at her. "There wasn't any library."

"What?"

"I needed to make you mad enough to ring the bell," he explained.

She muttered a word that Ji was surprised she knew—then a groan from outside caught his attention. Oh, no. *Sally*. With his heart in his throat, Ji ran from the tower and scanned the avenue.

One swordsman lay limply on the cobblestones, and Sally cowered near him, paws raised to block a clay hatchet eight inches over her head. But the hatchet wasn't moving. Flowerface the terra-cotta warrior stood motionless over her, frozen in midblow—another two seconds, and his hatchet would've split Sally in half.

A dizzy weakness rose from Ji's legs and into his head. Another two seconds and Sally would've died. The thought sickened him and the evening dimmed. . . .

"Ji!" she yelped. "You did it!"

"Roz did." He took a deep breath. "Are . . . you okay?"

Her muzzle lifted into a fierce grin. "Who cares about flying? I can *fight*."

"I'll take that as a yes," he said faintly. "Where's Chibo?"

"Here!" Chibo called from above, then slammed into

the ground. "Ow! My landings need work."

Sally rolled out from under Flowerface. "And Nin can *sting*. He chased the other soldiers away. And look!—" She kicked Flowerface in the shin. "We stopped the terracotta warriors."

"Yeah," Ji said. "And now we have to—"

Bunnyrun! Nin's voices piped up. *You saved the goblins.*

"Roz saved them," Ji said. "Using her love of books."

"Serves me right for trusting a liar," Roz groaned, sitting on the tower steps with her head in her hands.

A louder blare of trumpets sounded, and Ji said, "Quick! Run to Ti-Lin-Su's house!"

"I can't run," Roz grunted. "I'm not entirely sure I can crawl."

"You need to," Ji said, trotting closer to her.

"Let me catch my breath!" she said with a half sob.

"Sorry. I didn't mean to rush you."

"Except that we're in a rush."

"Yeah, except that." He took her stony hand. "C'mon, before anyone sees us."

She groaned and rose shakily to her feet. The sound of soldiers marching came from higher on the mountain, and Ji looked toward the wall with the seaweed-and-coral-reef mosaics. The bronze-banded entrance to Ti-Lin-Su's property was only a block away.

"They're almost here," Sally growled. "Stay close, Chibo."

Roz made a rocky noise in her throat, then grabbed the

top of the urn. When Ji took her free hand and pulled her down the block, the urn rattled and clinked across the cobblestones.

"You can do this, Roz," Ji said. "You can do *anything*."

"She can't fly!" Chibo fluted.

"They're here," Sally said.

A dozen black-clad soldiers jogged onto the avenue fifty feet away, drawing scimitars and clubs. Too close. Too fast. A lump of failure curdled in Ji's stomach, and his eyes stung with unshed tears.

"What should we do?" Chibo asked. "They saw us."

"Stick to the plan," Ji said, pulling harder on Roz's hand. "Get behind Ti-Lin-Su's walls and—"

"We're not going to make it," Sally growled.

You run, Nin's voices chimed, loud and insistent. *We'll hold them off.*

"They're too many of them," Sally said.

Ant lions poured from the urn, dropping onto the avenue like a rose bush shedding petals. *You saved goblins. Now ogre saves you.*

"No way," Ji said. "We stay together. Whatever happens, we stay together."

Missroz, Sallynx . . . take care of Sneakyji.

"You're an ogre of honor, Nin," Sally said, and jumped on Ji's face.

Blinded by the sudden furball, Ji reeled backward, away from the soldiers, shouting muffled swears at Sally. He staggered a few steps. Then Roz's hand grabbed his shoulder and Sally leaped away.

"—doolally fuzz-faced hobgoblin!" he screamed.

Roz tugged him toward the bronze-banded door with one hand and dragged Nin's urn with the other. The clay rattled and dirt spilled onto the ground. Only a few ant lions still clung to the papaya seedlings: hundreds more fanned across the avenue.

"Let me go!" Ji snarled, struggling in Roz's grip.

"Sincere . . . apologies," she rumbled, trudging closer to the bronze-banded door.

Ji punched her arm, and pain burst in his knuckles. "Ow! Sally! Help me!"

"What do you think I'm doing?" Sally asked, backpedaling between him and the soldiers. "Hey!" she called to them. "I challenge you to a duel!"

"The monsters!" one of them said. "They *speak*."

"Let's see if they scream," another said.

"A duel of honor," Sally growled.

"Nobody duels an *animal*," the first soldier snarled.

Ji squirmed and kicked, but Roz didn't loosen her grip. She just pulled him closer to Ti-Lin-Su's bronze-banded door, panting with effort.

"How about jousting?" Sally asked the soldiers. "We could joust."

"We could skin you and use the fur for— *Aaaaaaah!*" The soldier screamed and pounded his calf with the hilt of his scimitar. "Scorpions! There's scorpions in my armor!"

336

Eat buttsting, human! Nin's voices crowed. *I'm inside your legholes, peeking your knees!*

The other soldiers started screaming and whacking at the ant lions inside their armor. Pain and panic scattered them . . . for a moment. Then one soldier grunted an order, and they started stomping on the cobblestones. Squashing ant lions.

Nin didn't say anything in mind-speak, but Ji felt bursts of pain each time another ant lion died.

"How many ant lions can Nin lose," he asked Roz, limp in her grip, "before the whole colony dies?"

Sneakyji? Nin sounded weak and faint. *Take care of everyone, stonefriend. . . .*

The ant lion voices faded into silence, and Roz dropped Ji beside the big bronze-banded door, then slumped against the wall.

"Nin?" Ji said, staring into the empty urn. *"Nin!"*

Roz struck the door with the side of her fist. "I'm too . . . weak, Ji. I can't break through the door."

Six black-clad soldiers stalked toward them, driving Sally backward with flashing blades—and Ji couldn't do anything. He couldn't do anything except watch with his stupid stinging eyes and his useless merman scales.

40

SCALDING TEARS FILLED Ji's eyes. His fists clenched in fear and frustration . . . and with a *creeeeak* the bronze-banded doors swung open. Green light spilled out like an emerald fog.

"Hurry!" Chibo fluted from inside. "There's more coming!"

Roz shouldered into Ti-Lin-Su's estate, the urn scraping the floor. Ji stumbled after her, into a cool breeze that smelled of marsh and rainfall.

"I flew over the wall!" Chibo announced, wings shimmering in pleasure.

"How's Nin?" Sally growled, bounding beside them. "Is he—they—still here?"

"The doors!" Ji shouted. "Bolt the doors!"

With a pained grunt, Roz shoved the doors closed a moment before the first black-clad soldiers arrived. The slam reverberated inside the high walls. Pounding sounded from outside as Ji and Sally slid three heavy metal bars across the doors. Then Roz hefted an even bigger bar into place.

"Nin?" Ji knelt beside the urn. "Nin! Say something!"

Silence. No mind-speak came from Nin. No red-and-gold ant lions boiling from the mound in the urn. Nothing but fluttering papaya leaves and four ant lions scratching in the dirt.

"Roz, you're bleeding," Sally said. "Are you okay?"

"A trifle tired," Roz said, wiping her split lip. "But not hurt."

"C'mon, you headbutton!" Ji begged the urn. "Tell me how to pickle beets! Say some aws or—"

A blare of trumpets shrilled through the night, and a tromp of boots echoed along the street outside.

"We're cornered." Sally put her paw on Ji's shoulder. "We're trapped and—"

Crack! Soldiers slammed the other side of the doors. The wood shuddered and the bars creaked.

"And *that*," she finished.

"Okay" Ji said, wiping his eyes. "We need another way out of here."

"The water garden," Roz said in an awed rumble.

Her hood had fallen, revealing her curved horn—and

her broad, granite-flecked face was alight with wonder.

When Ji turned away from the door, he saw why. Palm trees rose above walkways that twisted through an enormous water garden. Streams linked dozens of pools, some glittering with golden fish, some thick with seaweed, some steaming like hot springs. Gauzy canopies draped lush islands scattered with cherry trees and seashells and driftwood. Canals flowed through archways into the triple-domed main house.

"That's not a water *garden*," Sally said. "That's a water *forest*."

When Chibo spread his wings, emerald light shone on pillars rising from one pool and illuminated the bookshelves between them.

"This is where Ti-Lin-Su writes," Roz said, her voice soft. "All her greatest works of poetry and zozology and—"

"Who cares about her?" Ji snapped, above the pounding on the door. "What about Nin?"

"If there is a single ant-lion queen left alive," a woman's voice said from the water garden, "the colony might survive."

Chibo's wings flared brighter, and Ji's heart thumped. "You ready for another fight?" he muttered to Sally.

"I'm not going to hob some damp old lady," she said. "Not even for you."

Ji followed her big-eyed gaze toward a woman with long white hair, standing waist-deep in the water beside a walkway. The woman fixed a veil around her face, then waded closer, wearing a flowing blue dress that shed water.

"M-my lady Ti-Lin-Su," Roz sputtered. "We—we *do* apologize for bursting inside so rudely, and—and for how we look but, but—"

A *slam-slam-SLAM* sounded from the boulevard, and Ti-Li-Su said, "But there is another queen who worries you?"

"Yes, milady," Roz said. "Her Majesty's army is hunting us."

"So if you've got a back door," Ji said, "we'll get out of your hair."

"After you break the spell on us," Sally growled.

"The spell?" Ti-Lin-Su asked. "Oh, of course! You survived the Diadem Rite? But not before it transferred some of your essence into the heir."

"The rite made us less than human," Roz said, her voice thick, "to make Brace more than human."

"I cannot break this spell," Ti-Lin Su said. "Its power runs too deep."

Roz's shoulders' slumped. Chibo's wings sagged and Sally growled, "Then who *can* break it?"

"That doesn't matter right now!" Ji said, looking toward the shuddering front doors. "If we don't get out of here fast, we're dead."

Ti-Lin-Su eyed him through her veil. "Ah! I presume

that you are the one who rang the black-glazed bell?"

"I barely made it up the stairs," he told her. "Roz rang the bell."

The white-haired lady turned toward Roz. "The same Miss Roz who called on me the other day? I've lived alone for many years, my dear, in quiet meditation. And now you've shattered my peace."

"I apologize." Roz lifted her head. "However, we hadn't a choice."

"I turn away all callers," Ti-Lin-Su said, wading to the edge of the walkway. "And yet, meeting the four of you is—"

"Five of us," Ji said, putting a hand on Nin's urn and trying not to scream in frustration. Why were they just standing around talking? But he couldn't push this lady too hard—they needed her help.

"Meeting the *five* of you," Ti-Lin-Su said, accepting the correction, "is the consummation of my most dearly held ambition."

"Huh?" Sally growled.

"She's happy to meet us," Roz explained.

Ji eyed the shuddering doors. "I'll be happier when we're gone."

"You are part . . . sprite?" Ti-Lin-Su's veiled face turned toward Chibo. "I'm not sure I've ever seen anything so breathtaking. May I feel one of your wings?"

"Yes, ma'am," Chibo said, and shifted a sheet of green light toward her.

Ti-Lin-Su brushed the wavering rays with her fingers. "They truly are made of light," she said with childlike wonder. "How do they hold you aloft?"

"I don't know, ma'am," Chibo said, oddly shy. "All I know is I can *fly*."

"That's a tremendous gift."

"I know! That's what I keep telling them! It's the best thing ever!"

"We're kind of in a rush," Ji said, as the pounding grew louder and the front doors shook. "So if you could tell us how to get out of—"

"Jiyong!" Roz rumbled. "Hush!"

"Indulge me for another moment, young man," Ti-Lin-Su told Ji, "and I will show you how to leave undetected."

"There's a way out?"

"There is indeed."

"Thank summer," Ji said, faint with relief. "And, uh, *do* you know who can break this spell?"

"Whyever would you want to?" Ti-Lin-Su asked, still waist-deep in the water.

"Just look at us!"

"Very well." She turned her head, and her breath caught when her veiled gaze fell on Sally. "A hobgoblin!"

"Yes, ma'am," Sally said.

"Strong, fast, acrobatic. Not to mention sleek and stunning. And, I must say, hobgoblins are entirely f—"

"Fuzzy?" Ji guessed.

"*Formidable*." Ti-Lin-Su rested her elbows on the

343

walkway. "One must never underestimate a hobgoblin. And you," she said, looking to Roz. "A troll. So rare and beautiful, and rooted so deeply in the earth."

"Th-thank you, milady," Roz said, and managed to blush.

"And not even in my most fanciful imaginings," Ti-Lin-Su said, looking back to Ji, "did I dream of *you*."

"Yeah, yeah," Ji muttered, with a glance at the shuddering front doors. "I'm a merman who can't swim."

"A merman?" Ti-Lin-Su's laughter sounded like wind chimes. "You're no merman. If anyone can assure you of that fact, it is I."

Roz pressed her hand to her throat. "You!" she gasped to Ti-Lin-Su. *"You!"*

"Indeed, you clever young lady."

"What in the moons are you nattering about?" Ji asked. "And can we please, *please* run away now?"

"She's a mermaid!" Roz said, her voice thrumming with excitement.

Ti-Lin-Su laughed again and glided through the water. Her tail broke the surface behind her, then splashed back down with a slap.

Sally's tufted ears pricked up and Chibo's wings fluttered and Ji's breath caught. Whoa. Ti-Lin-Su was an actual mermaid! Swimming through the water garden, completely full of both mer *and* maid. He gave a low whistle. Maybe she really would know who could to turn them human again.

"Perhaps this is a sign that I've hidden for too long," Ti-Lin-Su said, removing her veil to reveal a wrinkled mermaidy face. "Perhaps it's past time for me to return home."

"Wait a minute," Sally said. "If Ji's not a merman, what is he?"

"The answer to my outstanding question, I very much hope."

Ji frowned. "The only question I care about is how do we get out of here?"

"Your outstanding question . . . ," Roz whispered, her eyes widening.

"You are the rarest of beasts," Ti-Lin-Su told Ji. "The proud echo of an ancient song that has quieted almost to silence."

"So now I'm a song?" Ji scoffed.

"What she means," Roz said, "is that you're a *dragon*."

41

ANOTHER CRASH SOUNDED at the bronze-banded door, and Ji calmly said, "Well, I guess that explains the scales." Then he uncalmly shouted: *"Can we go now?"*

"If only you knew how special—" Ti-Lin-Su stopped at a louder *BANG-crash-smash-bang.* "Well, perhaps you *should* follow me."

Roz looked a little shaky, so Ji stayed beside her, holding her elbow when she stumbled. They trotted along walkways between springs and grottos to the largest pool in the garden. When they reached a display of driftwood statues, Ti-Lin-Su dived underwater, her tail driving her deeper with powerful strokes.

"Are we supposed to swim after her?" Sally asked, crouching on a boulder beside the pool.

"Of course not," Roz rumbled. "Lady Ti-Lin-Su knows we can't breathe underwater."

"Plus if you went underwater," Ji told Sally, "you'd smell like wet dog for a week."

"Go shed your skin, lizardboy," she said, flashing a few fangs.

"Is something happening?" Chibo frowned toward the pool where Ti-Lin-Su had disappeared. "Sounds like something's happening."

Ripples appeared in the water, and then a whirlpool formed in the center. A sudden current lapped against rocks, then splashed the banks. As shouts sounded from the boulevard, the entire pool started slowly draining away. Very slowly.

Ti-Lin-Su broke the surface near Sally. Water sheeted down her white hair, and her eyes were golden, with oval pupils. Her tail splashed beside a hummock of sea grass that seemed to grow larger as water emptied from the pool.

"This pool drains through an underground river to the coast," she said. "When you jump in, the current will carry you to freedom. You won't be comfortable, but you'll survive."

Across the water garden, the bronze-banded doors shook and the metal bars creaked. "Survive" sounded pretty good to Ji.

"Thank you so much," Roz rumbled. "And when we

reach the coast, you'll tell us about breaking the spell?"

"Only the Summer Queen can reverse the effects of the Diadem Rite—and the Ice Witch, if she is not merely a myth."

"But you think she *is* a myth," Roz said. "I read your article about her."

"Apparently the world is even stranger and more wonderful than I imagined," Ti-Lin-Su said, her golden eyes glinting. "And while magic is not always—"

"We'd love to hear more," Ji interrupted, "after we escape."

Ti-Lin-Su laughed again. "Dragons!"

"Yeah," Sally said. "Reptiles have no manners."

A louder *bang* sounded at the doors. Then two more: *bang-bang*.

"I'll swim first to clear the way." Ti-Lin-Su pointed to a pale, submerged boulder on the bank of the pond. "Follow me when the water reaches the bottom of that rock, and you'll have enough room to breathe."

"Breathing is good," Ji said. "We like brea—"

With a slap of her tail, Ti-Lin-Su vanished into the swirling current. The whirlpool circled more quickly, revealing the muddy banks . . . and a strong fishy smell.

Roz sighed. "She even *swims* elegantly."

A sudden crash shook the doors, and one of the metal bars snapped with a sound like a bone breaking. Chibo whimpered and Sally's ruff rose into a spiky mane.

"She's a mermaid," Ji told Roz, staring impatiently at the water level in the pool. "Of course she swims well."

"I can't believe I actually met Ti-Lin-Su," Roz said, her voice soft with awe.

"Just don't let go of Nin's urn. Maybe there's a queen in there."

Soldiers shouted outside, voices hoarse and determined. Another slam rang out across the water garden, mixed with the squeal of bending metal. For a moment, none of them spoke. Then Chibo wrinkled his nose at the pool and said, "Smells like rotting seaweed. Why don't I just fly to the coast and meet you there?"

"You couldn't *see* the coast." Ji watched the water level drop—slowly—along the pale rock. "Just follow the plan."

"Why does a scholar need an escape route?"

"Because they would've cooked her into chowder if they'd realized she wasn't huma—"

The bronze-banded doors burst open with a blast of debris.

Dust billowed into the water garden. Chibo squeaked and Sally spun into a fighting stance. A splinter stabbed Ji's shoulder, but he barely felt the sting of pain, too busy feeling a stab of panic: the water level wasn't low enough yet. They couldn't hold their breath all the way to the coast—and they were out of time.

The clang of weapons rang from the avenue, and hoarse shouts sounded inside the water garden.

"Oh, *badness*!" Chibo piped. "Here they come!"

Ji stepped toward the mucky bank of pool. "I'll go first in case the water's too high to bre—" He paused, remembering that he wasn't a merman. Still, *someone* had to go first. "Then Roz, then Chibo. Sally, you come last, so you can watch our backs."

"You got it," she growled, her ears flattening.

"The lady said wait!" Chibo fluted at Ji. "The water's not low enough!"

Ji crossed toward the draining whirlpool, slimy muck oozing inside his sandals. "Dragons don't need to breathe."

"I'm pretty sure they do."

"See you at the coast," Ji said, and bent to jump into the water.

"Wait!" Brace called from the dust cloud at the shattered doors. "Ji, *wait*!"

His voice rang across the water garden, firm and commanding. So commanding that Ji actually obeyed. He straightened, ankle-deep in the mud, and peered toward the entrance.

Brace strode into view on a walkway between the big pool and the front doors. He looked different, and not just because of the silvery diadem on his forehead. He also looked . . . *more*. More powerful, more confident, more honest and good and true. The twins flanked him, while Mr. Ioso and Proctor followed a few paces behind. The dim shapes of soldiers moved through the dust cloud at the doors.

Ji's heart shriveled like a frightened raisin. "Oh, no," he breathed. "Proctor and Ioso."

"Here?" Chibo asked. "Where? Do they look mad?"

"They don't look happy," Sally growled.

"Stay there!" Ji shouted, his voice wavering with panic.

"Don't worry." Brace paused on the walkway. "I just want to talk." He called over his shoulder. "You soldiers, stay back!"

"Back is good," Ji murmured. "But we still need to buy time for the water to fall."

"So keep him talking," Roz said. "And I'll watch the pool."

"Okay!" Ji called to Brace, sloshing onto dry ground. "We're listening."

Brace raised a finger, telling Proctor, Mr. Ioso, and the twins to wait as he strolled along the walkway. "Look at you, Ji. What are you? A snake?" Brace's blue gaze flicked to Roz. "And you're even worse, Roz. You're big and thick . . . and is that a horn? You're a rhino."

When Roz ducked her head in shame, Ji felt a hot barb of anger.

"But you don't have to stay this way," Brace continued, his voice chiming with hope. "The queen can change you back. Her Majesty will make you human again."

"She's trying to kill us," Ji said. "*You're* trying to kill us."

"Not me!" Brace said. "I swear on my parents, Ji, I didn't know the Rite was going to kill you. Proctor never told me."

"Yeah, well . . ." Ji shifted his weight. "Then why're you chasing us?"

"Because we need you," Brace told him. "But we don't need your deaths. There's another way."

"What's that?" Sally called.

"The water's low enough," Roz murmured.

"And smells like oyster armpit," Chibo added.

"Instead of fighting me," Brace said, "serve me."

"We're not servants," Ji told him. "Not anymore. Chibo, *jump!*"

Three things happened at once:

First, Chibo swooped toward the center of the pool.

Second, Brace raised his arms and said, "You *will* serve the realm."

And third, the whirlpool froze in midwhirl.

The water thickened, like the pond in the pavilion. Chibo hit the surface with a *thump* and lay there moaning and rubbing his side.

"The Diadem Rite gave Lord Brace power," Roz gasped, her hand pressing her chest. "He turned the pool solid."

42

"DON'T KILL THE creatures." Proctor stalked closer with the twins, while the soldiers waited farther back. "We need them alive."

"Don't worry," Lady Nosey said, with a razor edge in her voice. "We'll just *wound* them at little."

She fired her crossbow: *schwap!*

The bolt flew at Ji, and fear turned his knees boneless. He stood there like a lump of fat—until Roz shoved him out of the way. He stumbled sideways, and instead of piercing his leg, the bolt shattered against Roz's calf.

"Please, my lady," Roz said. "Let's not resort to physical viol—"

Schwap, schwap! Two more bolts broke against Roz, and Lady Nosey said, "Keep your grunts to yourself."

"Save a few for the goblin thing," Lord Pickle told his sister, glaring at Sally.

"She's not a goblin," Ji said.

"And she's certainly not a *thing*," Roz rumbled.

"She's a hobgoblin," Ji said. "And she's about to kick you cross-eyed."

Sally launched forward from behind him. She landed on Roz's shoulder, then bounded at Nosey and Pickle. Another crossbow bolt flew, but Sally plucked it from the air and hurled it at Proctor, who was throwing his dagger at Roz.

Proctor ducked and his dagger missed Roz by inches, then buried itself hilt-deep in a boulder. A chill touched Ji. That was no ordinary dagger.

"It's a magic knife!" Chibo piped. "Watch out, Roz!"

Ji hefted a piece of driftwood. He gulped as Mr. Ioso's fists started glowing white, and he made himself step beside Roz. He didn't know to fight, but he knew how to try.

"Please," Roz begged, spreading her four-fingered hands. "Can't we discuss this like rational—"

"Freaks?" Lord Pickle asked. "Beasts?"

"I'm sorry," Brace told Ji, swinging his sword. "If you won't serve me willingly—"

"I beg you, Lord Brace," Roz said. "Surely we can—"

"Roz!" Ji raised his driftwood to block the sword. "Less talking and more trolling!"

"If you even touch the prince," Proctor warned, "you shall pay dearly."

"You're the prince now?" Ji asked Brace.

"One day I'll be king," Brace said, shifting his grip on his sword. "And Roz is right—there's no need for this. Pledge yourselves to me and—"

"Stay still, you filthy squirrel!" Lady Nosey snarled, stabbing at Sally.

Sally backflipped away, hurling a rock at Nosey's forehead with one foot. *Thunk*. Nosey dropped to her knees. A howling Lord Pickle attacked, his blade a blur of slashes. Sally twirled and leaped and punched him in the eye. He fell and—

A beam of white light struck Sally. The impact slammed her to the floor. The light recoiled to Mr. Ioso's fists, and a palm tree withered behind him.

Sally lay still, her fur singed . . . and Proctor kicked her in the side.

"Bad Proctor!" Chibo's wings glowed as brightly as an emerald sun. "You get away from her!"

Brace recoiled from the blinding light while Proctor raised a hand to shield his face.

"You're being terribly rude!" Roz roared, and leaped through the green glare to backhand Proctor.

Her blow struck his chest with a meaty thud. His beard shook and his mouth opened in a scream as he was flung through the air and slammed into Mr. Ioso. They tumbled off the walkway together, dropping in a tangle to the mucky bank of the half-empty, fish-stinking pool.

The light dimmed as Chibo fell exhausted to his knees,

and Brace pointed his sword at Ji. "I'm trying to save the realm!"

"I'm trying to save *us*," Ji said.

"This isn't about you, Ji," Brace said solemnly. "It's not about me, either. It's about the survival of humankind."

"I guess you just got lucky, huh?" Ji asked. "Humankind needs you in a crown, but it wants us in chains."

"Look around." Brace gestured toward the soldiers on the walkways, waiting for the command to attack. "You have a good eye for strategy, Jiyong. You know you can't fight a whole army."

"We can fight them," Ji said.

"But you can't beat them."

"There's more to life than winning," Ji said.

"And you can't get away, not with the water frozen."

"So unfreeze it and let us go."

"I can't. I need you. *We* need you. You know me, Ji." Brace's voice sounded raw and honest. "Join me. Please. I'm not asking as the new heir, I'm asking as an old friend. How many hours did we spend in my room, fighting ogres and goblins?"

"Lots," Ji said. "Lots of hours."

"I know what it's like to be weak." Brace looked to Roz. "I know what it's like to be bullied. How many kings can say that?"

"Not many," Roz said.

"Am I cruel?" Brace asked. "Am I greedy?"

"You never used to be," Ji said.

"I haven't changed," Brace said. "I'm still me."

"If we join you, Prince Brace," Roz rumbled, "will Her Majesty truly reverse the effects of the Rite?"

"She will," Brace promised, and sheathed his blade. "She'll turn you human again."

Ji glanced at Roz and saw the longing and hope in her eyes.

"There's a long war being fought between humans and beasts," Brace said, "and the Summer Crown is our only defense. It's the only thing keeping the monsters from killing us all. There's exactly one way to save the realm. Exactly one way to save every crafter and clerk and farmer, every mother and father and child."

"Yeah," Ji said. "And that way is 'finish sacrificing us to the water tree.'"

"No!" Brace said. "No, that was wrong, that was terrible."

"We didn't like it much, either," Sally growled, limping closer, holding hands with Chibo.

"Pledge yourselves to me," Brace said. "Serve me. Help me."

"And if we do," Ji said, "the queen will break the spell?"

"You have my word," Brace told him.

Nobody spoke for a moment. The trickle of water in the garden mixed with the creak of the soldiers' armor. Ji watched Lady Nosey and Lord Pickle on the other side of the pond, helping a muddy Proctor drag a limping Mr. Ioso onto a walkway.

"Being servants isn't so bad," Sally growled.

"It's not freedom," Chibo fluted.

Ji looked to Roz. He needed to talk to her, he needed to tell her what he feared. She returned his gaze steadily. Maybe reassuring him, maybe encouraging him. Maybe just trusting him.

When Ji ducked his head, his gaze dropped to Brace's court boots: the stingray leather, the gleaming turquoise, clusters of garnets, topazes, and fire opals. And two sparkly new baubles, glittering with emeralds, rubies, and pearls.

With an aching hunger, Ji wanted them.

For a long moment, he stood there, feeling this sudden craving. Whatever he did right now might save him and Roz, Sally and Chibo, and even Nin—or kill them all. He thought about battling ogres with Brace, and sacrificing knights. He thought about friendship and honor and betrayal.

Then he fell to his knees.

He dropped his forehead to the walkway, inches in front of Brace's jewel-encrusted boots, and said, "We'll join you, my prince. We're yours to command."

43

"Move in!" Proctor shouted. "Separate them from the prince! We need them alive!"

"Alive is good," Chibo whispered. "Maybe we'll be freed later, right?"

Still kowtowing, Ji didn't answer. He just clenched his scaly fists and listened to his heart thumping in his chest.

The soldiers swarmed, shouting and scowling. Two yanked Ji to his feet and dragged him to the edge of the pool. Ten more shoved the others beside him, their faces masks of fear and hatred.

Proctor limped beside Brace while Ji waited with a reptile stillness. Thoughts rose and fell in his mind: *the outstanding question, the price of freedom. A water tree, a mermaid, a treasure hoard. A servant, a dragon, and a pair of stupid boots.*

"We agreed to serve you, my lord Brace," Roz rumbled, bowing her head. "And we shall abide by our agreement."

"Because we have honor," Sally growled.

"You're peasants," Proctor said with a chilly chuckle. "You don't need honor, only obedience."

"This is how you'll serve me," Brace said, his voice ringing out. "And how you'll serve the realm. . . ."

He raised his arms, and water spouted from the center of the pool. The geyser twisted and coiled, braiding into a gnarled trunk, then branching into a tree. It was half the size of the one in the Forbidden Palace but still towering, deadly, and magical.

"H-how?" Chibo stammered to Brace, his wings shrunken into his hunchback. "Serve you how, m-m'lord?"

"A king must make hard choices." Brace turned his palms upward. "He must protect the many by sacrificing the few."

Branches of the water tree lengthened, sharpening into spears. The largest one flowed toward Roz—then paused like a cobra ready to strike.

Blood simmered in Ji's head and his pulse thudded in his fists.

"At Prince Brace's whim," Proctor told them, "the tree will pierce you and complete the rite, securing Brace's place as prince once and for all. The realm will be safe in the hands of its rightful heir."

"You—" Roz looked in horror at Brace. "You said you wanted us to join you."

"And so you shall," Brace told her, a hint of sadness in his voice. "Your spirits will strengthen mine. And Roz, you won't be a monster any longer."

"You will die," Proctor said, "that the prince may live."

"I'm sorry," Brace said, his eyes wet with tears. "I'm so sorry."

"My lord prince," Proctor said, "finish this."

When Brace moved his hands, the water tree shifted. Sally growled, and the silvery branches drew back to strike.

"You . . . you lied to us!" Roz told Brace.

And Ji finally spoke. "He's not the only one."

44

"WE'RE NOT YOURS to command," Ji told Brace, and opened his fists to show two boot baubles, glittering with emeralds, rubies, and pearls.

"Those—" Brace looked at his court boots. "Those are mine!"

"He took them when he kowtowed," Chibo fluted in surprise.

"You want to know why dragons hoard treasure?" Ji asked Roz, drawing on the heat of the gems in his hands. "Because we need jewels to make fire."

Lava surged through his arms to his chest, rising like a volcano into his head. The world turned red, and Proctor screamed, "Take them, prince, *now*! Kill them!"

The water spear thrust toward Roz—and pillars of

flame erupted from Ji's eyes and roared across the pool.

Brace stiffened in terror, and the water spear stopped inches from Roz. Sally tackled Chibo away from another branch while Proctor jumped in front of the flames to protect Brace—and a shield of Mr. Ioso's white light crackled into place around both of them.

Ji's flames dimmed when they struck the shield. A palm tree withered behind Mr. Ioso, and he fired arrows of white light at Ji.

Sally bounded forward to protect Ji. But for once, he didn't need protection. The gems turned to coals in his fists and the flames erupting from his eyes burned the arrows into vapor. More tree limbs slashed at him, but he swept his gaze in a burning arc, shriveling the branches with lashes of flame.

Proctor prowled closer, his dagger held high. When Ji blasted him, the blade absorbed the fire. Ji poured more heat into his flames—and iron darts whipped past his ear. He grunted in alarm and swept his fiery gaze around the pool, scattering soldiers and dart throwers. A palm tree exploded into flames and one of Brace's sleeves caught fire.

Mr. Ioso raised his white-light shield and Brace clenched his fists—

"Ji!" Roz rumbled. "Watch out!"

When Ji spun sideways, a water spear thrust past his shoulder. He unleashed another barrage of flames, but

Proctor still battled closer, his beard smoldering and his eyes as black as death.

"On my honor!" Sally growled, bounding at Proctor. "You shall not touch him!"

Her ears flat against her furry head, she vaulted one writhing tree limb, hurdled another—and a bolt of white light blasted her. She staggered, blood trickling down her snout. The tip of a thrusting water spear pierced her side—and Roz scooped her into her granite-flecked arms.

Proctor slashed at Roz, opening a cut on her forearm with his red-glowing dagger. "Kill the snake first, my prince!" he snarled.

Brace thrust two more water spears at Ji. One tore through the air an inch from Ji's head, and he blasted the other one before trying to force Proctor backward with whips of fire. Flames licked at Proctor's jacket and his hand blistered on his dagger, but he kept coming.

Roz bellowed, "Sally—knees, *knees!*"

Which, frankly, didn't help. Even as a volcano spewed from his eyeballs, Ji wondered what in the moons Roz was babbling about.

Proctor blocked a column of flame, then loomed in front of Ji. A watery branch unfurled behind Ji, cutting off his retreat. As Proctor sliced toward his throat, the water spear thrust at Ji's spine and—

"Now!" Roz yelled.

A furball rammed into the back of Ji's knees. He

sprawled to the ground just as the branch surged forward in a killing strike. It flashed over his head and stabbed Proctor in the chest.

Brace shrieked and Proctor gasped. The skin on his face wrinkled. His teeth lengthened and fused together. His shirt bulged—and two belly-arms burst through the silk.

Turning him into a goblin.

The Diadem Rite drained Proctor's life, and his humanity flowed into Brace. He shrank and writhed, turning into a misshapen goblin. Finally, the branch withdrew from his chest, and he crumpled lifelessly to the ground.

"Stab the beasts!" Mr. Ioso bellowed. "Kill them!"

"I will protect the realm." Brace's words carried over the crackle of flames and the shouts of soldiers. "I will protect my people. Whatever the cost."

Mr. Ioso's eyes glowed white. "You'll never take the throne while they live!"

"Then they shall die," Brace said, his silver diadem glimmering.

He seemed to shine with purpose: more real than real, more human than human. He raised his arms and dozens of branches surged from the water tree; an unstoppable flood, an onslaught of spears.

Ji heard the roar of a thousand dragons. His flesh turned to lava, his mind turned to flames. He gathered all his fear and rage—all his love and hope—into one scorching glare. But instead of blasting the branches, he aimed at the trunk of the watery tree.

The blackened gems burned to ash in his fists and the tree boiled into vapor. Every branch, every twig, every inch of the tree frothed into an unearthly white mist. The world turned silver and scalding. Soldiers screamed curses, Brace shouted orders, water hissed and spewed. Steam billowed, blindingly thick.

Ji couldn't see—he couldn't stand. The pool wobbled and he fell to his knees on the rippling surface, a husk of himself, exhausted but unburned.

"This way!" Chibo fluted, hidden by the billowing steam. "Follow me!"

"You can't see!" Sally said.

"My wings can feel the way!"

"Stay close!" Roz said, and Ji felt her four-fingered hand wrapping his arm. "I have Ji."

The pool turned to jelly beneath them. "Nin," he gasped.

"I have the urn too," Roz said, dragging Ji through the fog.

"The water's low enough," Sally's voice growled. "Let's dive in!"

"No," Ji whispered.

"What?"

"We're not leaving," he said, dizzy and weak. "Not yet."

Sally growled. "What are you talking about, you doolally lizard?"

"Make lots of noise like . . . we're jumping in," he told Sally.

For a moment, nothing happened. The steam billowed and the water sloshed. Then Sally shouted: "This way, quick! Everyone dive into the pool! Dive in!"

"Throw in . . . driftwood," Ji murmured to Roz. "So they hear . . . splashes. And once they think we're gone, follow Chibo . . . to the street."

"Why aren't we leaving?" Roz asked.

"Because we're not done here," Ji said. "Not yet."

45

AS THE MOONS shone down from a cloudless sky, the steam from the vaporized tree covered the city in a dense fog.

Soldiers ransacked every room of Ti-Lin-Su's estate, and elite squads ventured into the long, reeking tunnel toward the coast. In the Forbidden Palace, bucket crews poured water on the smoldering fires. Work crews returned sleeping terra-cotta warriors to their pedestals. And a young goblin peeked from a canal drain and daydreamed about combs.

Lower on the mountainside, Ji limped toward a neighborhood packed with canals and waterwheels. Roz walked beside him, her face hidden in her hood, holding Nin's urn under one arm. Chibo held her other hand—then stopped suddenly.

"This is the Oilpress!" he fluted. "We're a stone's throw from the tapestry weavers."

"And this time," Ji said, "we're not leaving anyone in chains."

Sally bounded down from a nearby wall. "The coast is clear."

"You—" Chibo beamed at Ji, his green eyes glowing. "I *told* them we'd come back! I knew you'd save them!"

Sally prowled closer. "What happens when we get there?"

"We tear down the looms," Ji told her, a savage note in his voice. "We release the kids. And we stomp anyone who gets in our way."

"Then we'll sneak out of the city?" Sally asked.

"Yeah, we need to hide for a while. Until it's safe to search for Ti-Lin-Su."

"Hiding won't be easy," Roz rumbled. "We're not exactly human anymore."

"That's true," Ji told her. "But we *are* exactly free."

Chibo fluted a laugh, Sally growled in triumph—and Roz's smile still looked like the sun coming out from behind the clouds.

Ji kicked his tattered sandals off his clawed feet. He didn't know if they could escape the realm; he didn't know if they could break the spell. But he knew one thing: he'd never be a servant again.

And deep in his heart, a dragon roared.

Acknowledgments

MANY THANKS TO Caitlin Blasdell, Alyson Day, Renée Cafiero, Alana Whitman, Lindsey Karl, Brian Thompson, Tessa Meischeid, and Joel Tippie.

Joel Ross is the author of *The Fog Diver*, which received the Cybils Award and the YouPer Award from the Michigan Library Association and was named to the Texas Bluebonnet Award Master List. He is also the author of *The Lost Compass* as well as two World War II thrillers for adults (*Double Cross Blind* and *White Flag Down*). He lives in Santa Barbara, California, with his wife, Lee Nichols, who is also a full-time writer, and their son, Ben, who is a full-time kid. To find out more information, go to www.fogdiver.com.